UNLEASH THIS DOG, LORD...

Worldly Glory is Temporary...
Eternal Glory is Forever...

ALAN TRUJILLO

Printed in the United States of America

ISBN 979-8-89114-025-7 (sc)
ISBN 979-8-89114-026-4 (e)

Library of Congress Control Number: 9798891140257

2024.05.22

MainSpring Books
5901 W. Century Blvd
Suite 750
Los Angeles, CA, US, 90045

www.mainspringbooks.com

Based on a true story, only the names have been changed to protect the identities.

I dedicate this book to Christina, my love.
You have always supported me, even
when the outlook was bleak…
I love you with all my heart. You are as close
to perfect as there is. Forever yours…

CONTENTS

PREFACE

It became evident to me that I must write this book, not only to tell my story, but to prove the duality that is this world. A world where good fights evil, that the devil and his demons are real. Growing up, I wondered why God would subject me to such evil, and why he allowed me to see the things I saw? I often asked Him this question after seeing what I saw. After many times repeating this question to God, He revealed why. "If there is a devil, there is a God." This is the message I am to portray.

It astonishes me the number of people who don't know if there is a God, but are likely to say there is a devil, and demons. They don't realize that if there are demons and the devil, there is a God. The younger generation acknowledges they are spiritual, but aren't sure if there is a God. I'm writing this book not for myself, but to prove God's existence through my life. I seriously contemplated using a pen name. I was withholding certain stories out of embarrassment. I realized people need to hear the truth, and it must not be filtered. I must be bold and not afraid. I'm doing this for God's glory, not mine. At the time of writing this story I was ridiculed by friends, which seemed logical from their perspective, but they couldn't feel the urgency God put in my heart to tell my story. Everything written in this story is true, only the names of the characters have been changed to protect their identity. Time will tell the prudence of my actions...

While a friend was reading this story on her tablet, a black figure came out of the tablet. It started as a black shadow on the screen, flew out, and entered the room. While reading the story it is possible for demons to attack the reader. It has happened to me several times while watching movies based on true events. Mostly, movies that involve a possession. In order to protect the readers and prevent any attacks, I strongly recommend anyone reading this book say this prayer before reading; "Dear lord Protect me and my family from all evil, let no evil near us, and let me finish this book. I bind all evil in this story in the name of Jesus Christ. With the blood from calvary I bind up all attempts against me, my family, and my home in the name of Jesus Christ!" I realize some reading may not believe in God. If one does not want to say the prayer for lack of believing in Jesus, read at your own risk, and know that you were warned, but I pray for God's protection over you in Jesus Christ's name! I'm not responsible for what if one chooses not to read and accept the prayer in their heart…

I tell these stories not for entertainment, nor boasting, but that they may help. Some of these stories are humiliating, but I have to see beyond my own feelings, and I do it for the Glory of God, and His Kingdom. May they help whomever is suffering in a similar way, and know that you aren't alone. They are written to expose the ways of the devil in order for the reader to discern his works through patterns. He operates in patterns and cycles, always playing the same hand. Recognize the patterns of his hand, and ask God for the grace to overcome it.

As I was originally writing this book I faced many obstacles, and it became very evident that the devil himself was terrified of becoming exposed. One day while writing, The Holy Spirit spoke to me, "Back up your work." I went out and bought a thumb drive. Weeks later the desktop I was typing on caught fire in the tower. I unplugged the computer and the fire fizzled out.

Thankfully I saved all my work on the jump drive. I bought a brand new desktop and laptop. While writing this book my wife and I were expecting, and I was in a paramedic program, as well working forty hours a week at a nursing home as a CNA. The night before a paper was due I came to a crossroad; Either finish the book, or type my paper that was due. The Holy Spirit moved me so powerfully, I was compelled to finish the book. My fingers punched away at the keys on the laptop. As I hit the period key the laptop froze. The cursor flew the pages backward. I tried pressing delete, and the power button. Ctrl, alt, delete did nothing. I tried to power it down, but it wouldn't change anything. I pulled the battery out of the laptop for a hard reboot, but nothing worked, the cursor flew backwards through the book. The walls cracked and it felt as though the walls were crushing in on us. Demons ran on the roof, and cackled outside of the windows. There were hundreds of demons around the house in a frenzy. I ran to the desktop to upload the file of the book that I had saved earlier. The last page was missing, but I could send it later. I knew the demons didn't want the book released, so I tried everything I could to send it to the publisher. The file couldn't load to the desktop.

Finally the Holy Spirit spoke, "You must pray three Rosaries with your wife." I followed the command. As soon as we finished the last prayer, The walls stopped caving in, and the demons went silent. I couldn't hear them running on the roof, or cackling. I went to the laptop. The cursor wasn't running backwards through the book anymore. I downloaded the file to the jump drive, and transferred it to the desktop. I sent it to the publisher, and it was accomplished. May this book reach believers and unbelievers alike, may the truth reveal God. This is All For You My Love, Jesus Christ Most Holy!!!...

Chapter 1

The dim light of my cell phone illuminated the room, and I could feel the vibration of the shaking of the top of the nightstand against the bed frame. "Hello…" "hey, I need you to come to my house now." It was almost Midnight. I grabbed a small plastic bottle of Holy water that was on my dresser, and threw on my Rosary. Rushing to the kitchen I grabbed a container of salt. A surge of energy from the Holy Spirit burned from my heart, and nothing can stop me, except God himself. On the way out, I was met by my wife standing in front of the door. "Where do you think you're going?" "I'm going to Russell's house, he needs help." "No you're not. if you leave, I won't be here when you get back." "I'm sorry, I love you, but I have to go."

I hopped in my truck, and I was off. As I started my drive I began to praise God, the Holy Spirit urged me to say a series of Our Fathers and Hail Mary's. The Holy Spirit burned in my chest and radiated to my head and out through my arms. As I approached the dirt road that led to his house, I could hear all the dogs in the neighborhood howling and barking. I pulled into his driveway. The garage was closed. That's strange, I thought to myself. He always had the garage door open, as most backyard mechanics do. When he wasn't working on cars, he was hanging out with his brother and friends in the garage. I parked my truck, and walked along the sidewalk to his front door. to the left there was a small tree, bats were swarming the tree. they were swooping down in every direction. I walked to the door, and rang the doorbell. No answer, I rang it again.

The garage door began to open, so I made my way to the side of the house back to the garage. Russell met me, with a heartfelt handshake hug combo. "I'm so glad you're here." It was uncharacteristic for Russell to be so distraught. He was from a hard place. He left home at sixteen, and lived in the ghetto in the worst parts of California where he struggled on the streets submerged in ganglife. "What happened?" "Barbara and I were about to lay down for bed, I had music playing on my cell phone. the lights began to flicker and the phone froze. I picked it up and on the screen was a cartoon picture of the devil. I tried turning it off, and it wouldn't turn off. Then Barbara began to have some sort of seizure. I picked her up and slapped her a couple times to wake her up, and she wouldn't wake up. Then I called you. Before you got here it felt like my feet were in blocks of cement, my feet were so heavy I could barely walk."

"Alright, I'm going to Bless your house." I began to throw Holy water in the shape of the cross as we walked, repeating, "I cast you out in the name of the Father Son and the Holy Spirit." As we walked I saw a shadow figure the shape of a black handkerchief fly into a picture on the wall. I asked him who was in the picture? "Those are my grandparents," he replied. I blessed the picture and the figure went into his bedroom. We walked into the bedroom and I could feel a dark heavy presence. The figure flew into a picture on his nightstand. Before I could ask him who was in the picture, he said, "Get that picture." "Can you see it, I asked him?" "Yes," he replied. I blessed the picture and it flew into the closet. I blessed the closet and it flew across the hall into his children's room. I blessed the room, and it flew into the closet. I blessed the closet and it went through the floor and into the basement. We made our way to the basement. The basement was cold and dark. The heavy omnibus presence was in the corner. As we blessed it, the figure flew out of the basement window, and I sealed the house with the sign of The Cross on the window. We went upstairs and I blessed the salt I had brought with me. I laid a perimeter of salt around his property, which was about an acre. As we walked back to his house in the cool night air, a sense of peace was palpable. The neighborhood was peaceful again, all the dogs had stopped barking. As we walked back into the garage I looked at the small tree in front of his house, there wasn't a bat in sight. "Alan, a lot of crazy shit has happened this week."

"Earlier this week I was shooting the shit with the guys in the garage. As we were talking a rattlesnake slithered into his garage. You know, there are rattlesnakes in this area, so I wasn't shocked. This was not a typical rattlesnake. It made its way into the garage charging us, I grabbed the machete from the wall. Whack, I hacked its head off. The snake grew another head, and began to strike at us. I grabbed a can of brake cleaner from the shelf and a lighter, and torched that mother fucker. I'm not trippin, everyone saw it. Alan, I don't know where that demon came from, but it seems that the snake was connected to what happened tonight?"

It wasn't until several years later that I realized where it came from. I didn't think to question, all I knew was what I had to do, to help him out. That was the first house I cleared. Looking back, I know exactly where the demon came from. Russell's brother, Alonzo was 22 years old. He lived in his basement. He tells a story of vivid nightmares he was having that week. He said, " I was laying on my bed in the basement where my room is, and as I was sleeping. I could see myself rise out of my body. There was a giant hand I was laying on, not my bed. The hand head had sharp nails and was so powerful. I could feel it trying to squish me, and I woke up in a cold sweat. The Source finally dawned on me, I knew exactly where it came from. I'm getting ahead of myself… let me start from the beginning, back where it all started.

Chapter 11

My spiritual journey started at a young age, I must have been around seven or eight years old. I remember my grandmother sitting with my mom in the kitchen. a cigarette in one hand and a cup of coffee in the other. She spoke so passionately about The Bible and The Revelations. Kneeling on the floor by the table I memorized every thing she said, feeling that I needed to memorize every word. It consumed me as if I needed to know everything she was saying, in order to prepare. as she spoke I could see a vision of a group of men in brown cloaks, and a green background. I couldn't see their entire body, only from their legs down. None of them were wearing shoes. I could hear a holy frequency radiating, the humming bass of what now I can only describe as a Gregorian chant and it filled my heart, my mind, and my soul with ecstasy. At that time I had no idea what I was experiencing, I knew it was good, and I knew it was from God. It wasn't until I was older that I realized; I had seen Franciscan monks. Their bare feet symbolizing; walking, evangelizing The Word of God, and the spiritual war between the Almighty, and the wicked.

My grandmother would tell my mother the story of her mother. "Your grandmother Samantha and grandfather Paul were in love. Grandpa would play in a band at a local bar on the weekends. He was a great guitar player. Grandma noticed that Grandpa was becoming more distant. He stopped coming home on the weekends after his shows. Eventually, he stops coming home at all. Grandma went to see a culandeda/witch doctor, a witch or warlock that practices white magic. It is said that after a long time of practicing black magic, they start doing white magic to make up for their karma before they die, but they charge a fee. She went to this man's house, "A lady from the bar has fallen in love with him. She has put a spell on him to fall in love with her. She has cursed you through your shadow when you were hanging laundry." He explained to her everything she needed to do. He told her to place a glass of water underneath her bed. He prescribed her a list of prayers that she needed to complete. He told her that she would run into the lady that had cursed them. He said that she would know because she would panic and run away. He will leave her and come back to you but she has taken part of him that can't be given back. she did as he instructed, in three days the glass underneath her bed contained a huge white pearl.

The Warlock instructed her to throw it in her backyard and not watch where it fell. Soon after Grandma ran into the lady that had cursed her, and it was true she ran away. and it was also true what he said about Grandpa. he had a stroke, and was never the same. He wasn't able to remember how to play the guitar again. He ended up having to have surgery to have a tumor removed from his brain, and they lived their life well for some time. Many years later he ended up getting brain cancer again and dying from that. A few years later Grandma Samantha died as well.

As my grandmother Verna told my mom these stories we listened intently. My grandmother Verna had her own story of a witch she battled. Ironically, my mom, Angelica, would tell her kids about her mom, and how she was cursed. Mom would tell the story of how her parents were together over twenty years, and divorced. Shortly after, he met Bertha. Bertha seemed kind. The way she told the story, it sounded a lot like the same scenario. She came between their marriage. It wasn't until recently that I learned that grandma Verna and grandpa Ron stayed together until their kids were older, and decided to separate. Nonetheless, Bertha was into magic. She had a daughter from a previous marriage, little Bertha. As my father was discharged from the army we moved around quite a bit in order for my dad to find work. We moved from Colorado to Nevada a couple times.

We seemed to follow my mother's father Ron, and Bertha. With great caution, my mother told me and my siblings of her first experiences with Bertha. "One day I went outside and I heard Bertha speaking to little Bertha over the fence. But they weren't speaking english, or Spanish. They were speaking in demonic tongues. Then one day she asked if I wanted my cards read. I felt bad saying no, and I was curious, so I agreed. As she read my past and my present your dad walked in the bedroom and threw the cards off the table." "What the fuck are you doing!" He yelled. My dad, Adam, is very passionate, and very protective of my mother. My mother was a hard worker, she had two jobs, and five kids to care for. After getting her tarot cards read she came down with an autoimmune disease. At that time there was only one other person in America diagnosed with it at a young age of 28. This disease usually shows up when a person is in their mid fifties. She was unable to work, and couldn't drive due to her double vision. Eventually, her eyes would close, and if she wanted to see, she would have to prop them open with a small hair clip. If she would prop both of them open, one eye would focus, and the other would wander. Only one eye propped open would cause depth perception problems. "The last thing my dad said to me before we left Nevada was; "I love your eyes. They are beautiful. They remind me of your mom's eyes." Then I came back to Colorado and was diagnosed with myasthenia gravis and lost control of my eyes."

Shortly before all that happened I was about five years old, and all I could remember was Bertha being nice to me. I remember she took me to this place and dropped me off. It reminded me of a library, our preschool. It was only for a day, but I remember it very vividly. she said it's down for storytime. All the children gathered around to listen to the story. It was very similar to Hansel and Gretel, but it had a strange twist. The witch in the story was the protagonist, and painted in a good light. The children in the story chose to live with her in the forest. in a weird way it was condoning leaving your parents to live with the witch. Even at that age I thought it was strange, good always wins, and the bad guy should never win. It was my first memory of her. Shortly after that my youngest sister was about to be born. There was my oldest sister Jesse. Three years later I was born. Three years later Maggie was born, then Victor, and finally Anne. Each sibling has been born in Christianity with certain gifts, passed down from genealogy, but also from God. As God has said, *"The wind bloweth where it will, and thou hearest the sound thereof, but canst not tell whence it cometh and whiterit goeth: so is everyone that is born in the spirit."* John 3:8.

Anne and I were born with certain spiritual gifts. When Anne was about to be born Bertha had an odd request for my mother. Somehow she asked my mother to give her Anne to raise as her own after her delivery. She wanted a baby girl to raise as her own. It was never talked about why she asked for her out of all the children. It is my intuition and understanding now that I am older, that tells me she wanted Anne to develop her. She wanted to groom her in witchcraft. Born with the gifts she already has, Anne would have been a power for the darkside. Spirits sees spirit, and Bertha knew Anne would be strong. Obviously, my mother refused to give her child away. After the refusal would come the hard part. My mother's labor with Anne was one of the toughest things my mother would go through. During the delivery the doctor turned towards my father, "You have to choose, Your wife or the baby?" My father replied, "Angelica." My mother yelled, "No Alex, you save the baby!" He conceded. The doctor explained that the baby had the cord wrapped around her neck, and they needed to rush them to surgery for a C-section. The doctor was able to save the baby, but my mom died. She was without a heart beat for six minutes, but fully recovered after CPR.

Bertha was a short lady, definitely under five feet tall. She always has her hair dyed red. Her hair is thinning out, and the scalp is visible from every direction. In order to cover up balding, she teases it upward, nearly a foot high. Her tiny black eyes showing who she really is. Her pointed nose curling towards her lips doesn't disguise the witch that she is. I could not understand why my grandfather was with her. There was always talk about that floating around the family. All three of my uncles, my mom's brothers, worked with him. They worked for a construction company, and had a habit of going to the bar after work. My uncle admitted to having a conversation with my grandfather about him leaving her. He said to my uncle, "John, I have tried to leave her, but every time I do one of my you get very sick. I have to stay with her." One day my mother, my uncle John, grandfather Ron, and my grandmother Verna were talking about the curse. My grandmother had just bought a crystal Rosary from a jewelry store. The conversation arose about him attempting to leave, but something happened to each of their children when he did. That night Ron decided that he was going to stay with her to protect his children, and if anyone would be hurt, it would be him, and he would bear the curse. That night Verna prayed the Rosary to protect her children. After that night she never found that Rosary again. It completely disappeared as if it never existed.

My grandfather got to the point of having to sleep with the lights on. This was very uncharacteristic of him, he is and was a tough guy. I don't know if it was because Ron and Bertha got into a fight one night, or what exactly happened, but the story goes like this; It was late in the evening, right before bedtime, and he turned out the light on the lamp on his nightstand. Just as he layed in bed to lay down, several little green men rushed into the room. They pulled at him from the side of the bed, jumping up to pull him off the bed. Hooded brown cloaks hide their dark faces, But their gloss black eyes and sharp teeth could not be ignored. Ever since then, he has slept with the light on. He never broke up with her. Now that I am older and wiser, I have a different opinion than the one I had when I was growing up. My grandfather was always so nice. He was a good man, generous and loving. He always made me feel special. I have one brother and three sisters. I have over 13 first cousins from my mom's side. With this many grandchildren around, how can he show any of his grandchildren any attention, but he found a way. His love for us was palpable. He always managed to. We all had financial struggles. Grandpa Ron always found a way to buy us Christmas gifts. Even as a Child I found this special. It was rare to get a consistent birthday gift or Christmas present from any uncle, aunt, or grandparent. Most people couldn't afford to buy all the children a gift, there were just too many kids.

My grandfather's gifts were always nice too, nothing cheap. It always seemed to follow trends, a nice watch for me and my brother, and a bracelet or necklace for my sisters. I could never understand why, or how they would break. Shortly after putting them on, they would either break, or I would fall and get injured. I was frustrated that they would break so fast. Especially, because they were always expensive quality brands. It wasn't until I was older and talking with my siblings that it made sense. It also made sense when I learned the rules of magic. I wasn't the only child who realized that every time I put on one of the gifts, it broke, or I fell, and then it broke. I watched my sister do the same thing. What a crazy coincidence I used to think. Anne would also say, "It seems like whenever we put on the gifts, we always get hurt right after putting them on." After learning more about Magic, spiritualism, and santeria, it all made sense. In all these religions the Shamen, witch doctor, wiccan, warlock, witch ect. can place a curse on the item, and it will curse the person that puts it on. They can also Bless a bracelet or necklace for protection. There can be many purposes for the jewelry worn, and created for a purpose. This is why we would end up getting hurt. When it would break, the Holy Spirit was protecting us, breaking the curse meant for harm. There is another type of jewelry breaking. Some people wear an evil eye, or some sort of talisman. This is meant for protection, but is also considered magic. The culture I was born into says there are two kinds of magic, white and black. Now that I'm older I know that all magic is bad, as it is not done through Jesus Christ.

Even now, when wearing a crucifix, or Rosary, and it breaks, it takes a hit for the wearer. It absorbs the spiritual blow. Does that mean every time it breaks it has to have a spiritual attack? Of course not, but there are things unexplainable to physics when it comes to a spiritual attack. I have had Rosaries fall apart in my hand like it was made of water. Each bead falling apart as my hands shuffle underneath to catch the remnants of beads and metal. If it doesn't fall apart, it gets so knotted up that it is nearly impossible to untangle it. I've spent hours untangling a rosary. Sometimes it gets tangled and breaks in sections at the same time. When this happens it couples with the feeling of hopelessness and desolate feelings.

As I was growing up, I understood that my grandparents broke up because of Bertha. It was only until recently that my mother told me the truth. One day my mother explained it to me, "I was about sixteen, right before I left to live with your father on base in Hawaii, and I asked my dad something about him and mom staying together forever. He said, "There are things about me and your mother that you just don't know." inferring that he and her mother were just staying together until the kids grew up and moved away, only to then, get divorced. Knowing that now, it's nice to know that she wasn't the wedge that drove my grandparents apart. I used to try to imagine what it would be like if they were still together. I'm under the impression that my grandfather must love Bertha, since he is still with her. He must, if he allows her to cast spells on his children and grandchildren. If that's not it, then He is a coward who is afraid, and chooses not to protect the rest of his family, and does nothing. Similar to the sin of a Pilot, to stand neutral in the sight of evil, and not do anything to stop it, especially if one has the power to stop it from happening. How can a man allow his children to be hurt by witchcraft and stand by idly? Both can be true; he can love her, and be afraid of confronting her. I used to give him the benefit of the doubt, and think, maybe he doesn't know. Now I know he is aware of what she is doing. Perhaps, one can go years of hiding their practice of the black arts. It would be hard to do while hiding all the rituals, and planning of spells around astrological events(moon phases, and solstices), but it might be possible. Perhaps he developed Stockholm Syndrome; which is where the captive develops positive feelings towards their capture. Either way, I now know that he eventually chose Bertha and her children over us. There were two stories that confirmed my thoughts.

Many years ago my mother trand father were invited to a local bar to have drinks with Ron, Bertha, Bertha's daughter (little Bertha) and her husband, who incidentally, is my uncle Jason. Uncle Jason had married little Bertha. She was Bertha's daughter from a different marriage, even though it was weird, they are not blood relatives. When they met at this bar, Ron had a request for my mother. He asked that she call Bertha mom. My mother was flabbergasted, "I only have one mom, and that's Verna. I would never call someone dad, even if they marry mom. I have only one dad, and one mom, and that is you and mom." My mother's oldest sibling Ariel and her youngest sibling Audrey could not understand. They were quick to call her mom. The day Ron and Bertha invented my mom to go for a drink, happened to be on my mother's birthday. Ron must not have realized it was her birthday. While they were having drinks Ron called the bartender over, "Can you bring my daughter over a special drink? It's her birthday!" Overjoyed, my mother felt special. As the bartender arrived with the drink, he asked, who it was for? Ron replied, "Her," he pointed to little Bertha. "In a couple of weeks it will be her birthday." He said proudly. My mothers heart sank. He completely forgot it was my mother's birthday. He could have asked for two drinks, one for little Bertha, and one for my mom, but he didn't. It was then that my mother realized that Bertha was his daughter.

I was telling Russell about everything that had happened to me. The family curse, and Bertha. Russell said you know Billy does that stuff, he can help you. "Does what stuff?" "You know, santeria." Billy was our co-worker. We all worked for a local auto parts store, and Billy had only been working with us for a couple months. After meeting with Billy everything that was chalked up to coincidence, was now confirmed. All my life I second guessed myself and tried to use logic, and rationalized to explain everything that had happened to me and my family. After a while, things are too numerous to be explained purely as coincidence, and all my intuition that I had ignored for so long, was proven. Billy told me everything I had felt since childhood, but I'll come back to that thought at a later time. After meeting with him Russell and I had a deep conversation. We were working at an auto parts store at this time, and Russell and I were sent to another location to count all the inventory just as all the other managers from our district. Russell was standing on the stair ladder next to me as I was kneeling and scanning the items on the bottom shelves. He said, "You know, I'm not like you. I wouldn't let that happen to me. If I knew someone was hurting me or my family I would confront them." "What do you mean?" "I would tell them to take it off." "And what if they didn't?" "You know. Like I said, I'm not like you," As soon as he said that I knew what he meant. I thought to myself. Am I weak? Am I not a man, a coward that can't protect himself or his family? I must be. While standing there, a vision of a cross appeared in front of my already open eyes. The cross was made of round posts, both the vertical and horizontal were the same circumference, and nearly the same circumference as a telephone pole. I couldn't see the entire cross, just where the posts met in the middle, as if it was a foot in front of my face and I was holding it. It was a view as if I was bearing it. Was this my cross, I asked myself? Was the vision telling me to bare my cross? Jesus bore his cross, but he embraced it. I shook it off. That was weird, why did that happen, I thought to myself?

Russell continued, "You know I can help you with that." "What do you mean?" "I can take care of business, and nobody would know." I sat there letting it sink in, and again the vision of the cross flashed before my eyes. I started to let the rush of the idea wash over me like; how would we do it, and when? Again the vision flashed, and it hit me like a ton of bricks. Jesus was showing me that the whole scenario was my cross, and I must bear it. I must bear my cross like he bore his. "I appreciate that Russell, but I'll figure it out. Thank you, you're a good friend."

A day later, Ron passed on a message to me, through the family. He said, "If anyone thinks of harming one hair on Bertha, Little Bertha, or little Bertha's daughter, I won't think twice about putting a bullet in him." That was precisely when I knew he had been aware of her attacks on his children, and grandchildren. Why would he know, and how would he know about a conversation I had with someone neither of them should have known. It was 4 towns away, and completely confidential. His threat on my life was proof enough that he is aware of her attacks on me and my family. At the time I didn't know how magic/wicca/witchcraft worked. The person that practices, has demons who listen to their enemies' conversations. It doesn't have to be an enemy, but whoever is speaking about the practitioner. The demon then repeats the conversation to the practitioner to warn them.

It was disheartening to hear my own grandfather threaten my life, it definitely showed who he truly loves. How did we get here? Twenty years before that conversation took place my father was in the Army. We needed a place to live when we moved to colorado. Ron and Bertha bought a second house, and moved out of their current house in order to rent it to tenants. We were offered their old house, so we moved in. I was only three to four years old at that time. The house is unique and a little on the older side. Across the street was a tall brick Baptist church. As one would walk up the sidewalk to the steps entering the house, the living room was on the right side. There was a walkway with a decorative ledge to the left. It had a scenery of the mountains and a lake painted on the wall behind the ledge. The ledge held mulch, rocks and pine cones as if it was the ground of the scenery. There was a step up to the right, where the living room was. Off to the right of that, was a pavement patio. It was about ten feet by ten feet, and about four feet off the ground.

Walking past the living room was the dining room. Straight ahead was a sliding glass door that led to a wooden deck and the backyard. To the right of the dining room was the kitchen. At the end of the kitchen was another door that led outside, and to the left of that was a staircase that led to a dirt basement with an old furnace. Standing in the dining room facing the sliding glass door, to the right was a mirror that was at least six feet long and four feet tall that covered the wall. To the left, was a step down, and one would be in the hallway. On the right of the hall was the master bedroom, and to the left was the other bedroom, with a bathroom in the middle. Halfway down the hall, across from the bathroom was a full size body mirror. Further down the hall was Mine and Jesse's bedroom.

This was the first house I had a supernatural experience in. My mom sent my sister and I to bed. At this time we were the only two children. We had a bunk bed in the corner of our bedroom. I was lying in bed on my back on the bottom bunk. My sister was on the top bunk lying on her stomach with her left arm hanging off the bed. My mother walked into the room, shut the lights off, and started walking towards us to give us a kiss, suddenly she changed her mind, turned around and walked back out of the room. As soon as the door closed behind her a man walked in. She didn't see him, they passed each other in the doorway. He was a light blue in color, but transparent. He was wearing a suit and a round brim hat. Curls descending from each ear. In shock I closed my eyes tight to appear as if I was sleeping, but I kept them open enough to see everything. He walked towards us. He stopped bedside, and reached out for Jessie's hand. He held it for a moment, and became aware that I was awake. He let go of her hand, he bent down inside of the bed. Staring at me face to face, an inch away he continued to stare. It probably lasted about thirty seconds, but that is a long time to be face to face with a spirit, but it felt a lot longer. All of a sudden he stands up and walks to the door. As he reaches the door, my mother walks back into the room directly passing him without a clue he was there. She walks to the bed and places Jesse's arm back on the bed. "Mommy your hand was cold," Jesse murmured. I lay there quite, acting asleep, and shocked. Looking back now I don't know if I should have been scared. He didn't hurt me or her. I was afraid, but should I have been? He appeared to have been comforting my sister, and he looked like a Rabbi. However, staring into my eyes was pretty creepy.

That house was haunted without a doubt. I remember walking down the hall past the mirror. I would walk past it, and my reflection would walk the other direction. My sister and I would stop and stare into the mirror at our reflections. The reflection looked like us, but at the same time, it didn't. It would look like someone else pretending to be us. It was an ominous version of ourselves. I remember we would test it out. We would raise our right arm, and the left arm would raise, and we would run away to tell our parents. They didn't have anything to say, but their silence and lack of response was enough to know that they believed us, what could they say?

One morning mom screamed for my father from the patio, "Alan!" We rushed to the outside to see a name written on the cement. It read; "Satin John." My mom tried washing it away. She tried every cleanser in the house, but nothing worked. It appeared to be written in charcoal. After hours of scrubbing, mom called her father. Ron and Bertha came over, and mom explained how she had tried everything, but nothing would work. Bertha grabbed a cloth and wet it with water, and wiped it clean as though it was an eraser wiping away a dry erase marker. It was way too easy for her.

One thing Bertha has in every house besides the southwest decorum was an owl. Every house she has lived in, she always had a stuffed owl. One day my mom noticed that a small stuffed owl the size of a baseball had been left by Bertha. It was sitting on the ledge in the walkway of the living room. She gave it to my father to destroy. We walked to the side of the house to the sidewalk with him. He wrapped it up into a paper towel and lit it on fire. The paper towel caught fire, it burned and the fire consumed it, but the owl was left completely unharmed. He went back into the house and came out with a hammer. He wrapped the owl again, lit it on fire, and hit it with a hammer. The owl was left unscathed, and the paper towel fizzled to ashes. All of us were shocked as we stared at the little indestructible owl. My mom ran into the house, and returned with a large glass bottle of Holy Water. My dad wrapped the owl in a paper towel, and my mother poured Holy Water on it. My dad lit it on fire. The paper towel burned and the owl disappeared. All that was left was just a small remnant of ashes from the paper towel.

One day my dad was on base, and my uncle Sam came over to help us organize the house and hang pictures. Mom and uncle Sam were astonished when they tried hammering nails into the walls. The nails were bending as if the walls were made of concrete. It was as if the house had a mind of its own. There were many nights my mom swooped me and Jackie up in a frenzy and rushed us to my great grandmother's house to sleep while my dad wasn't home. Granma Ronda was Ron's mother. I remember sleeping on the couch a few nights while my mom and grandma talked late into the night about what my mom had seen and experienced in that house.

One morning my mother was making her bed. She threw the blanket up and as it floated up, she saw a gigantic baby crawling away through the doorway. The baby was the size of a full grown German Shepard. It was wearing only a cloth diaper. Its hair was black as cole, and spiked into a single point. The baby began to crawl away, and as the blanket floated to the bed, she was hoping it would be gone when the blanket landed on the bed. It made its way to the hallway and crawled up the step and to the left. She could see the chubby creased leg slither into the dinning room. All she could think of was Jesse and I were playing in the living room, and it's heading right for us. She had to run right where the baby was to get to us. She went for it, hoping not to see it again. She ran scooping Jackie and me up from the floor with tears in her eyes. She put us in the car and we spent all day and night at grandma Ronda's.

When my father was gone the evil amplified. Occurrences would still happen when he was there, but they were less frequent and usually less scary. One night, we were asleep when there was a pounding at the front door. Dad jumped out of bed, and quickly walked to the door because it sounded urgent. The bangs were loud enough to wake all of us. When he got to the front door, nobody was there. He walked around to both sides of the house, figuring it was teenagers pulling a prank. He locked the door and went back to bed. as soon as he laid down there was a pounding on the front door again. When he got to the door there was nobody there. Then he heard a pound on the side door. He ran to that door and there was nobody there. Then there was pounding on the back sliding glass door. The backyard was blocked off by a privacy fence, and it would have been difficult to jump the fence so quickly to pound on that door. When he got to the sliding glass door there was nobody there, and the pounding started on the front door again. Eventually, He stopped answering the doors and went back to his room. There was nothing we could do, the pounding eventually stopped.

His shifts on base changed from time to time. it wasn't uncommon that he had to do graveyard shifts. One morning my mom and grandmother were visiting in the dining room, and my dad was sleeping for a night shift. the door slammed open from his bedroom, "What in the hell are you guys slamming? I'm trying to get some sleep. I have to work tonight!" my mother replied, "we're just sitting here talking." my dad closed the door and went back to bed. a couple minutes later he came back out of the room to yell, "God damn it, Keep it down!" Mom and Grandma were whispering at this point. When he went to bed, he could hear pounding, yelling, and doors slamming. He didn't get any sleep that day.

We didn't stay in that house very long. Eventually, we had to move. I remember sitting by the window staring at the church across the street. Looking at the beige bricks stacked like a fort. It was a giant church. Staring at it I wondered how a holy place like that could be so close to an evil place like this. It was like heaven and hell shared the same street. We ended up moving into a fourplex. It didn't seem to be haunted like the last place, but that's not to say that nothing happened there. I remember Jesse's and my bedroom was right next to the bathroom, and every time I walked to my bedroom, I had to pass by the bathroom. There was one thing I always remembered about that place. Every time I walked past the bathroom I could see a man sitting in the bathtub.

He was white and gray in color. He was tall, skinny, and caucasian. He had the most atrocious scowl on his face, evil permeated through. He did not look transparent, but he was ashen, and looked like he had already died. On his face was an expression of someone who wanted to kill. He had long wavy salt and pepper hair that flowed into his long beard. He was not stationary, because every time I walked by his head would follow me, letting me know that he saw me. He never had any clothes on, but I couldn't see from the waist down. He was sitting in the tub as if he was taking a bath. The scariest part for me was when my mom would give me a bath. I was still only between 3 and 4 years old, so she had to help me. I was reluctant to take a bath because

I knew I had to face him. Every time I stepped in that bathtub I hesitated, hoping this man would go away, but he didn't. I was in his bathtub. As I sat in the bathtub he was behind me. when my mother told me to rinse my hair out by dunking my head. I had a feeling that he was going to drown me. A panic rushed through me as I hurried to complete the task. Every time I went below the water I felt panic as if I was drowning. Years later my sister told me a story about how she used to see a man sitting in the bathtub. She described him the same way. I had kept that story all to myself, never telling anyone. After Twenty Years of keeping it to myself, she explained it to me in detail. She explained how he looked, and how he had his left arm propped up on the side of the bathtub as his head followed her every movement.

Life for my family was always uncertain. We had many financial problems, just like a lot of people do. My dad was honorably discharged from the army, but always had trouble finding a decent stable job. At times we were homeless, and had to move in with family until we could get on our feet. We moved around a lot. Once things became stable, they eventually became unstable. Eventually, My dad was able to get a job that paid well, but it was a temporary job. It was expected to end after 3-4 years. By then we had moved into a three-bedroom trailer. It was a very old single wide trailer, but it was ours. We had a lot of good memories there. It probably looked like trash to most people, but it felt as if we were living in a mansion. We were able to do things that we hadn't before, go to the movies when we wanted, all sorts of things that make life better.

One of the things we really liked to do was to camp-out in the living room. We would turn off all the lights, and tell ghost stories. One night we laid a mattress on the living room floor. Those that couldn't fit on the mattress were laying on blankets. This Was one of the scariest nights I've ever had up until this point. There have been three times in my entire life where I have been terrified. This was the first time I had ever been that scared. We began our routine of telling ghost stories. Most of the time while we were telling ghost stories we would see a flash of light somewhere in the room, as though someone had just snapped a picture. At the time I thought it was strange, but now I know it was the presence of a demon.

Time went on, and just like normal, when we would start telling ghost stories, everyone would start hearing things: the house creaks, the wind blows, and every sound seems related to the story being told. My mom and sisters let out a scream each time they would hear a noise. Then we started to talk about my sister's doll collection. While we started the conversation in a new direction, it is important to understand the set up of the trailer. The trailer was set up as follows; walking in the front door was an entry into the living room, to the left was the kitchen. The kitchen was connected to a long hallway that led to mine and Greg's room, the second room down the hallway was my sister's bedroom, then the bathroom that was next to their room. To the right of the front room was my parents room. My sisters received collectable porcelain dolls for christmas from Ron and Bertha.

These vintage collectable dolls were creepy. They were adorned with old fashion dresses. My sisters and I would joke about how creepy they were. Several times they would tell us how when they left their room and returned, the dolls were in different positions. They lined the top of their dresser. There was one doll in particular that seemed really expensive, and it was taller than the rest. It was about 18 inches tall. It always felt like it was watching me. While the stories kept coming, I heard tiny little porcelain footsteps creep down the hall. "Shhh, do you hear that?" "What?" Tiny porcelain footsteps tapped down the hall. They made their way into the kitchen and stopped. The only thing between it and us was a love seat. Nobody moved. The quietness was only to be broken by four more footsteps skipping down the hall. I couldn't move, I was paralyzed with fear. Just as everybody else was. I had to remind myself to breathe, and even then I was controlling my breath to not make a noise. I didn't want to let them know where I was, and I avoided any movement. Once the other dolls reached the dolls in the kitchen, they stopped. They began to giggle and whisper, I couldn't make out what they were saying, but they're voices were that of little girls. The scariest part to me was that my mom and dad were completely silent. Even they didn't get up to flip the light switch on. Even they were terrified. Finally, my father yelled, "Mother fuckers go away!" We waited silently to hear a response. The level of fear doubled when they laughed at him and continued to whisper and giggle. They continued to run up and down the hall. We were helpless, all we could do was lay there.

Soon after we talked about throwing them away. My sisters consented to throwing them away. I grabbed the big doll and walked it to the trash can outside. The next day the doll was sitting on the dresser. Everyone swore they didn't collect her from the trash can, but there she was, sitting on the dresser smiling. I grabbed her, took her to the dumpster, and smashed her to pieces. She never returned. My sisters got rid of most of them, but there was a couple my mom insisted they keep. She explained they might be worth something. I didn't think it was important enough to keep. They stored them on the top shelf of their closet.

That wasn't the only doll phenomenon. They say that spirits can enter dolls, and I believe that to be true. One day my mom was home alone, all the kids were at school, and my dad was at work. She walked by the living room and there was a doll sitting on the floor as if it was a person, nothing was holding it up in a sitting position. It wasn't propped up against anything. It was a famous stuffed doll from the eighties. It was made of cloth and stuffing.

This doll was not made to sit, and it was stuffed and made to be in a standing position. To sit down, someone would have to be holding it and pushings it downward for the legs to fold. As she stared at it, it slowly turned its head towards her, and she ran back to her room.

Another day she was in the living room watching TV, and she saw a shadow approaching from behind. The living room picture window behind the couch, which was at her back, as well as the porch. The shadow looked as though it was walking up to the window which was right next to the living room door. She turned around, and there wasn't anyone to be found. She stood up and went to the door to peer out. Nobody was there. She turned to the TV and the shadow of a man's body got closer. She turned around, and again, there was nobody there. She turned off the TV, hoping it was the station having interference. And the Shadow was still there. As usual, she ran to her bedroom. Just because she made it to her bedroom, didn't always mean she was safe. There were times when something followed her to her room and sat on her bed. She could see an imprint of its body sitting on the comforter beside her.

Chapter III

I remember wanting to play tackle football, and asking my parents. I was one of the few 4 year olds glued to the television. I remember not being able to track the football on the TV screen, just the commotion around it. I remember my favorite team getting to the Super Bowl year after year, but not winning. The heartbreak of their failure. I remember the first year I was eligible, but unfortunately, my mother missed the sign up date. I would watch the boys geared up in their equipment walk past the window, and the heartbreak as I couldn't participate.

I never had a big brother growing up. The closest thing I had was a cousin who was 5 years older than me, his name is Marty. There were times we were inseparable. He was little for his age, but he was in great shape. I could never understand why he was the only person besides my dad who had never called me fat. Everyone had pointed it out as if I didn't realize. Even my mother would let one out when she was mad once in a while. He was Ariel's son, my mom's oldest sister. She had three kids. He was the oldest, and had a different father than the other two. Interesting family dynamics to say the least. He was raised by our grandmother Verna.

My mom's brother, my uncle Jordan, would babysit all of us once in a while. Sometimes my Aunt Audrey's two children,

Aubrey who was two years younger than me and Wanda, who was four years younger than me, would be over at the same time. Now that I am an adult, that scenario sounds like a babysitting nightmare, but he wouldn't win any awards for being uncle of the year. My cousin Marty's half brother and sister were Velma, who was a year older than me, and Arnold who was a few months younger than me. At times he would babysit ten children. That wasn't all my cousins on my mothers side. There are about 8 more first cousins, but we rarely are in the same place except on special occasions. However, the 10 of us were around each other often. Like I said, my uncle Jordan was not going to win an uncle of the year award. Sure he was funny and cool, that was the consensus. Not that I like lowriders, but he owned one. Not many other uncles could relate to the younger generation. How many other uncles would listen to Snoop, Dre, and Warren G at that time. Uncle Jordan was always funny, loud, the life of the party, not to mention brutally honest. When all the kids were together, and the other grown ups were gone he would make us fight. Separating us into two age groups. I was in a group of Marty who was five years older than me, Jesse who was three years older than me, Velma who was a year older than me but outweighed me by nearly 80 pounds, and Arnold who was close to me in age and size. 1 year made a huge difference in strength and development. The sad part is trying to fight someone who didn't want to fight you back. It's much easier defending yourself when someone is attacking, but I didn't feel comfortable fighting Arnold. He was sensitive. I learned a lot about fighting.

Not all my family was like that. My dad's brother, Uncle Shane, is awesome. He was like a second dad to me. He showed me what it was like to have an adult show you interest. In a family with so many children, it was hard to get quality attention from an adult. He would take Jesse and I on his motorcycle. I fell in love with motorcycles. Jesse had to ruin it for both of us after burning her leg on the exhaust pipe. I'm joking, and I did feel bad when she got hurt.

I was also thankful for my cousin Marty, but he had his downside like everyone does. He felt it necessary to toughen me up. He never called me fat, but he would say, "Alan, you need to get better at skills when you play football, you can't rely on your size to keep doing good." When we would play basketball in the park he would spot a kid younger than me, and brag on them. "You should be like that, he is two years younger than you and so much better." I should have let it motivate me like he intended, but all it did was make me hate basketball. We would play catch with a football out in the street. He was amazed at my ability to catch, and how if I needed to I would dive on the pavement to make a catch. One day he called his friend over from the end of the block to show him how I could catch. Jed was amazed. Jed was Marty's age, and full of bad influence. I remember him smoking joints often. That was more than 25 years ago, back before it was legal in our state. Jed thought I was cool, and I was too young to understand I didn't need his approval.

One day Marty was at my house, and Jed made his way down the street. I was staring at my bike. "How did your front rim get all jacked up?" I replied, "I tried popping a wheelie while riding up the curb." "Aww man that sucks." "Yeah, but the back tire is flat, I wouldn't be able to ride anyway." "What are you guys talking about?" Jed chimed in as he walked up. "Alan's bike is all jacked up." "We could fix it. Old man Johnson's yard is full of junk and old bicycles. I'll jump the fence and grab one, no problem." Before I could say anything he and Marty were walking to our neighbors house. We could have knocked on the door and asked to pay for a rim, but somehow, that never crossed our minds. The yard was jam packed with metal and many old bikes. Jed jumped the fence and before I knew it, he was climbing back over with a rim.

My bike was up and running an hour later. The sentiment was really nice, but we stole. As soon as my mom saw my bike, she was so thankful he helped me. "Where did you get that rim? Jed helped you put it together? That is so sweet. I need to pay him." "No mom, you don't have to do that." "Yes we do, he went out of his way to fix your bike. Get my purse" "No, mom, please." What could I say to not have her reward him. We stole, and now she was going to pay him. I can't let that happen. I had to tell her. "We stole the rim from Mr. Johnson's backyard." Mom did what most moms would do. She went and told Mr. Johnson, and Jeds parents. All I could do was just stare at the bike. It was so tainted that I couldn't ride it. Of course, my honesty wasn't making me popular with Jed and Marty. It spread through the family too. All my cousins would walk by me and say, "Snitch." My grandmother Verna, who was raising Marty, even had to give her opinion. Looking at me in shame as she talked to my mother, "He should take the rim off that bike, if he stole it. He is riding his bike like there is no problem, but he is willing to tell on the other boys." I was eight, the most I could do was unscrew the valve stem cap. I never rode that bike again.

Grandma Verna had a bias, and all us grandchildren could see it. She raised Marty as if he was her's, and an only child. He received all the special treatment. Even when I would go over to their house to have a sleepover with Marty, I felt like Marty's friend having a sleepover, not like another grandchild. Grandma Verna was sweet, and loved all of us, but there are about at least 18 first cousins. I also watched as my grandma Verna pitted her daughters against each other to win her love. Showing off a birthday present from my mom to her other children, and watching the competition unfold. How she would finish a phone conversation with aunt Audrey, and turn to aunt Ariel who was sitting right there, and gossip about everything Audrey had just told her. My mother had to see it too. She had to know that as soon as she left she would do the same, but a child doesn't stop loving their parents, and still yearn for their approval. She had her good moments. She bought me my first football helmet the following year because we could not afford it.

Jed and Marty would get their revenge. They played on my weakness. Marty knew that I missed the sign up date for football. One afternoon he said, "Hey do you want to go play football? Jed has pads, here you can use these." He handed me a golden football helmet that looked like it belonged to a kicker from the 50's, and a pair of shoulder pads. I couldn't wait. I didn't hesitate. I got dressed and we headed to Jed's house. Jed had his gear on and was standing in the middle of his yard. I was impressed, he had an actual jersey over his pads, and actual football pants with pads in them. He looked even bigger than normal. He was big for his age. He was around 13 years old and he was at least 5'10" and 220 lbs. Definitely not all muscle, but still a big teenager. I walked to the grass and Marty tossed me the football. I caught it, and looked to Jed to see what's next. The crown of his helmet was already under my chin as the plastic of his helmet struck my chin and throat. I didn't know my body could do a backbend into a flip, and I didn't have to move a muscle. There is something that happens to a young boy when playing football. If the boy is lucky he gets a stinger early into playing. A stinger is where someone hits you just right and hard enough to make your arm go numb. Maybe hard enough to knock your breath out, or to see a scrambled TV channel for a second when your head gets hit. It's not good to have any of those happen, but it is probably better that it happens early into playing. This lets one decide if they want to continue playing. The person either responds in three ways. One; they get up and try just as hard, or even harder. Two; they begin to play gentilly. Going to the ground before getting hit, avoiding contact. Three; they decide football is not for them.

I have always had a high tolerance for pain. I noticed years prior when Marty and Jesse would make me always be the seeker, while playing hide and seek. I don't ever remember hiding. If they had to seek, they would get irritated and stop playing. When I would find them they would punch me in the stomach. I usually didn't react, and they continued until I reacted or they got bored.

Jed got his revenge. Jed looked at me from the ground wondering if I was going to get back up with a grin on his face. He only tackled me once and a bead of sweat streaked down his red hair that peeked out from his forehead. It trickled to his pale freckled face. I stood up, and before I could pick up the ball he hit me again. It was an endless cycle of me standing up, and him demolishing me with his man size body. At one point there was not even a ball to be found. After 15 minutes of getting my teeth kicked in, the walk back to my house was quiet as Marty and I walked back, I wasn't going to let him see me cry, and I was too exhausted to even try to cry.

A month later Marty was at my house, "Hey, do you want to play outside?" "Ok." Were out there for a couple of minutes and a kid Marty's age was walking by with his younger brother. Marty had a football in his hand, "You guys want to play football?" Finally, a game. There were four of us, and I wasn't smart enough to see that Marty was standing on the side of the yard along with his little brother. Or see the pattern of what had just happened. The kid was not nearly as heavy as Jed, but just as tall and athletic. Marty Tossed me the ball and, all too familiar, I felt the back of my head touch my back as he hit me with such force that it sent him into a front handspring. Eventually my body caught up to my head that was folded under both of us. This time I didn't have an option to hold in the tears, they were instant. I got up and ran into the house crying as I choked on the dirt. Marty remarked, "At least you held onto the football, you didn't fumble."

I had to be punished for being a snitch. Sometime later Marty was at my house and our parents were gone. Jesse, Maggie, Greg, and Anne were there. Marty was fascinated with a lighter he had just found. He was sitting on the top step of the stairs that led to the basement. I was sitting a step below him. He dangled a pom pom strand over an ash-tray as he watched the flame melt the strand to a blue liquid. All a sudden he reached his arms out to drip the residue on my wrist. I screamed as the blue puddle sizzled my skin. I couldn't wipe it off with my other hand, the blue liquid was still hotter than wax. I still have a scar on my wrist 30 years later. After he apologized, to not get in trouble, he invited us downstairs. He brought with him the glass ashtray, and a few birthday candles. He lit them and set them in the center of the ash-tray. Then he started lighting twisted paper towels. He lit one thing after another. Finally, the ash-tray shattered into three pieces from the heat. Marty collected everything and threw the ash-tray in the trash. He didn't do a good job of hiding the remnants. All the kids were called upstairs to discuss what had happened. My aunt Ariel and my mom glared at us. "Tell us what happened to the ashtray. All the kids stayed quiet. Nobody spoke up. Finally my mom said, "Alan will tell us. Alan what happened?" Of course, I couldn't lie, "We were lighting candles in the ashtray, and it got too hot, and then it broke." My mother grinned at her sister with pride. I'm glad she was happy, she just painted another target on my back.

My family was and is very dysfunctional. We were the most normal, if there is such a thing. Maybe, the most stable out of all our family. Perhaps that is why I don't associate with family, except my immediate family, and even that can be challenging at times.

One day we were in a pool and everyone had gotten out except for my third cousin Natalie who was my age, and Anne who was three years old. She was sitting in a floating baby inner tube. It had a baby seat attached which kept her from sliding through the innertube. I walked back outside to see what the commotion was. I could see Anne's feet kicking, the intertube still secure around her waist. She was completely upside down and stuck in a way that she could not pull her legs out of the inner tube seat. Natalie was pointing and laughing hysterically. I ran over and dove into the pool, and flipped her right side up. I looked at Natalie and she was still laughing like a psychopath. I'm surprised none of us kids died, or ended up being severely debilitated.

Jesse learned a lot from Marty. My mom's cousin introduced her to gambling in the form of bingo. Another good thing to add to the list of trauma growing up. The more I share my story, the more common I find it that almost all people have grown up with some form of trauma, whether its Abuse, sexual abuse, drugs, alcohol or some form of trauma. All of those disgusting things have touched too many lifes. If one can say they have never experienced those, that's wonderful, that is the way it should be. When my mom went to bingo, it left us with three unadulterated hours. Me and my younger siblings had to endure Jesse's wrath. My father would be at work, and my mom would be at Bingo.

This was the time we were to spend cleaning, or cooking dinner so it would be ready when mom and dad would get home. We spent twenty minutes doing chores and Jesse and I spent the rest of the time fist fighting. I never wanted to fight, but it was my obligation to protect the younger kids from her. She loved to pick on the younger kids. I remember the first time I was able to beat her in a fight. She quickly learned that her time of torment was over. She turned to me and said, "Let's pick on the little kids." I stopped dead in my tracts. I hesitated, and stood there thinking, what just happened. Maggie was quick to remind me that I always helped them, and fought for them as she screamed and walked away crying. That was all I needed. Jesse's time of torment was over, at least while I was around. Sometimes my mom would pick one of us to take to bingo. It was a nice way to get quality time with a parent. Quality time is difficult when your father works a lot, and your mom has five children. I enjoyed going with her, and every once in a while I would win. After going, I realized that when I was gone, Jesse was picking on the little kids. Eventually, I chose to stop going, I didn't want to live with that guilt.

Chapter IV

As I have mentioned before, I was overweight, but that wasn't for lack of trying. I was always playing sports or riding my bike. I was faster than most of the boys and girls in my class. I made it a point to stay outside, and to run, and play to lose weight. I would come in after dark and plop on the couch because my legs and feet hurt. I remember I couldn't wait to get home for a reprieve, a reprieve from kids at school calling me fat. Eventually, I was accepted for my athletic abilities, my size was overlooked, and I made a lot of friends. School became a good place to be. Things at home became the place of disappointment, and completely flip flopped with school. I now yearned to be at school, and hated being at home. My father had been honorably discharged from the Army roughly nine years at that point in my life, and like many soldiers, the military leaves its mark on the former soldier in the form of alcoholism. Many reasons they pick up the bottle, Boordom, nothing else to do, or unhealthy coping skills. However, it became worse and worse. He began beating my mother.

One night it was really bad. Drunk, he started in, and I felt like I had to intervene. I ran and tackled him, and between my mom, Jesse and I we hog tied him with the telephone cord. After that event, my father stopped drinking for a long time, things got better, and we moved past it. The devil moves in gentilly, so you compromise and say it's not hurting anybody. Gambling doesn't seem too bad, people say they have a handle on it, look how much strife it caused my brother and sisters. You don't have to gamble away your house to be hurt by it. Alcoholism hurts families who don't refrain. Look at all the people who have been hurt by it, their loved ones killed by drunk drivers. The point is; all sin is gateway sin. Don't ever compromise, if you compromise with the devil, you lose a little bit of your soul each moment that passes, because he is a liar. He works in patterns and cycles as well. The addiction can get better, and then before you know it you're wallowing in vomit again. He has the same hand of cards, and will play them over and over, and break us down. Whomever has perseverance will overcome, the beauty is, we have Christ to replenish us daily, cling to Jesus Christ.

I am not proud of anything I have shared thus far, but in my humiliation, I share to help others to recognize sin/the devil, and fight back. My father has many good qualities. I can share many bad things about my family or parents, but the truth is; there are many good things too. Even when most of my family was confused and trying to search for different churches, My dad held fast, and brought us back to our church. He had many metals and accomplishments from the military, he gave a lot of his metals to his friends. I would listen to his stories with admiration. I wanted to be just like him. I wanted to be a soldier. Time after time he would say, "Don't be like me, go to college, don't join the Army." One night he was tucking me in, "Dad, I don't want to be like you, I'll go to college." That night I probably broke my dad's heart, but the truth of the matter is that I did want to, I just wanted to assure him that I wanted to make him proud. It wasn't the only time I put my foot in my own mouth, and wasn't the last.

As I have said before my mother with her illness was unable to hold a job due to her illness, her muscles would give out after physically exerting herself. She couldn't drive well. Her eyes would need to be propped open, and only one would be able to focus causing depth perception problems. I prayed for years, and so fervently. I asked God to heal her illness, and could not understand why he wouldn't. I prayed every night, and did so for twenty years before I gained knowledge.

Life got better for me. I was now in the seventh grade. I still wasn't happy with my chubby body. I resorted to anything possible, which can be an unhealthy way to resort to working out. I asked my mom for a weight bench, and she said I shouldn't lift weights until I am 13 years old. I was very impressionable, and took her words to heart, just like the wise-tale that picking up frogs will cause warts. Obviously it was not true, as I know now. Boys can start lifting younger than that if they have a proper coach to instruct proper form. It was only one year away, I thought to myself. I started doing natural exercise like push-ups and sit-ups. I was able to work myself to sets of 100 for push ups, and 1000 crunches. Before I knew it, it was a year later, and I received my bench press and weights, one of the best gifts I had received. I hit the weights hard, and started running at least six miles a day. Along with the exercise, I developed an eating disorder. I realized I was shedding weight, and realized it was easier if I was doing all these exercises and only eating one meal a day. My parents became concerned. They tried to talk to me about the danger of my actions, and I did what most teenagers would do, ignored them. It wasn't until my grandmother Verna had sought me out to have a serious conversation, that I changed my behavior. My parents must have asked her to speak with me. I think I responded to her concern because of the third party perspective, rather than listening to my two authority figures.

I eventually got the body I wanted. Everything came together at once. I didn't completely understand it then but it all started when My mom took me and Arnold to Catechism classes. It was amazing, they taught us about God, prayers, scripture, and routinely got a chance to play basketball in the gym. Father Michael was such a good guy. He looked at my necklace that I could not be separated from. My mother gave it to me. It was a crucifix on a gold chain. I treasured it. A disturbing thought, but I guarded it with my life. I was worried my mother would die at an early age from her illness. That necklace was the object I would treasure the most, and it would be the object by which I would remember her." Can I see your necklace?" Father Michael asked. "Yes." I replied as I handed it over. "Interesting," he said as he turned it over. "Bethlehem, that's really cool," as he read the inscription on the back. Father Michael would leave a huge impression on my life forever. Life became too hectic to continue taking me and Arnold to class, but it was not in vain. God gave me that short amount of time one of the greatest gems one can find, just after finding Jesus Christ as one's savior. Father Michael said, "I'm going to give you all something very important. It's a gift, but there is a stipulation. You have to promise me that you are going to use it at least once a week." We all agreed to the stipulation as he handed us out our own personal Rosary. Many Christians would gasp at the Rosary. "Doesn't God say, you shouldn't be caught up in repetitive prayer. Don't worship saints, you shouldn't wear a Rosary." To all the naysayers I say this; When the disciples asked Jesus, *"Lord teach us to pray, as John taught his disciples." Luke 11:1.* What did he say? He recited The Our Father. Jesus didn't say, "Say this prayer once and only once, for I don't want you to get caught up in repetitive prayer." If you have said The Our Father more than once, you have repeated it. To set the story straight, true devout Catholics don't worship saints. They honor them. They were an example on earth, so when someone says, "I'm not perfect, Jesus was, I can't be like him, he made me this way, I'm allowed to sin so I can't repent." These saints are living proof of God's grace, that even though we are not perfect, we can do miraculous things through our Savior. We ask saints to pray for us, as Christians ask each other. Moses is a saint, and was a mediator for the jews. Now we have Jesus as our mediator. Much is said about the prayer of a just man, there are plenty of supporting scriptures about the prayer of saints in heaven, and even in The Book of Job. Job was told to pray for his friends by God himself, because his prayer is different from his friends.

We just believe the saints have a little more pull since they are already with the Big Man upstairs. Catholics don't worship Mary. We honor her, as she is the second Tabernacle, the second Arch of the covenant, She held The Bread of life in her Whom, Do you hear Christians criticize the Jews for carrying around the original Ark of the Covenant. If another unknowing tribe of people seen the Jews carrying around the Arch of the Covenant like God instructed them, they certainly would assume that box was their God as they had directed a select people to carry it, and a special cloth tent or veil, made for it, and directed only a select people to carry the veil. The hierarchy goes, Father, Son, Holy Spirit, which is the Holy Trinity, and One God with three parts. All that is important is that Jesus is the Lord and Savior, If anyone believes anything else they will spend their life searching for the peace that God brings, and never have that empty hole fulfilled.

Even the wisest Evangelists still get this wrong. They preach about the differences between each Chrisrian sect. And sects are dangerous. Let me explain it to you from the devil's perspective. The devil knows that he can not prosper against unity. If all the Christian religions combined their focus on the devil rather than each other, he would be in a world of hurt. He knows that if all the militants are fighting each other, they are not fighting the common enemy, him. That is why Saint Paul explained the body of Christ, and how it has all its parts. Starting from the heart, which was Judaism, which is the start of man's relationship with God. Christians and Jewish should realize, we are all worshiping the same God. Catholicism has a long history of corruption and isn't perfect, but it is the fullness of Christianity. It is run by man, and men sin, just like every Christian Church has some form of corruption. By God's Grace and Majesty he reaches people bypassing the corruption, and the Church stands proclaiming the Gospel, growing year after year. There are only two sides, Good and Evil, God or the devil.

I have seen many fruits of the Rosary. I started praying it once a week. It only takes 20-30 minutes to complete, and I have seen it do countless miracles. One can write volumes of books about just about one topic, the Rosary. It is the Apex spiritual weapon. It is the spiritual sword as it reestablishes the Word of the Lord. It is a spiritual assault rifle in my opinion. It has power, so some who practice santeria use it in a ceremony. Obviously, if it can be used for good, the devil will use it for evil. For Christians speak in tongues, and devil worshipers speak in demonic tongues. Evil mirrors good. There is a Holy hour observed by Catholics when Jesus died on the Cross at 3:00 P.M., and Evil has their hour at 3:00 A.M. One should not wear a Rosary for jewelry. The person wearing a Rosary is in prayer, so if sinning, they are condemning themselves. Even some Catholics don't know the exact rules of wearing a Rosary. Some orders of priests and nuns wear Rosaries, as they should. It's a great way to evangelize. So there is much good from the Rosary which then points to Christ from his mother's eyes. It has changed my life, and is the most important devotion besides taking part in the Eucherist, and adoration of the Eucherist. After starting this devotion I lived in bliss. I had never felt so wholesome. Every day brought a perfect day, I had so many perfect days I didn't remember what a bad day felt like anymore. I was completely happy. I realized that; one can't have bliss without knowing what a bad day felt like. Even though a bad day is most unpleasant, still, it has a meaningful purpose.

I realized that Rosary helped me detach from all the things that made me fat. Not just food, but all the junk food I was consuming, and it worked. I gave up pop for lent, and never started drinking it again. I was shocked how people treated me after shedding all the fat. Not only did girls treat me better, but males treated me better than ever, and people instantly respected me, even strangers. It was eye opening. I was now in eighth grade, and things were good at home and at school.

Our first day of school, we were to report to the auditorium. It was electric, everyone was ecstatic to be there. Teenagers don't always know how to channel excitement appropriately, we got out of hand. The teacher on the stage trying to orchestrate our schedules couldn't get a word in. The ambiance of the chatter only got louder as she tried to speak with the microphone. She began to get louder, but so did the laughter. Defeated, she let the hand holding the mic drop, as she looked around in desperation. The auditorium roared even louder. A man walked up to the lady, grabbed the microphone, and began to yell, "Give her some respect! She is up here trying to help you!" His face was beat red. The entire auditorium went silent. Who was this guy? None of us had ever seen him before, was he our new principal? Whomever he was, we all knew not to mess with him. He meant business. After getting our schedules we went to our homeroom. I looked at my schedule, math seventh hour. The day went by pretty fast and I was already walking into the last hour of the day. Guess who I see standing at the blackboard. The guy from the assembly, he was calm and a little less red than earlier. Great, this guy was my teacher, lucky me. "Grab a seat, I'm Mr. Bernard. According to testing, you kids are the cream of the crop. I have been chosen to roll out an algebra for the eighth grade. Other schools have been doing this for years, and it's our turn to get an early start." The school I was enrolled in was ghetto. I didn't have to worry so much this year, but the past two years I had to keep my head on a swivel. When I went to school I had to be prepared to fight. One thing I learned was, a bully gets tired of picking on you when you constantly defend yourself. If they see a weakness, or you let them, they will continue to own you.

Algebra was a difficult subject, but I liked math, so I wasn't too worried about it. That changed really quick. The Math assignments took me an average of three to four hours. They brought me to tears every night. My parents tried to help, but they couldn't help. Mr. Bernard created a study hall on Saturdays to give us extra help. I attended but still needed at least three hours for my math homework. After talking to him about my struggles with the homework he asked me, "How are things coming along, is it taking more than three hours to do your homework?" I didn't want him to think it wasn't helping his Saturday study, so I lied to him, "Yeah, it takes me about two hours." I hated lying, but I felt awful. Mr. Bernard created a chess club, and I didn't hesitate to join. He ended up being one of my favorite teachers. He was strict, but the most influential teacher I had ever had.

Before I knew it, Christmas break was approaching. The last few days before break were fun. In class we would just watch movies or play games. My friends and I were huddled up in a circle. Mr. Bernard walked by, "That is so cool. I told the principal I wanted to watch this program, and he is playing it for us on the school TV." Meanwhile me and the fellas were deep into an interesting game of truth or dare. The girls had their game going on. Last hour Malinda had planted a soft peck on my check. I didn't know how to react, so I played it cool, and kept a poker face.

Inside I was jumping for joy. I had liked this girl for the past three years. I would have never asked her in sixth or seventh grade, but this year, I would ask her out at any opportunity. This year I had confidence, which probably stemmed from me being comfortable in my own body for once. The opportunity never arose, and she was back and forth between the two same guys. As soon as she would break up with one, she would be right back with the other.

Our game was getting interesting. My friend Von chose dare. It was my turn to figure out what his dare would be. "Next time Mr. Bernard comes around, you have to ask him where babies come from." The guys chuckled, Von shook his head and he thought it was a stupid dare. Here came Mr. Bernard, right into the trap. "Mr. Bernard, can I ask you a question?" "Shoot." "Where do babies come from?" Without hesitation and with the best poker face one could have, he replied, "Babies are a gift from God." "No, but I mean, where do they come from?" "Each baby is a miracle, and a gift from God." The fun was taken right out of all our faces, and he could probably tell. We were not going to embarrass him, or play him for a fool. Back in that time a teacher could reference God without being afraid of getting fired. He always gave us such sound advice. He was in the special forces, and retired from the military, he knew how to handle us. Even though he was a math teacher he gave us pearls of wisdom. Some of it was directly from the military. "Don't ever trap yourself in. When you enter a room, find all the exits. Make sure there is always a way out." Some of this advice may have stemmed from a little PTSD, we all knew he had fought in a war, if not several.

A kid asked a question while he was switching the projector sheet. "I bet you don't know the football player with the most receptions?" Mr. Bernard replied with the correct answer. "You don't know everything though? Who was the first peanut salesman in the football league?" "Stanley West." All of our jaws dropped.

How in the world did he know that? The classroom was amazed in silence. "If you reply with a direct answer, keep a straight face, and show confidence, anyone will believe you." He explained.

The game of truth and dare was getting interesting. Now it was my turn. I'll be brave, school is almost over and there is only two minutes left in class. It was the seventh hour too, so there was just enough time to knock out a dare and go onto Christmas vacation. My friend Doug was going to dish me out a dare. There was a group of four of us. Doug was the one friend I considered my best friend. He was funny, and cool. We played football together. "You have to grab Karen's boob." "That's crazy, I'm not doing that." "Yes, you have to, you chose dare." Everyone laughed. The bell rang and I was home free. I got out of that one. I was so relieved.

Christmas break was over and we were getting right back into the swing of being back at school. We were at lunch and Doug was focused on me. Hey Alan you have to finish your dare. "No, I'm not doing that. Have you been worrying about that over break?" "You just have to finish what you promised to do." "No." We were at that awkward phase in life where we would get done with lunch, and have to decide if we wanted to play basketball, which we did, or stand around and BS, and act cool. If we stood around and talked, we wouldn't be all sweaty, and it would give us time to flirt with the girls. We were standing around in a circle talking. There was a group of popular girls sitting on a bench partially in the circle deep in conversation. Her Doug came, "Hey you have to do your dare." He would not stop, constantly in my ear, and I just started to ignore him.

The more he said it, the more the girls on the bench started to listen. "Shut up Doug." The girls didn't know about the dare, but they were tuning into our conversation. Karen was a teacher's pet. She was the type of kid that would remind the teacher that they didn't assign us homework, and then the teacher would pile on the homework. She was nice, but always needed attention from the teacher. She wasn't ugly, just annoying. Earlier that year she had asked me to one of the dances, the dance where the girls ask the guys. I politely said no, but I felt bad. It had to be more embarrassing for her. She was nice, and I was a stupid teenager that cared what other people thought, and I truly didn't like her. "Come on, just do it," Doug said, he was relentless. Just at that time Karen came strolling up. Doug shoved me towards her, he wasn't going to stop. I instinctively put my hand out, and with an upward motion I touched her boob. It didn't help that she wasn't wearing a bra. She shoved me away and stormed off. Everybody burst out into laughter and then tears. I felt horrible, I couldn't imagine how awful she felt. Doug gripped onto me as if his legs couldn't support his weight and he couldn't hold back the tears.

Later that day I was in class, when the counselor sent for me. "Come in," she said, "grab a seat." I knew what was about to happen. We were going to talk about what had just happened with Karen. I didn't know what to say. "So I brought you here to ask you about Karen. She told me that you touched her." What was I going to say? Right, I'll tell her that she liked me, and I didn't return her advancements. It was partially true, could it work? It was the only way out of this. I'll tell her that she was angry, because I didn't like her back, so she made up this story. As soon as those words left my mouth, I felt awful. She could tell I was lying. "Have a seat in the office. I walked to a chair outside of her office. What was going to happen next?

Into the office walked Doug. The counselor sent for him. Whew, great he'll have my back. He surely isn't stupid enough to tell me, and himself. All he had to do was deny it, he didn't see anything. After only a couple of minutes the door opened, and He walked out smiling. What is going on here, he looks happy.

"Thank you Doug, I appreciate you being honest with me." He walked back out of the office. "Alan, can you come back into my office?" She sat down with a stern look on her face. "Have a seat. I don't appreciate you lying to me. Doug told me everything." Did he tell you it was his idea? Did he tell you he harped on me until I finally broke down through peer pressure? Did he tell you that he is a traitor? I sat there in silence. "You can go back to your class, I will call your parents." In shame I walked back to class. On the way out of the office Von ran into me. "What are you doing here?" Von was an office aide during that hour. "I had to talk to the counselor about what happened with Karen." As I told him I could feel the tears well up. "Are you in trouble?" "I don't know." Just then Melinda walked up, great, don't cry, don't cry. "What are you guys doing?" Melinda was also an office aide this hour. I walked back to class as the tears filled up my eyes, and Von filled in Melinda.

I walked out of the school in shock of everything that happened that day. The van pulled up. Weird, all the kids had been picked up already, and both of my parents were in the van. It started to make sense as I closed the van door, and my mother started to speak. "You sick son of a bitch!" That's not an ideal choice of curse words. It doesn't paint you in a good light, I thought to myself. I wouldn't dare say anything like that, I don't want my face beat in. "I had to go to the office and argue with the principal to not suspend you. I had to argue that you are a straight A student, but you're a little pervert. If you want to grab a girls breast, get a girlfriend you sick little fucker." She was right, it was awful. At the time I felt bad, but I can't imagine what Karen was feeling, and Karen's parents. Karen's parents probably wanted to find me and hurt me, and they would have been justified. As soon as the van pulled into our driveway, I walked to my bedroom and layed on the bed. I wanted to die. I wanted to disappear and never be seen again.

After a few hours of solitude, my father walked into my room. I was laying on my belly in silence staring at the wall. "Hey, I know you feel bad, and you feel like it's the end of the world, but it's not. Soon enough this won't feel like it does now. We just want you to be safe, and if you are with a girl, you are safe," He walked out of my room, and I felt better instantly. I was able to show my shameful face outside of my bedroom. I couldn't believe Doug, he verbally berated me until I did what he wanted, and then he easily stabbed me in the back, and he never got in trouble. Maybe they don't know that he was the one daring me to do it, but either way he left the office smiling, no guilt for betraying a friend. If I would have been honest, he wouldn't have had to betray me, but at least I knew how loyal he was to me. It made my transition to high school easier. I would attend a different high school than all the kids at that middle school.

Chapter V

Eighth grade went by with a flash just like life does. One interesting thing happened at school besides the introduction of bell bottoms, in the form of Janco pants. We had a food fight. We were eating lunch, and I was just about finished, when groups of kids started standing up throughout the cafeteria. "Food fight!" someone screamed. Von and I stood up and looked at each other. "I don't feel like getting hit with any food." "Me neither." We ran to the hall, and the food started to fly. A couple of my friends didn't fare so well. One of them got a scratched cornea from a chicken nugget, and the other a banana pepper in the eye. Sounds like I'm making it up, but it was so ridiculous, it's true. The principal questioned everyone. Anyone who was witnessed throwing food was suspended. Five people were suspended, Melinda was one of five. The school year came to an end, and it came with such sadness, as I knew I would not see these friends again. They were off to Central, and I was off to East, as that was right where we lived, and it would be easier for my parents to not have to drive all the way across town to drop us off or pick us up. I was sad I would not see Melinda every school day. Extending the olive branch I asked Karen if she wanted to sign my yearbook. She signed her name and wrote, "Sorry for being such a bitch." I was sad that she felt like she needed to apologize, to me, I was the one who was way out of line.

Before I knew it I was in highschool. The summer leading into highschool I was worried about getting into football, and summer weightlifting. One morning I walked to the school and into the office. "Where do I need to go for summer workouts with the football team?" I asked the school secretary. "They are out there now. You can go join them. It's right out the side of the building in the portable gym, you'll hear a lot of racket, just let yourself in." I made my way there. The door to the portable gym was cracked open with a ten pound weight. I let myself in. There were only five people in the gym. Three lanky guys, and one really tall hefty guy, and one older man. I walked up to him and introduced myself and said I was excited to start practicing and lifting weights with the team. He looked at me a little puzzled and replied, "Hi I'm coach Smith. We meet here around nine, and I open the gym on Tuesdays and Thursdays." "OK, sounds good, thank you." I was still puzzled, was this summer work out not mandatory, and if so, why was there only four people. He said he was the coach, so I guess he is just really lax with his players. It was kind of a lazy work out for them. Barely any energy, no instruction from the coach, and they only did a couple of things and sat around. The summer came to an abrupt end.

One day I went to the gym, and nobody was there. I told myself I'll try tomorrow on a Wednesday. Sure enough I could hear that there were many people in the gym today. The boombox was cranked up playing rock and roll. A guy answered the door. "Can I help you?" This guy was ripped, and looked like a bodybuilder. "I wanted to workout with the football team, my name is Alan." "I'm coach Blaine, the Varsity football coach. Why haven't you come all summer?" "I have." "I haven't seen you." "I've been coming all summer with coach Smith." He looked puzzled. Later I learned that Coach Smith was the track coach, and everything started to make sense.

I walked into the gym and started looking at the equipment, I could see a distinct age difference in some of the guys. you can tell the freshman from the upperclassmen. All the freshmen seem to have a shaved head. I fit right in, a few weeks prior, my sister tried to give me a haircut and failed drastically. The only way to cover up the mistake was to get a buzz cut. As I was sitting in the chair Victor and Marty were laughing and pointing at my haircut. For whatever reason my mom said, "what are you guys laughing at? You're next." We all got buzzcuts. Marty decided to do a haircut he had been wanting to try. At that time there were a couple of teenagers walking around with one of the stupidest hairstyles ever. Marty left his bangs. He parted them down the middle, and it looked like a mustache right on his forehead. He must have liked it. He repeated the hairstyle for over a couple of years.

Apparently, all the freshmen football players were hazed by the upperclassmen during the summer workouts. One of the things they did was to shave their head bald, then drove the Freshman to a prairie so they could walk home. By the looks of my haircut, the upperclassman assumed I had already been hazed. It was a definite silver lining. One of the freshmen pointed out my haircut and knew that it wasn't from hazing. He replied that I must wear my hair like that. One of the upperclassmen had his own hazing. He made sure every freshman got a swirly from him. School toilets aren't as deep as I thought, but anyone in their right mind wouldn't voluntarily stick their head in a toilet. It was kind of nice that all the other freshmen had a haircut like mine, it made me feel part of the team, and it made it a lot easier to wash my head After I was forced to get a swirly.

Our freshman football team was very small, we had 13 kids. Our freshman coach constantly preached that no one can get hurt, as if it was a choice. It didn't help that one of the boys on the football team was developmentally delayed. The one game that stuck out the most was when we played the rival team. This team was the high school where all my middle school friends went. The game took a turn for the worst. Two people got hurt, one was the special Ed kid, and the quarterback. Our backup quarterback went in and got her as well. The coach called a timeout, "Alan, you're going to be the quarterback. You're going to be in a shotgun. when you hike the ball, pick an open Lane and run." That was the first time the Wildcat offense had made an appearance as far as I know. I got in place, reached my hands out, and Yelled hike. The ball hit my hands and I dropped back. I looked for the first receiver and he was open, but he never looked back. I looked to the second receiver and he was open but he never looked back. None of the receivers were looking back so I dodged the first defender. I broke the tackle of the second Defender and the 3rd and 4th. I scrambled around the pocket and nobody would look back and then the pocket collapsed and I got sacked. The coach called another time out, and ran to the huddle. "Alan, I told you to get in the shotgun position, hike the ball, pick a lane and run the ball." "Sorry."

I got back in the position, and yelled hike. I found an open Lane and ran for fifteen yards. The next play, the same thing for 20 yards. Our team had never moved the ball this consistently. The quarter came to an end. The coach called me to the sideline, "do you think you can throw?" "Yes." "Okay I want you to pick a receiver and throw it to him." The next play, I dropped back and threw it to the flank, and the receiver picked up 15 yards. This was amazing for us as a team. All season we never scored a touchdown. For the first time we were moving the ball up and down the field. It was the funnest game I ever played. It felt like I was playing a video game. There was no other feeling like it. The next day at practice the coach had me take snaps as the quarterback. The shoulderpads I had been checked out were at least ten years old and every time I stepped back to throw a pass, it was a little off. The coach shook his head. I was too shy to speak up. I should have taken off my shoulder pads, and showed him how I could throw, or asked for a pair of shoulder pads made for quarterbacks, they are made for full range of motion for the arm. I wasn't a good advocate for myself, and that ended my time as the quarterback.

Home life was great, it was the best it had ever been. My dad finally landed a stable, well paying job at a steel mill. We applied for a loan for a house. It was something we had been praying for a long time. In the process of closing on the house, the steel mill went on a strike. The employees were exhausted and frustrated with management. They would constantly force overtime. The crew would work a twelve hour shift, and be forced to stay another four hours whenever management felt it necessary. They would make the crew come in on their days off if orders came in. My father didn't care, he was delighted to get the overtime. It was the best paying job he ever had. He was faced with a decision to cross the picket line. He could cross and become what the union members called a scab, or strike. If he crossed he would continue to make good money. If he remained on strike with the union he would show loyalty. It was a difficult position to be in, but especially for only having worked there for a few months.

He weighed out the pros and cons. The pros for crossing were: Making consistent money for his family, all the overtime he wants, moving up in learning higher paying positions, and loyalty to the company. The cons for crossing were; unknown whether he would have a job if the strike ended. The union was pushing for all the scabs to be fired when they returned to work, and they made sure to put it into their negotiation contract, getting your car destroyed, getting death threats from union members on you and your family.

The union members had a list of all the employee's addresses, and emergency contacts. Pueblo is one of the most deceivingly ruthless small towns in America. It has ties to the mafia in the past. It has the highest teenage pregnancy, highest crime per capita, and the highest number of liquor stores per population, coupled with an opiate crisis, and a couple of providers that prescribe pain meds without reserve, The union members would throw eggs, and paint thinner on the vehicles as they drove into work. These union guys took it personally, and it's hard not too when it's your livelihood. My dad decided not to cross the picket line. The good part was that the union members paid a union due every pay day, and there was a huge fund to cover times like these. Unfortunately, the union board members were corrupt and cutting extra checks to the buddies. Each union member would walk into the union office to show statements of their bills, and get a check written to cover their bills. Because my father had only been a member for months, they would only give him a check for the mortgage, and complained about it. Some guys were getting two mortgage checks a month. Some ended up paying off their houses early. There was a lot of improper allocation of funds happening.

We were still blessed, and doing well. My father had to find another job in the meantime until the strike ended. We ended up getting the house of our dreams. My mother had been having nightmares about a certain house. In her nightmares she was being chased up a winding staircase. Surprisingly enough, the house we bought had four levels. There were four flights of stairs, and were like stairs in her dreams. The house offered us nearly enough for everybody to have their own room. Only Jesse and Maggie would share, and Jesse was in twelfth grade, so she would be moving out soon. The house was perfect, and it didn't feel like reality. The house had an inground swimming pool. We closed on the house on Friday, and we were to get the keys on Monday. Mom was concerned about our house, it was the first time we had something valuable that was ours. She was worried people would break in through the doggy door and vandalize. She said, "You, Greg, and Fred need to spend the weekend there, and protect the house. "One of you will crawl in through the doggy door, and let the other two in." Fred was Jesse's boyfriend. He was cool, and really fun to hang out with. "Mom, isn't that breaking and entering?" "No, we own the house, we're just waiting for the new keys from the realtor." "Ok, that sounds fun," We'll be the first to sleep in our new house, I thought to myself, even though it felt like a bad idea.

We made the most of it. We put a king size mattress on the floor and bunked out. We rented *The Blair Witch Project,* and camped out. At that time *The Blair Witch Project* was believed to be real, the World Wide Web was not what it is today. For years people believed that movie was a true story. After watching that movie as was our tradition, we started telling our personal ghost stories. We were in the family room. It had a big fireplace that stretched all the way across the room. To the right was the sliding glass door that we had propped open. The sliding screen door was closed, but we felt secure the way the house was built. Right outside of the sliding door was a big screened in patio that had another screen door that was locked. As the lights were off, Greg, Fred and I began telling ghost stories. I could not stop looking at the ceiling fan I was laying under. It looked like the human stick figures from *The Blair Witch Project*. As the stories went on we heard a noise on the back patio that jolted us into silence. It stopped making noise. "Did you hear that?" Greg whispered. We lay there puzzled, we made it a point to lock the outer patio door earlier that day. It had two locks, a sliding lock, and hook and latch lock, and both were checked before we started the movie. The only way onto the patio was if something walked right passed us in the family room onto the patio. I was a foot away from the sliding glass door, and nothing passed me. Then we heard it again and it wasn't a question that it was on the inside of the screened in patio. The silhouette of its figure appeared on the sliding glass door as it blotted out the moonlight. Its back was nearly three feet tall, and as it ran by, it oinked. We lay there stunned, none of us dared to say a word as the pig snarled and ran by again. There was no way any of us could doubt it was there, and we were in awe of how it could get inside a locked patio. The house was in city limits without any type of rural farm life. In fact, it was and still is illegal to have farm animals inside of city limits. We ran to the door and closed the sliding glass door, and locked it. It ran by again. The night took forever to come to an end. I layed there praying for the sunlight to come up. We layed in silence until the sun rose, and we were able to get some sleep. In the morning it was gone. There was no way it could have let itself out. There were no droppings to be found.

Ironically, mom had a recurrent dream before we got that house. Her dream always repeated a recurring theme of running down the stairs in the dark with something chasing her. She ran down one flight of stairs as she noticed that there were mirrors everywhere. She turned left and randown another flight of stairs, and saw another full size mirror. Then she turned left and ran down another flight of stairs. Her dream continued to show her the same thing. The first time we saw the house we fell in love with it. It was a four story home. As soon as one entered the front door, they were in the living room. Straight ahead was the kitchen. On the right the living room connected to a dining room. The ceiling was vaulted, and on the right living room wall was a gigantic mirror that spanned the entire living room and dining room wall. The mirror started about three feet from the ground, and went all the way to the vaulted ceiling. On the left side of the living room was a staircase. At the top of that staircase was a bathroom on the left that had a mirror that covered one entire wall from the floor to the ceiling. After stepping into the hallway from the bathroom was a full size mirror that went from the floor to the ceiling. To the left of the mirror was the master bedroom. The entire closet from the floor to the ceiling was…You guessed it, two sliding closet doors made entirely of mirrors. Stepping out from the master bedroom was a smaller bedroom. This bedroom was Jesse's.

To the right of Jesse's room was another small bedroom, and this was Maggie's and Anne's bedroom. Walking back down the stairs led to the living room, to the left was the kitchen. While standing in the kitchen, the dining room was visible with a giant interior wall opening and an open doorway with a door to the left. Once standing in the dining room, there was a sliding glass door that led to a wooden deck. This deck was one story high, as the staircase dropped to the left and led to the closed outdoor screened patio. While standing back inside the kitchen, if one was standing at the entrance of the kitchen, they can turn left and go down a short staircase which led to the downstairs family room previously mentioned. At the bottom of that staircase to the right was a full size mirror that went from the floor to the ceiling covering that entire wall. As mentioned earlier, to the right was a sliding glass door that led to the enclosed patio. Opposite from the stairs was the fireplace. To the left of the fireplace was a wet bar with an interior wall opening. Where the fireplace met the wet bar was the doggy door and a long skinny window that spanned from the ceiling to right above the doggy door. Standing back at the bottom of the staircase looking into the family room, there was a small hallway to the left. The first door to the left was another small staircase that went in another family room, but was used as my room. Standing at the bottom of the stairs in my room was two doors to the right. The first was a small water heater room to the right, and then Greg's room. To get to Greg's room, one had to walk through my room, a small inconvenience, but it was well worth it since I had the biggest room in the house.

Walking back upstairs from my room to the second family room turning left was the small hallway previously mentioned. To the left was a small half bath. Opposite of that doorway was a closet that housed the washer and dryer. To the left of the half bathroom was a door that led to the garage. In the backyard it was beautiful. Trees and bushes everywhere. In the center of the yard was an inground swimming pool. The deep side only went to five and a half feet, but it was perfect. The entire pool could be utilized at all times. It was our dream house. It wasn't until after a couple of months that my mom realized that the nightmares she was having about running down stairs and seeing mirrors everywhere, was coming true.

One night she was getting ready to go to bed. She heard my dad call her from downstairs, so she made her way downstairs from the living room. She turned the corner into the kitchen and then down the stairs to the family room. She looked around the family room, nobody to be seen. She got an irie feeling as she turned the corner. The door flew open from the staircase leading from my room, and I ran into her, colliding and pushing her backward. "What the hell...?" she mumbled. I turned around and looked at her, then I disappeared. She stood there shocked. She looked around then at the bathroom. The light was on and the door was closed. The door swung open, and my dad walked out of the bathroom. A moment later he too disappeared. She walked into the bathroom, looking for him, as there had to be a reasonable explanation for what just happened. The bathroom was empty. Chills went down her spine. She knew what she saw, and that she felt me run into her. She walked into the garage. Both my dad's car and mine were gone. The garage was empty. She walked down to my room, then Greg's. They were both empty. She ran up to her room. On the way she saw that Maggie was in her room, getting her clothes ready for the next day. "Alan isn't home yet?" Maggie replied, "No it's just you and me. Anne said she would call when you need to pick her up."

From time to time it would sound like my mom would call me, "Alan!" The voice sometimes was in distress. It happened to all of us, my brother and sisters have the same exact stories. My brother and sisters would all come running to my mom and say, "What." "I never called you," she replied. That was a true sign it was not just a ghost. In my experience, if there is a random spirit, it can move things, or flush the toilet. It will take your car keys, and you will spend an hour looking for them, and you will go right back to the place where you know you left them, and the first place you looked, and they will be there. It's like they pull the item into another dimension temporarily. I got to the point that I started asking St. Anthony to help me find whatever I was looking for. He has a prayer that helps with this. Or when trying to print out a report for school, the printer will keep locking up unexplainably. I learned to bless whatever electronic device is locked up, and it starts working immediately after.

Electronics are run on energy. In my experience spirit is energy. It is known that energy can not be created nor destroyed, but only change form. We are spiritual beings with electricity running through us. An electrical signal from our brain to our muscles causes action/motor function. Our heart beats due to an electrical pathway cause the heart muscles to contract. Spirit is the same way, a spirit is energy. We would experience spirits/dark figures walk by, and be amazed at what we saw. We were able to distinguish between a spirit, and an evil spirit/demon. Demons would try to strike fear in the subject. They would mimic our voices, even take on our appearance. Just like my mom's experience with the previous story. Anne would experience Greg sitting in front of the family room mirror staring at her with an omnivis grin, and would not talk to her, just stare. It was not uncommon for any of us to be in our room and hear many people talking and creating a ruckus in another part of the house. I would come up from my room as I heard a commotion in the kitchen, and when I would get upstairs, I would find that I was the only one home.

One day it was really bad. I was a senior in highschool, and I went out with some friends. In the meantime, mom, Greg, Anne, and Maggie were at the house visiting with my grandmother Verna and my aunt Ariel. After their visit, they were getting ready to leave, and started backing out of the driveway. They felt something crash into the car as if they hit a large dog. Aunt Ariel put the car in park, and jumped out. There was nothing there. She went back to the house to tell my mom, "Keep an eye out, I don't know if something is wounded and ran off? I hit something with my car really hard when I was backing up. It was so creepy, and so loud like it hit us. I'm going to take mom home." After they left my mom went to the back patio door to let the dog out. As she approached the door she could see a small brown animal, about the size of a large racoon on the back patio looking in. It jumped to the door handle on the outside as if it was trying to get in. She yelled for my dad and locked the door from the inside. She never saw a creature like it. The only creature I could think of how to describe is like a whistle pig. Which looks like an oversized gopher. Dad ran downstairs, and ran onto the patio deck, but couldn't find anything. He searched under the deck and in the backyard, nothing to be found. He had to go to work, he was working the night shift. However, nothing calmed down. My mom, Maggie, Greg, and Anne were in the living room when they started hearing laughter. The booming crack of a loud man's voice was sinister, and directly in the middle of the room where nobody was, but all new it came from something they couldn't see. They started to hear whispering and TVs turning on in the upstairs bedrooms.

All of sudden at the front door there was a pound that reverated throughout the house. Greg went to the front door and opened it. "Who is it? My mom shouted from the kitchen." Greg looked around. Nobody was there. Then a pound came from the dining room sliding glass door where the creature had been. Greg shut the front door and locked it. Everyone ran to the sliding glass door, and flipped on the back porch light. Nobody was there. The back yard had a six foot privacy fence and the sliding glass door was one story high where the deck led to the door. Even if there were multiple people playing a prank, they would have had a hard time running off the deck to hide in the trees and bushes, or jumping a privacy fence. It was not an easy task without being caught. The front door began to bang again nonstop pounding, and vigorously. Sending chills down their spines. They realized; this was not a person they were encountering. They ran to the front room window and peered out. They saw a black figure jump off the porch landing on the hedge, and to the side of the house. They all ran down to my room for refuge. They could hear the pounding on the doors upstairs. They could hear people walking around upstairs. About an hour later I pulled up with Harold. "Have a good night, thanks for the ride." I said as I exited his SUV. I walked up to the door. As I approached the door I noticed the hedge was badly smashed in. It looked as though a small car had run over the bushes and left a gap. I forget my house keys on my dresser. I knocked on the door. Nobody came, I waited, I knew they were home. I pounded even harder. I could hear a commotion from the basement window that was next to the porch, that was Greg's bedroom window. I knocked again, and I could hear my mom, Anne, Maggie shriek. I guess I'll have to go through the window on the side of the house I thought to myself. I wasn't happy about it, but I knew that Greg kept his side window unlocked as it was guarded from the street and sidewalk by ten feet of thick bushes and trees. That entire side of the house was completely covered. It was fall and there were leaves on the ground. Hopefully that window was still open I thought to myself as I made my way around the winding porch steps.

The right side of the house was covered with evergreen trees and evergreen bushes. It would have been a perfect hideout for a child to use as a fort as they could duck under the first tree branch and have cover from anyone passing by on the sidewalk. I made my way to the side of the house. The corner of the house blocked the light from the porch. As I made my way to the corner I got a creepy feeling, just then, something stepped from my left directly in front of me and into the darkness where I was heading. I didn't see the entire body. I only saw from the calf down. It looked like a naked human leg and barefoot. The difference was that the entire leg was covered in short black hair. The hair resembled that of a black doberman's hair, in length and texture. The leg pulled into the darkness. As it stepped into the darkness I could hear its footsteps on the fallen leaves, except; it didn't have the sound of having two feet. It sounded like it had six feet as I heard the leaves crunch under its feet, and then I heard it scurry up the wall, and the footsteps thudded as it ran on the stucco wall of the house, and then back onto the ground crunching the leaves under its six feet.

That stunned me for a moment, and I was scared, but I didn't have any options, because I left my keys in the house, and everyone refused to let me in. I took a deep breath and hunched under the trees into the darkness. My eyes were trying to focus in the dark. I felt the darkness smoother me as I tried to hurry to the safety of the house. I hopped down into the basement window well. The window was open, I popped the screen off and slid in through the window. I closed the window and locked it behind me. I walked through Greg's room and into mine. "Ahhhhh!" They screamed as I made my way into my bedroom. They were curled up on my bed holding each other. "Why didn't you guys answer the door when I knocked?" "Something had been pounding on the doors for an hour nonstop." Mom exclaimed. "Then it jumped off the porch and into the bushes. It ran to the side of the house." "What did it look like?" We didn't see all of it, but the bottom half of its body looked like a giant panther, only way bigger…" I told them what I saw, and they only became more terrified. "Why would you go into the dark behind the devil himself?" "Well, I had to get in, and you guys weren't going to let me in." This was before everyone had access to a cell phone, So I couldn't call, I didn't have a phone. The bushes where that thing jumped on, died. It left a gap in the bushes from that point on.

Chapter VI

W e had grown accustomed to strange things happening in that house. It was so bitter sweet. For the first time in my life we have a steady home, and we didn't have to live with family in their home, or switch from one school to the next. Everyone had their own room except for Maggie and Anne, but Jesse would be moving out soon. It was an actual house, and not a mobile home. We were truly blessed. As happy as we were, the devil and Bertha wanted to rip it away, as it was our pride and joy. There are a lot of superstitions regarding mirrors and spiraling staircases. It is thought by some that a spiraling staircase allows spirits to ascend and descend up and down it. Mirrors have been said to be a portal in which demons can pass through and peer through as a window. Some who practice magic/the occult won't put a mirror on the outside wall of their house unless it's on the east side of the house. The sun rises on the east, and somehow prevents evil from entering or peering in. This is a controversial topic and debatable, but as an wiseman once said, "Superstition is a name the ignorant give to their ignorance." This house had a winding staircase and plenty of mirrors. I have read a book *Out of the Devil's Cauldron A Journey from Darkness to Light,* written by John Ramirez, and it is a must read. He was a devil worshiper who converted, and he does a great job at exposing the ways of the devil and his demons. In that book he mentions that demons hate to see themselves in the mirror, and when he and his fellow practitioners would summon them, they would make it a point not to have a mirror in that room except, on a certain feast day for a particular demon.

I have had my own attacks by demons, so many that I have lost count. When I have been spiritually attacked, looking in the mirror was hard for me to do. I didn't want to look at myself in the mirror. It was almost painful, and I could see that it wasn't me looking at myself in return. Perhaps, the spirit can tell at that point that something is gravely wrong, and the demon inside doesn't want to be found. A person like this usually goes into a depression, goes months without looking in a mirror, and can go weeks without showering. There is something that reflects on a spiritual level with cleansing the soul and the body externally that has power. Hence, water is used for Baptism. Then again, Jesus also points out that cleaning the outside of the vessel doesn't mean the inside is pure as well. In my experience it is a good indicator that there is much trouble inside, spiritually speaking, if the outer is not cleaned frequently. My point of saying all this is; this house we just moved into had more mirrors than I had ever seen, and perhaps it was an outdated decorative design that made rooms appear larger than they were, but they were not helpful to us, looking back. It was a perfect storm for us spiritually. I know now that the demons had been following us from way before, ever since my mother had her tarot cards read. As I had mentioned, John Ramirez explains the twenty one paths to hell. Fortune telling is one of the paths to hell.

My mother constantly had nightmares, and they were so vivid. At this point I know now that frequent vivid nightmares of horrendous things is a sign of demonic disturbance. One night my mother had a dream that a three foot tall girl was attacking me and my siblings. She said, "She was only three feet tall, but lanky. She was so skinny, but had long legs and elongated fingers. For being so short her arms and legs were so skinny and long. She had jet black hair and sunken black eyes. Her nose was long, sharp, and pointed downward. All of her teeth were long and sharp. Her hair was pulled back into a ponytail, she was wearing pink shorts, and a white button up sleeveless blouse. Her feet were bare and just like her fingers, her toe nails had long claws like nails. She had a curved back and you could see her spine poking through her blouse. All a sudden she jumped on you kids and was attacking you in the living room. Then she jumped on you Alan, and knocked you onto your stomach. You were crying, "Mom, please help!" as she ripped the meat off you back with her teeth and claws, I could see your ribs exposed.

Then I saw your decapitated head calling for me as a biker drove away with your head. It was one of the worst dreams I had. That's not all…after the dream I was laying there thinking about how awful it was. My right hand was hanging off of the bed. It was just a dream I told myself. At that moment I felt the smallest hand grasp my index and middle finger. I was so cold. It felt like I was touching a roll of cold hamburger meat. I yanked my hand under the covers, and flipped to my back. Then the blankets were slowly being pulled off of me. I looked down at the foot of the bed, and there wasn't anyone there. I grabbed the blanket thinking maybe your dad was pulling them off of me. I Looked to the right and he was sleeping, snoring away. But he was on his back and he wasn't moving. I grasped the blanket firmly and pulled up, but something had tension on the comforter. I yanked harder and pulled the blanket over my chest, and that's when I saw it. On the opposite side of the room through the reflection of my mirrored closet doors, I saw her… The girl from my dream. Every time I pulled up on the blanket I could see her reflection slide into eyesight. Her feet were anchored against the side of the mattress, and her hands gripped the comforter. Everytime, her back arched and her legs straightened, the blanket nearly ripped out of my hands. I yelled, "Alan!" and elbowed him in his ribs with my right elbow. He woke up startled, "What!" he yelled. As soon as he woke, the blanket's tension released.

I turned on the lamp on my nightstand, and quickly scanned the room and the floor, using the closet's reflection to find her. I couldn't see her anywhere, but there was no way in hell I would step off that bed. Dad said, "Go to bed. You're seeing shit again." I wasn't having a nightmare. I was awake when it grabbed me, and when it was pulling the blankets off of me. I couldn't sleep, but dad had to work in the morning so I turned off the light. I layed there terrified. I couldn't go back to sleep, and if by some miracle I did fall asleep, she might be in my dreams. I layed there petrified. The Sun came up, and I layed there for hours. I couldn't avoid what was about to happen. I needed to pee so bad. I had two choices, wet the bed, or make a run for the bathroom. I sat up slowly and looked around the room and didn't see anything. I thought to myself, I have to be fast and run all the way around the bed, as the bathroom is on the right side of the room. I could crawl over your dad, but he already wasn't sleeping well from earlier, and he had to work. I looked in the closet to see the bottom half of the room. It was clear. I told myself, "I just need to run to the bathroom and lock the door behind me, and I will be fine." I sat up even more and got to my knees. I slide the covers completely off. I put one foot on the floor, and then the next, waiting for a hand to come out from under the bed and grab me. I ran around the bed, and slammed the door behind me, everything became blurry as I tried to focus on the door. I made it. I locked the door behind me. And sat down on the toilet. I was hurrying as fast as I could. I looked to the left at the shower. Both doors were closed, but through the smoked shower glass doors I could see a black silhouette standing in the corner. It was about five feet tall. I blinked to focus my eyes. As I opened my eyes, it was still there. I hurried and finished cleaning up, and washed my hands as if I didn't see it. Maybe it was a towel someone left in there. It wasn't moving or making a noise. I need to confront my fear. It's day time now, I told myself, nothing evil sticks around in the day time. I slowly walked to the shower. I put my hand on the shower door, and slowly opened it.

The squeaking of the door felt as loud as sirens in my head, I didn't want to make whatever it was, move. The door thumped, as it came to a stop. In the corner of the shower was a little old lady with white hair staring into the corner of the shower. She was completely dressed in long black tattered drapes. She had a black tattered head cover as well. I blinked my eyes hoping I was seeing things, and there she was quietly staring into the corner. I backed away slowly and turned to make my exit. The thought crossed my head, maybe if I turn around now, she will be gone. I turned to look as I unlocked and opened the door, but there she was. She was not a figment of my imagination. I shoved the door open and leaped onto the bed, hitting your father as I bounced to my side of the bed. "Son of a bitch. What are you doing?!" he yelled. I crawled into bed pulling the covers over my head. I couldn't sleep that morning. I uncovered my head. This was ridiculous, I thought to myself. I sat up, and looked around the room. In front of my closet mirror was a little girl sitting with her legs crossed, and her back was to me. She was looking at her reflection in the mirror. I could see the front part of her body through the reflection of the mirror, and she was turned toward me at a 45 degree angle. She was wearing a pretty white dress. Her face was covered by a white lace veil. I stared at her to see what she was doing. As she lifted her veil, and her face was an old lady's face. I buried my head under the blankets.

What's even crazier, two months after I saw her. The movie *The Others* came out. In that movie the same scene happened, I about died. How can they portray such a thing that I saw two months earlier." One thing I learned about the devil and demons, they are copycats. They have no new tricks. There is a Holy hour at 3 PM, the devil's hour is at 3 AM. There are speaking tongues for God, there are demonic tongues for the demons. There are holy candles used at Mass, there are evil candles for their ceremonies. There is an Altar in a Church, there is an altar for them as well. Churches sometimes use wooden altars as well as stone, usually granite for its supernatural powers, same for the devil and his demons, they use both as well. There is prayer for Christians, and curses for the demons. There is a Holy Bible for Christians, and a black bible for devil worshipers. My point is, demons watch what we do all the time, and influence us to sin. If a man creates a story like the movie *The Others* and a demon sees his vision while filming, he will steal it and use it as his own way to terrify someone. I'm not saying that is what happened in this instance, but it's not out of the realm of possibilities.

One night my mom was up by herself. She told us what happened, "Everyone else was in bed, I was watching a movie. I was sitting on the couch in the front room watching TV. I heard a loud crash in the kitchen. It sounded like someone was holding a stack of glass plates, and then threw them to the floor, busting into a million pieces. I walked the entire house in the dark looking for someone, or broken glass. I found nothing. Meanwhile, for some reason I didn't turn on the light. I wasn't afraid. So I went back into the living room to watch TV. A minute later, out of the side of my eye, I saw a shadow. The shadow was in the shape of a bear. It was four feet tall, and it started walking from the dining room and was coming straight for me. I turned my head toward the shadow to make sure I wasn't seeing things. It tiptoed through the dining room slowly. I watched it in terror as it creeped from the dining room into the front room and the floor creaked under its feet. It reached the front room, took a right before it reached me. I headed toward the staircase, and climbed up slowly. Stairs creaked under its feet. As it reached the top of the staircase it remained still.

The bear stood up on two legs, and the figure transformed from a bear into a silhouette of a man and started walking to the end of the hall. I left the TV on and bolted to the staircase. I was headed in the same direction the figure walked, but I didn't know what to do. I was afraid that it was waiting there for me at the top of the stairs, but I didn't want to stay in the front room by myself, and I didn't want to go downstairs, all I could think about was getting to your dad who was asleep in our room. I reached the top of the stairs, and I couldn't see anything, but I was trying not to look for anything, because I didn't want to see it. I barely felt the floor under my feet, and I turned left to run into my room, and I grabbed me. I felt it grab my left shoulder, and I ripped my shoulder away from its grasp as I felt my shirt pull from its fingertips. I made it into my room and I leaped into my bed. Bam, I landed directly on your father. He was laying on his back. I knocked the air right out of him."

Mom wasn't the only one experiencing things. I was getting ready for bed one night. I got in bed, and I could hear someone walking around in the kitchen above my room. I crawled into bed. The footsteps started down the stairs from the kitchen to the family room. Then I heard my door to my room open. Greg was already asleep in his room, I figured it was my mom coming down to talk to me. The stairs creaked as it headed downstairs. I turned My head to see who was headed my way. As the footsteps made it to the bottom of the stairs, nobody was there, but the footsteps continued to walk towards me. The carpet crumpled underneath its feet. I could see the outline of the shoe prints as they approached my bed. They stopped right at the edge of my bed and stood right next to me. I couldn't see anybody, but I was waiting with anticipation. It was so quiet I could hear a pin drop. What was going to happen. The hair on the back of my neck stood up. Then all of a sudden the footsteps turned around, and walked back up my stairs and into the kitchen. I don't know what was supposed to happen, but it was sort of uneventful, but maybe it was trying to scare me, and if that was the goal, I guess it worked.

We were always having something scary happen. One thing that always happened was; birds always flew into our windows. Not just once in a while, but all the time, and not just one at a time multiple times a day birds would crash into the windows. It was not uncommon for us to find several dead birds on the ground. This is a sign of demonic presence in a house. Birds navigate with a mechanism in their head that operates using the magnetic field, and somehow the magnetic field is disrupted, or stronger where demons are, as their energy changes the magnetic principles. Demonic interactions with this planet heightens during certain lunar phases. During the approach of a full moon, during a full moon, and days after a full moon, demonic influence is higher than normal. During small crescent moons it can be the same, or sometimes worse than full moons. During, or around eclipses spiritual activity is super high as well. This has to do with gravitational pull, and laws of the spiritual nature. It's not just spiritual warfare that is affected by this. Medical conditions are exacerbated, women who are close to term pregnancy, go into labor, psych patient's mental illness exacerbates. Just ask any EMT, or nurse about changes involving lunar activity. I have heard soldiers say the same thing. When there is a full moon, or small crescent moon, their camps were bombed. Of course armies are going to use the light of the full moon to their advantage, or the lack of moonlight to attack in a stealthy manner. Moon phases are deeply watched by devil worshipers and any type of witchcraft. During certain moon phases they practice certain rituals and ceremonies. Our experience as a family with evil was way more intense than anyone I knew. We didn't do a lot to stop it in hindsight. We should have had our house blessed, and ourselves. It would have helped if we would have stopped talking about ghost stories. It was routine for us to camp out in the living room and tell ghost stories. It seemed to invite evil as we spoke about it.

One night we had all the lights out in the house and layed a mattress on the floor against the loveseat and couch. Greg, Maggie, and I were sitting on the mattress with our backs leaning against the couch. As we told ghost stories the house started to creak. All the stories we told were the true stories of things that happened to all of us, we were just recalling them, and resharing them with each other. Somebody would tell a story, and I would ask questions about all the details, which seemed to make them even more scary. As we told them, our dog Abby would start growling, and barking at the creaking of the house. She was laying next to Maggie on the mattress, and Maggie would continually pet her in order to comfort her. I mentioned the devil, just then, we heard the nails of a dog run across the kitchen floor. It wasn't our dog. Maggie was petting her. The clanking of the nails scratching the kitchen floor as it ran down the stairs into the family room, and the nails could be heard popping the carpet fibers as it ran across the family room. This thing had long nails. Just then, we heard hooves gallop across the roof. Whatever was on the roof was heavy, the whole living room shook. It trampled across the roof and jumped two stories to the ground in the backyard, it leaped over the six foot privacy fence and onto the sidewalk. We trembled with fear as we looked at each other for a reaction. "Did you guys hear that?" Greg shrieked. Just as he said that we could hear it gallop down the street. Clopping upon the asphalt and away from our house. We sat in silence. Anne screamed, "Look," she pointed to the staircase that leads into the kitchen.

We looked to the staircase where she pointed. "What is it? I asked. "It was a head that came out from around the corner just under the ceiling of the kitchen, and looked at us." "What did it look like?" I asked. It was bald, its ears were pointed, it had sharp teeth and building red eyes." Its legs were not visible to us, which means it was standing at least two to three steps from the top of the staircase. Which meant, it had to be at least eight to nine feet tall, assuming it was standing on the stairs.

One thing that confirmed that what happened the night before was not just in our head, happened the next morning. It was winter, and there was still snow on the ground from the previous day. After waking up the next morning, we went outside, and what we saw sent a chill down our back. In the snow, there were hoof prints on the ground in the backyard. We followed them to the fence, and looked over. The hoof prints continued on the other side of the fence. We could see where it leaped over the fence, landed, and continued down the street just as we heard. "We should look on the roof where it started." We climbed on the railing of the deck to see the roof. Sure enough, there were hoof prints on the roof, and whatever was on the roof was not of this world. The roof on that part of the house is two stories from the roof to the ground. The path from the roof to the ground crossed over the wooden deck. The deck is ten feet by ten feet, and it completely cleared it, and we could see where it landed from the roof. It had to be about 25-30 feet from the house and cleared the deck. A well trained horse could leap over a six foot privacy fence, but if it jumped from two stories high and 25-30 feet from that height, it most likely would have broken its legs. Not, making that jump, then leaping over a six foot fence and continuing down the street. One of the things I came to learn is; The supernatural are not confined to our laws of physics. They are completely unexplainable to our science.

One morning my mom dropped all of us off at school and went home. She locked the door behind her as she entered through the garage door. She was always worried about someone breaking in, so she was vigilant in keeping the doors locked. It wasn't very long after she returned home that she would barricade herself in her room until it was time to pick us up from school. She was walking out of her bedroom and got to the top of the stairs where she was making her way to the front room. Around the corner, somebody walked out from the kitchen and stood at the bottom of the stairs looking at her. She called out, "Maggie, Greg, Anne, Alan." My dad was at work, and all the kids were at school, but the reason she was calling out all of our names was because whoever was standing at the bottom of the stairs was wearing a mask. It was a weird mask that we had for a couple years. We used to scare each other from time to time. It looked like a homely female. The skin tone was dark brown, and the hairline was black rubber that stopped at the crown, where the bald spot was. The bald spot was dark brown and matched the skin tone. It also had jet black hair. The stringy hair had short bangs in front, and a short bob hair cut. The eyes were large, blue, and bulging out. The nose was large and bulbous. The lips were large, protruding, and feminine. The body that had the mask on was wearing navy blue sweatpants and a sweatshirt, but was not clear if it was a male or female.

There was a moment of silence, It stared at her, and it was not moving, just staring. Then it started running at her, and she turned to run away. She could hear footsteps chasing her. She yelled, "Stop, stop!" It was still chasing her. She turned left into her room and slammed the door. Quickly locking the door, and she heard a thump on the door as it hit the door. She jumped into her bed and crawled under the covers. She stared at the door as she could see the door knob shake as it was trying to open the door. After an hour of laying in bed terrified, she could hear someone walking up and down the hall. Up and down the stairs, and every once in a while the door knob would turn. Eventually, she had to come out to get us from school. She opened the bedroom door and she walked quietly down the hall. And as she passed Jesse's room, she could see it sitting on the bed looking at the wall. She ran downstairs and grabbed the car keys off the counter, ran into the garage and jumped in the car. She opened the garage door and left as fast as she could. After picking us up from school she told us what happened. Of course, when we got there, there wasn't anybody in our house.

We all experienced the unexplainable. One night Greg was hanging out with his friends in the front yard. He was about thirteen at that time. It was about ten o'clock on a summer night. As was their custom, they migrated across the street to the park. We were so lucky to have the park so close to our house. At the entrance of the park was a giant boulder with the name of the park etched in it. A couple of them were sitting on it, and a couple were milling around it when about a hundred yards away they saw two tall silhouettes walking in the park as if they appeared from nowhere. They were walking close together, and they had drastically long features. Their arms and legs were so long and cartoonishly skinny. Their abnormal height for their lankiness continued to capture their attention, as they made very harsh gestures. They were wearing trench coats and dressed all in black. The two figures came to a picnic table. One of the figures walked over to it and with one hand pulled up and flipped it over as if a normal person was flipping over a dinner plate. They all gasped, and watched as the figures disappeared into the night. Just as they appeared, from nowhere, that is how they made their exit. The boys rushed back to the house for shelter, and all confirmed what they had seen.

Another night Greg, Maggie, Anne, and I were in the family room talking. We had just finished dinner, and everybody went their separate ways. My mom was getting ready to leave, so she finished getting ready and left. My dad was at work, and Jesse went out with her friends. It was quiet in the house, the only sound in the house was our voices as we talked, not even the TV was on. I was sitting on one of the recliners facing the sliding glass door, and Maggie was on the other recliner facing the same direction. Greg was sitting on the fireplace facing the stairs and Anne was on the floor facing the same direction. I said, "You know what I picture… Sometimes I picture a giant dog the size of a doberman, a black body, and Bertha's head attached to it. I picture it running at me." Just as I said that, kaboom… Something smashed into the wall. The wall was stucco and wood on the outside, and it's a good thing it was. Whatever hit the house, hit with so much force, all the pictures on the wall lifted and banged back down to the wall in left in a crooked position. It sounded like a car was crashing through the wall. There is no way a person could hit the wall that hard. Possibly fifty men in a synchronized effort had a chance at replicating it. The area of the wall struck was in one small section, but it was about Six feet from the ground. The pictures in that section of the wall happened to be a picture of Jesus and the footprints in the sand prayer. It definitely felt like it hit that area to mock Jesus, but strangely enough, the house wasn't damaged, maybe that blessed image of Jesus helped the situation. Our first thought was that a car crashed into the house, but the pound hit the wall too high to make sense. The back yard had a privacy fence surrounding the entire yard, rocks, hundreds of trees and bushes, a deck, a closed in patio, and an in ground pool to avoid. There wasn't a way to run straight into the wall for more than thirty feet, much less get a car into the yard to hit the wall six feet high.

We ran to the door to see what was in the backyard. There was something back there, but the darkness of the night masked its presence. As we were standing by the door something slammed the wall behind us. We whipped our heads around to see what was happening behind us. As I turned my head I saw an arm of a white man wearing a white T shirt pull his arm back through the doggy door as the venetian blinds were still slamming into each other. The arm slowly snaked back through the doggy door. Hmm, "Who was that?" I whispered. I approached the doggy door, opened the blinds. And peered out. I couldn't see anything but the reflection of the wet bar behind me. I knelt down on the floor on all fours. I was going to look out of the doggy door to see who was messing with us. I creeped closer to the flap, and my head was right next to the flap. What am I doing... I jumped up to my feet, "Yeah, I wouldn't stick my head out there." Maggie gasped.

"Is mom here?" I asked, "Maybe she is messing with us." We ran to the garage, the van was gone. We checked every room in the house and nobody else was there. We retreated to my room until mom returned. The next morning we noticed our dog was missing. We walked around the entire back yard and around the neighborhood. The backyard was completely sealed by the privacy fence. Walking the neighborhood I looked up at the gray sky as the dark clouds trickled rain drops to the ground like an ominous sign. Mom and Dad circled the neighborhood in the van with the windows down to see through the drizzle of the fall day. We looked until the dark creeped in, and it was pointless to look any further. The next day we repeated the process with no avail. The third day the search was intense, and there was no way we could have not found her, we walked further and drove further than she could have possibly gone. Finally, we gave up and went home.

Jesse went outside. Suddenly Jesse screamed out from the backyard, "Ahhh! I found her!" We ran to the backyard to see why she was screaming. Jesse was next to the pool, she was on her knees fighting back the tears. The pool was winterized, and it was covered with a tarp. My dad stuck his hand in and pulled out the yorkie. As he lifted her out of the pool her body was limp, but her neck was even more limp, as if not connected to her body, and blood ran from her nose. He set her down, and we all started to cry. "Alex, did she drown?" my mom asked. "No, somebody snapped her neck, and threw her in the pool." I couldn't help but feel that she took my place. Maybe I was supposed to be killed when I stuck my head next to the doggy door. Whatever was attacking us was serious, and wanted blood.

Chapter VII

The dog incident was not one we would forget, and it wasn't quite over. Frequently, we had family time. Some nights we watched movies, others we told ghost stories as previously stated, and some nights were game nights. Once in a while on game night we would play hide and seek with the lights off, and the seeker was blindfolded. One night Maggie and Anne were running up the stairs looking for a place to hide. They screamed as they felt something chasing them. Mom peeked her head around the corner of the bedroom to see why they were screaming, "There is a black panther chasing you!" my mom screamed. Maggie and Anne ran into the same bedroom my mom was in, and took refuge. It was not uncommon for the demons to use animals to disguise themself. They know the fears of their victims. That is how they try to take over a person, by fragmenting a person's mind by fear. For Christians we have Faith, the reverse side would seem to be unbelief, but in the spiritual battle, it's fear.

We would entertain ourselves by telling ghost stories, and hide and seek, it was all fun and games until it gets real. It's fun and games for us, but not the demons. It invites them in. The last time we played hide and seek as a family, it was all a little too real. One night we started a game of hide and seek. Mom was the first to seek, so she put the blindfold on. The girls went upstairs, and Greg and I headed down stairs. I went into the water heater room just because everyone was afraid of going in there. I crawled on top of the boxes and Christmas decorations that were being stored, and leaned my back up against the wall. Greg went into his closet, and crawled on top of all the stuff in his closet and rested his back on the same wall I was leaning on. After a few minutes of sitting in the dark I felt the wall shake and three giant bangs at my back. They shook the house, and I could feel the vibration in my chest. Was Greg banging I thought to myself? No, that was so powerful. After The banging Greg got scared and crawled out of the closet and changed his hiding spot to under his bed. When he got settled he saw someone walk into his room. It looked around, then walked straight into the closet. After a few minutes nobody came out. He crawled out from under his bed and flipped on the light. He looked in the closet, and nobody was there. He thought it was weird that they walked straight into the closet. His closet was full of toys, sports equipment, and clothes all piled on top of a small desk that was in his closet. To walk into the closet, they would have to climb up onto the desk full of toys and sports equipment.

Meanwhile, my mom was looking for us in the family room. She couldn't hardly see anything in the dark as she stumbled around the room with her arms outstretched. She walked into the wet bar feeling around. She felt the cold countertop with her left hand, and with her right hand the cold metal of the microwave. She shuffled to the right and her right hand grazed what felt like hair. She patted it and she was right, it was fluffy and warm. It was at waist level, "I found you." she declared. She patted the head again, "I found you." She scooted over to the light switch and flipped it on. There was nobody there. She ran up the stairs and started turning on the lights. Everyone started coming out of their hiding spots. "What's wrong?" I asked, and she explained what happened. Greg and I shared our story of the shadow that walked into his closet and the pounding in the closet. We made our way up to my mom's room and I could smell something weird. I turned the lights to scope out the room. On the floor in the center of the room was a clot of hair. I walked over to the hair, and on the hair was dog feces. The hair was black, brown and silver. It was the same exact hair as our dog that had just died. Yorkshire terriers don't shed, this was a big chunk of hair, and she had been dead for a week. Where did this hair come from? I went to the bathroom to get tissue to pick up the clot of hair and stool. The stool is what I smelled when I first went in the room. Where did it come from, we hadn't had a dog for a week, and there wasn't a dog in our household. I was shocked when I picked up the stool, and it was warm. It was a fresh bowel movement.

Whatever was attacking me and my family wanted blood. They wanted us to die. My room in the basement was right next to the water heater room and the furnace. I kept smelling gas, and telling my mom about it. I kept getting massive headaches. She called the gas company, and they came out several times, but blamed the fumes from traffic from the neighborhood traffic. Nothing changed, I continued to get headaches. Finally, my mom called again, this time the service company came out and did a proper inspection. The technician said, "It's a good thing you called, if there was even a tiny spark, that furnace would have exploded. There was so much gas spewing out, I'm surprised nothing happened."

Our dog just died, what if she did take my place. Then the furnace problem got me thinking, how many times have I been near death? To start I nearly drowned three times as a child, I was electrocuted by a faulty power outlet. The shock threw me across the room and stopped my heart. Greg and I nearly flipped off a bridge after tailspinning on the interstate at highway speeds. It was nearly fatal. If we would have fallen off the four story drop of the bridge below, we definitely would have died as we were in a convertible. On that same stretch of the interstate driving in the other direction years later I was in a huge pile up. My brakes failed, and I was sandwiched between two cars, again at highway speeds, and I broke the windshield with my head after my face bounced off the steering wheel. I should have been wearing my seat belt. Nearly smashed by a semi on my motorcycle as it ran me off the road. A motorcycle accident that sent me over the handlebars of my motorcycle. The last near death experience I had, happened recently. It wasn't until this happened that it came with an epiphany.

I pulled up to Russell's house, the garage door was open, but he wasn't in the garage. I went to his front door and knocked a couple of times, and nothing. I walked into the garage and knocked, and nothing. I went back to the front door and knocked, and there was no response. I had just spoken to him on the phone, and he had told me to come over so we could run some errands. I was starting to worry, so I tried turning the front door knob to see if it was open, and it was. I walked into the house looking for him, hoping not to find him lying on the floor. I pulled out my phone and called his phone. He answered, "What's up?" "Where are you?" I asked. "Just at home getting ready." "Really, well I just got here. Did you know your SUV has two broken out windows?" I wanted to see him run out of his room frantically. "Really, I'll be right there," he said. He came flying out of his bedroom, and blew right past me. "Hey," I said to get his attention. He had tunnel vision, and was just reacting as I approached him. "Hey, it's me" I said again, as he stopped at the front door and turned to face me. I saw his arm go up, so I raised my arm, possibly to block a punch. He still didn't recognize me, and then I felt the cold steel touch my hand and realized he had a gun in his right hand. He pointed at my chest and made a stabbing motion with the gun three times. What was he doing I thought to myself, then my eyes drifted to the trigger and his finger. He was trying to pull the trigger down, but the gun wasn't firing. His face went white, "What the hell are you doing? I was trying to kill you! The safety isn't on, but the gun wouldn't fire, the trigger was stuck." "I was messing around with you, I didn't think you would run outside in the broad daylight and shoot someone." I learned, it was not smart to joke around with Russell, he had no subtleness about him. He had no restraint, just reaction.

I definitely learned my lesson in that regard, but it also came with an epiphany. It was at that moment I realized God was protecting me even more than I thought. He didn't want me dead, I had a purpose. All those other times I nearly died I felt God's presence, and the help of an angel. Nearly touched by death, I felt his presence. Not all of these scenarios could have ended fatally, some could have caused me to be severely disabled, but most could have definitely ended in death. There are shamans around the world who push themselves to limits near death. They do this multiple times. The reason they push the limits is so they can experience other realms. It pulls them between the reality we experience, but also the spirit realms. Regardless of me experiencing what I have, whether it served me in that matter or not, at least I knew that I was not going to die without fulfilling God's purpose. If one pays attention to every demonic movie/book that is based on a true story, there is a common theme, the demon does whatever it can to take human life, and as many as possible. Bertha definitely wanted us dead.

Chapter VIII

One night I was taking the garbage to the trash can, and I got an eerie feeling. I put the garbage in the dumpster. I looked around but all I could see was the black of the night. From the street an adult cat trotted towards me. It had its eyes fixed on me. It trotted towards me and I yelled, "Shewww!" It continued on its path, so I yelled again, and it kept coming towards me. As it got closer it picked up speed. A thought entered my head; what if Bertha was in the cat? If it's not her this cat is going to attack me regardless. I didn't want an infected cat scratch, or cat scratch fever. I decided to kick the cat because it ignored me yelling at it. It could not be redirected. I felt terrible, and didn't want to hurt any creature. God created all creatures, and each has a purpose. As it scurried off I said, "God bless you." I don't know why I said it, possibly to say sorry, and partially because I wanted to cast Bertha out of the animal she was possessing.

Next week my great grandmother Edna was in the hospital. She was Marty's mom. We went to visit her in the hospital. Bertha and my grandfather Marty were there. After our visit my mom made us give Marty and Bertha a hug. Showing manners we did as mom directed. We hugged our grandfather and got in line to hug and say goodbye to Bertha as well. I waited in line for my turn, I was last. As I hugged her and told her goodbye she whispered to me and only me, "God Bless." She didn't tell any of the other kids that. I hadn't told anyone what had happened with the cat. Just as evil does, it mocks using God's Words and Blessings. Not only was she mocking by being condescending, but she was confirming that her spirit was in the cat, and it only confirmed it for me. Many people either don't know about this. It's called astral projection, but it's true, do your own research, and form your own opinion. Again referencing John Ramirez, when he was a devil worshiper, he astral projected into a Black wolf, and sometimes in spirit form over a community to curse it.

I hated that we had to be cordial to Bertha. What was my mom thinking? We should have avoided her or confronted her completely, there is no middle. If you know someone is into magic, and they are actively harming you and your family, one shouldn't shake hands with the devil. We let down our defenses when you let the social rules force us to be polite through obligation. Don't ever compromise with the devil, he takes over slowly. There is no negotiating with him. We should have separated ourselves from her. And as John Ramirez says, "The devil can't love you or any of his practitioners, we are made in God's image, and he hates God," The devil is a liar, and has been from the beginning of time. My mom was trying to keep social etiquette alive, but conceding to evil is exactly the same as shaking hands with the devil. If you compromise with the devil he slowly kills you. We should have been genuine to our feelings, but we feel like we don't want to be rude. Never compromise or let evil in. There is a war and if you try to compromise he will still attack, and if we fight back, he will still attack. We retain more strength and power by not giving in, and by taking the fight to him. It is very disappointing that Catholics, like myself, are always playing defense against him. We should be on the attack. We should be playing offense. He can not win, because Jesus, The Almighty, is on our side, and even though there is a duality, the scales are tipped in our favor. The devil, all the demons, and all mankind on earth can not stand up against God. There is no defeating The Alpha and The Omega. He is always and will be Greater…

Shortly after That my great grandmother Edna died. Days after the funeral my nephew Chris and I were playing pool in the family room. We were playing eightball. It was Chris' turn, and all he had to do was tap the eighth ball in the corner pocket, it was hanging right in front of the corner pocket. He called his shot into the corner pocket and hit the Cue ball. It was a great shot and it was heading right for the eight ball. Right before it hit the eight ball it stopped about an inch in front of it then it circled the eight ball perfectly moving around it. Then it stopped, completely defying physics. It was as if somebody stopped it, and circled the cue ball around the eight ball with their hand. Chris and I dropped our cue sticks and ran up stairs. It happened in broad daylight, "What did that?" Chris said. "What happened?" mom asked. We told her what happened, "Alan, have you prayed for grandma Edna?" "No," I replied. I went to my room, and prayed. I thought it was ridiculous, but when I finished praying an Our Father, I had a vision of her smiling face and felt relief.

What just happened? I asked myself. Why did she come to me, there were so many people she was closer to than me, and certainly some were devout Christians. Spirit knows spirit, and once it transitions from this mortal world into eternal, it can see the Grace, merit, and gifts of spirit, and it knows where it needs to go for help. She was in purgatory. I know that, and I know many people don't believe in purgatory, and I know that even a lot of Catholics don't believe in purgatory. Some may not believe in earthquakes, but it doesn't mean that it doesn't exist. And it doesn't mean that the nonbeliever is safe from an earthquake if they don't believe it exists. After Adam and Eve sinned in the garden, God called for them. They hid their nakedness because the stain of sin was on their souls. This is the purpose of purgatory, purification of the soul. Everyone in purgatory will be in heaven some day when their soul is purified. Mother Angelica says, "If your teenage son wraps your car around a light pole, and says sorry. It is good, and what he should do, but saying sorry won't unscramble the car." We can talk about purgatory for years, that is not my intent. My intent is simply to tell my story, and there is plenty of research on the matter, one should research before arguing their point, this is prudency for discussion about any subject.

Two of the biggest lies the devil has are; he and hell don't exist. There is a rise in the belief of spiritualism. People acknowledge there may be a creator, but they go through life based on their feelings and how it relates to them. Their own experience, meditation. Secularism, which takes God out of the equation completely. If I focus on getting a nice house, a nice job, and a beautiful spouse, I'll be happy. That leads to nothing but a God shaped hole in the soul, and materialism leaves the person feeling wanting more and more, never satisfied. Yoga seems good for a person, but it's quite deceiving. Certain moves invoke demons, hence Alister Crowley endorsed yoga. By the way Alister Crowley was the author of the Black book, saintain's bible. Meditation can do well for healing and the psychic, but if not grounded in christianity, leads to self worship just like all the other isms. Relativism is dangerous and teaches that the rules are subjective, but that is a lie because the world is full of absolutes. The Absolute/ God created the world. One must navigate the occult carefully, crystals, spirit guides, will draw demons towards the practitioner, crystals/stones need to be cleansed or some will say charged by the moon and sun, or demons will cling to the stones. Witchcraft, santeria, palo mayombe, voodoo, are all forms of devil worship. As

I have heard a couple exorcists say, "One who is intrigued by the occult, and opens those doors, may not be strong enough to close the doors." Bertha definitely knew what she was doing with me and my family. She yearned for the day we would die. I felt death coming like an inescapable force.

Chapter IX

I was in my senior year now, and my main focus was on football. I desperately wanted to play college football. During the off season I stayed in shape lifting weights and running. As I was jogging around the football field, all I could think was; it's a shame, by this time next year I'll be dead. Oddly, it didn't scare me. The football season went by way too quickly. Midway through the season my dad suffered a heart attack. He was only forty four years old. Thank God! It was a close call, and he came out of it fine. It got me thinking, I need to spend more time with him. I thought to myself; the only time I should spend away from him is; when I'm training for football. I decided not to rejoin the wrestling team as I usually did after football season, because it meant time away from my dad. It would have been a good year for me, it came so naturally to me, and I would have done well, but I had to make a decision based on what's best for me and my family. The wrestling coaches were upset, and refused to talk to me, but I made the right choice.

I had run into Lanie, at the mall. I liked her, but I also didn't want a reason to be tied back to my hometown. I wanted to be able to focus on football. She had mentioned she was available at a graduation party, and I wanted to pursue a relationship, but part of me hesitated, and like I said, wanted to focus on football. Timing was just never right, but we both liked each other. My senior year came to an end, and I had received a couple offers to play football. One came from a school in Nebraska, they offered to pay half of my tuition with a football scholarship, but it was further from home than the other. That was based purely on video tapes sent from a team mate. If I would have submitted my grades, I could have drawn academic scholarships. The other college offered me a couple academic scholarships and a chance to walk on to the football team as the recruiting coach sent an invitation to walk on. I was leaving highschool with a couple of grants and scholarships of my own, so either way I was going to get college paid for, which is a good situation to be in, so I chose the latter.

The college I chose was a five and a half hour drive from home. It is the most dangerous route through Colorado, but it was also one of the most beautiful. My major was undecided so I wanted to get all my general studies out of the way. Listening to a random enrollment counselor, they suggested I pick a random history class to get the credit hours I needed to be a full time student. I wish I would have been more prudent with my decision, as this class was Western Civilization. It was the history of European nations. The book for the class was bigger than The Bible, and the course moved so quickly. This course and physics at the collegiate level was causing me grief. I had brought to college an ancient computer, and I was able to type papers I could print, and I wasn't able to save it to a disc and print it in the computer lab. I had to resort to the computer lab hours, just another obstacle, but it was do-able. I had been coming home at least every other weekend because I missed my family. At least I had the football try-outs coming to look forward to.

The day came for tryouts. I got ready and headed to the football field. As I approached the field I realized they were already suited up in pads and doing drills. There was no way that I was late. What was happening? I watched for a minute and started to walk around the facility. I came across a flier posted on the building. The flier had yesterday's date, and said, "Come tryout for our football team, Walk-ons welcome." I was crushed. They already had their equipment checked out and they were practicing. It was over, I had no shot. I had a recurring nightmare as a child, and I continued to get the nightmare until a few years ago. In this dream I walked into a locker room with my football gear. There were other players in the room getting ready. As I was getting I couldn't get ready fast enough, I struggled with the gear. My foot wouldn't fit in my cleats, I had to keep taking them off and loosening the shoe strings. As I was doing this, the room emptied. All the others were already suited up and playing. I looked out the window and no matter how hard I tried to get suited up, the sun started to set as the day passed by, and I missed the game. This dream first occurred after missing my 3rd grade football season, the first year boys are eligible to play tackle football. It was that feeling all over again. Obviously, my nightmares were a form of childhood trauma that would haunt me for most of my life. It was back again when I missed the walk-on date. Looking back now, I should have been persistent. I should have waited for practice to be done and talked to the coaching staff. But I was young, and crushed from missing the try-out date.

I received a notice from the academic board. The letter said I was to report to counseling to bring up my grade point average, I must maintain a 3.5 average to maintain my scholarships. I had a 3.4 as I was failing my history class, and had a C in physics. The feeling of impending death was in the back of my mind as I drove home for the four day weekends and back to college during the week. I was on the phone with my mom, "I need to stop coming back to town every weekend. I need to focus on school.

I'm in jeopardy of losing my scholarships." "Really, there must be something else you can do." I could tell I was breaking her heart, but I needed to focus on school. A week later my mom called me, "Hey, I need to tell you something." "Is everything OK, It sounds like you're crying?" "Yeah, your cousin Velma died in a car wreck on Wednesday. And yesterday they found your uncle Rick passed away in bed." "He wasn't old, what are they saying he died from?" "They don't know yet. They are ruling out an overdose. Alan things are bad here. Our car just broke down. We're down to only one car for everyone, your oldsmobile is the only thing running to get all of us to school and work." "I don't know what to say. That is a lot. I'll have to call you back later."

Should I leave college? My grades are subpar, I missed football try-outs, I feel like I wasted a year just because of that. Two family members died, and I want to be with my family. They are struggling with one vehicle, if I left school, and I can help them just by offering my car. My oldsmobile was the only thing working for them. It was my graduation present. I loved that muscle car. It needed work before I went to college, the shifter needed to be replaced, so I hadn't driven it yet. While I was at college my dad got the shifter replaced. There is one silver lining, if I leave college, at least I will be able to drive my oldsmobile.

I felt like I needed to go home, so that's what I did. After arriving home I felt the feeling of impending doom disappear. I realized it was; I was feeling the young death of my cousin. I had a feeling of empathy, and I was feeling it as if I was her. I don't know if she went to heaven, there was so much doubt. How sad it is, not only to me, but to God when someone chooses not Him. I felt the joy of my parents having me home, they treated me with such respect and love. It was at this point that I didn't understand what I was giving up. I was still in shock from death. While I went to college the bank on campus allowed me to open up a checking account along with a credit card. I never had a knowledge of managing money or an account, and having an account would come with a hard lesson to learn.

I noticed that the two hundred and thirty dollars would be in my account, and then it would be missing. I didn't understand what was happening to the money. I called my account again, and after a week the money was back in the account. I didn't realize that with the credit account, the bank would do that every month, for a short time it wouldn't be available to me. I continued to call the bank, but there was never anyone there to answer questions, so I withdrew all the money in the account. A short time after the account closed. Apparently I was supposed to have a certain amount of money in the account. It defaulted and went into collections. Collections would call and say, "I can reopen the account and you can make payments on it. You can pay ten dollars a month if that's all you can afford?" I agreed. And while the account was open, all the interest was accruing. What should have been only a few hundred, was now triple that. I closed the account. "Mom, what should I do?" "Just ignore them, don't reopen the account."

Another collector called, and wanted to settle, but now the amount was growing with interest and late fees. With the late fees and interest it just kept growing. The college I walked away from sent me a bill as well. It explained that since I left college a semester early, I needed to repay the scholarships they distributed to me. I needed to do something, I was now several thousand dollars in debt. My credit was demolished. It didn't help that my mom would open up an account under my name for the utilities when she went negative in the old account, again destroying my credit. I tried applying to a local university that had accepted me out of high school. I felt the urgency to get back into college. The university rejected me because of the unpaid balance of the unpaid scholarships from the other university.

I couldn't do anything right. The last thing I had to look forward to, my car. At least I could drive my oldsmobile. One morning I got in my car, and driving it for the first time I realized it wouldn't come out of second gear. The clutch was broken. The second time I drove it the same thing. My dad called a mechanic over and he fixed it. My dad had been driving it for a couple of days. Then I got it back. It was finally time for me to drive it. I got in it and drove it down the street, and something in the engine started clicking. I felt something in the engine go. This is impossible, The engine was rebuilt recently. It only had nine thousand miles on it. I know that when Jesse was in it, she was hot rodding it, but I was just driving it. I restarted the motor and drove it home. My dad met me in the driveway. "What the hell! Are you like a woman, jump in and drive, never checking the oil? The oil is low" he was right, I didn't check the oil. Years later he admitted that the day before he was speeding down the highway, and blew the engine. He made me feel like I blew the motor, but he was afraid to tell me. The saddest part is that he was afraid to tell me. I would have forgave him, he didn't do it on purpose. We were back to one car.

At this point I was driving my dad to work, my brother and sisters to school. I would pick them up from school, go get dinner, make dinner for them. Pick up my dad from work, and then run back to pick up my mom. That was my day. We took my car to a local mechanic. After a month my car was sitting there I started going by weekly to check on the progress, and he always had a different excuse. I stopped checking on it, and a year went by. Then he claims that he can't fix it, and we owe him 2500 dollars for storing it for a year, or he was going to keep it. There was nothing we could do. We went over with the money, and a tow truck, we left with the car, a dismantled engine, and four boxes full of dismantled engine parts. The motor had fresh gasket material on it, revealing he had the motor installed in another vehicle, because he thought we weren't going to come up with the money. We were out 2500 dollars. We took it to another mechanic and he started with the same pattern of events. After a few months we took the car home in pieces again.

I fell apart, what have I done? I left school and all the free money to get an education. I'm in debt, I can't play football, and I have no car. My days are spent as a housewife caring for everyone else. I fell into a depression. It was clear to me I would never play football again. Who was I? My life was football. Everything I did for the day was to play football. My workout routine, everything I put, or didn't put into my body. When I got back from college all I was trying to do with my diet was bulk up. I left college in the best shape of my life. I was 185 pounds of solid muscle, but even that was too light for my position. Who am I if I'm not playing football? At the time I didn't realize that every serious athlete goes through a crisis when they are no longer able to play their sport. My habits of trying to bulk up now controlled me. I was eating the same amount of food, but without working out. I slowly fell out of shape. I was going through depression. I started going to parties with friends, and they noticed that I was now drinking alcohol. I would go out and look for fights. I was waiting for someone strong to cross my path. I had nothing to look forward to anymore. I was charging down a destructive path that led to jail, or death. I vowed to God that I wouldn't have sex until I was in love with the women I was with. I wanted to make the vow realistic, I know that it would have been morally correct to vow to not have sex until marriage, but I made a realistic vow.

Along with all the other sins I was committing, I broke my vow. Of course I was not planning it to happen, and it might not have happened if I was drunk, but it lowered my inhibitions, and it happened. The next morning me and my friend drove around town to every planned parenthood looking for a plan B pill, even though I was sure I didn't need it, but I was worried. This pill was supposed to prevent pregnancy, so I was told. The only errand my friend had, was to buy a birthday present for his girlfriend. Her birthday was a few days away. With each stop he became more and more impatient. I felt like he was being so self-centered. We drove to three planned parent hoods. I couldn't find this stupid pill anywhere. The last planned parenthood was my last hope. I walked in and there were three ladies inside. The older lady standing greeted me, "What can we help you with?" I explained what I needed, and why I was there. "Do you realize, that is birth control, we don't just hand out pills, you should have been better prepared?" I felt her judgment, and the other two middle aged ladies sitting there. I thought to myself, "How can you baby killers be judging me? You guys are aborting babies, and really do harm, I am trying to use a pill to prevent pregnancy." Then The weight of what I was doing hit me like a ton of bricks. God showed me that even the plan B pill is just as evil as abortion of a baby/fetus. Once the cells are attached and conception starts, the soul is also placed in the womb. It took a person getting paid for assisted people with abortion to open my eyes to my own sin. I walked out of the building and asked God for forgiveness, I accepted that if she was pregnant, I would own my responsibility. "Lets go look for gifts for your girlfriend," and we were on our way.

I was heading down the wrong path quickly. I fell into what every young man struggles with, internet porn. I justified it by saying to myself, I'm not having premarital sex, and I not spreading sexual diseases around, but that doesn't mean it wasn't killing my soul. One night I couldn't go to sleep, it was about two or three in the morning. I walked up the bathroom in the downstairs bathroom, and in my sin. I could hear a loud growl at the door. It was the meanest growl I have ever heard. It was like the growl was a combination between a man and a lion, but more terrifying. I would rather have heard a lion. Then, on the door, a claw scratched the door that ran from the bottom to the top, and drug all the way to the bottom. It was the most terrified I had ever been in my life. It wasn't leaving. It was growling and breathing like a man beast, then it would scratch the door. I knew it was the devil. All I could think was, "I'm already sinning, leave me alone, and I'll keep on sinning." And, it left. I waited a few minutes to open the door, because it could be out there. I ran to my room. I didn't see anything in the dark, but I felt his presence.

I had absolutely nothing left to give. I couldn't even raise my head to the sky. While wallowing in my own self pity one night. I was laying in bed with the TV and the lights off, I could see a silhouette of Jessus standing next to me. When he was here, He let me know that he had been with me the whole time as I committed all the sins, but also my suffering. I committed sloth, gluttony, pride, lust, envy. I wasn't alone. Jesus was suffering my afflictions with me. I felt the urgency of going back to Church. Greg, Maggie, and Anne were not baptized yet. Sure we had been like most Catholics, we would go to Church on Good Friday, Easter, and Christmas, sometimes Palm Sunday. I was a cradle Catholic. It is debated by Christians, people should be baptized when they are of age to acknowledge that they actually want to follow Christ. That seems reasonable, but there are reasons why Catholics baptize babies. The first is; a Catholic that has been baptized in childhood is also given an exorcism, which is very important. The second is; if they die before Confirmation, they will not have to pass through purgatory. There is debate of the existence of purgatory, and I'm not going to debate that, but I will say a few things; First of all, it exists. There is a church dedicated to relics in which people have come from purgatory to reach out for prayers from the living and some of the relics are pillow cases, a wooden dining table, objects touched by the suffering that left scorched hand prints on these objects. And finally; I have been there…I will come back to that experience later. When a Catholic gets baptized as a child before they are of sound mind, they are promised to God, and have an anointing that most can not see, except for the some mystics. The fullness of the gifts of the Holy Spirit come at confirmation, and is undeniable.

Either way, I felt an urgency to get my entire family back to church. My father was the only one to have received the sacrament of Communion. These are the Sacraments; Baptism, Holy Communion/receiving the Eucherist, Reconciliation/Confession, Confirmation, Marriage, Holy Orders, Anointing of the sick. My father was the furthest along, he was the only one to have Communion. Me, my mom, and Jesse were just baptized. I remember going to Catholic mass and always feeling like an outsider. We didn't know how to follow along, and we were unable to celebrate communion, except for my dad.

My mom's brother Jason was involved in his Church, and was playing the part of Jesus in the Passion. It was a Christian non-denominational Church. Even though it was a small church, and a small production, it was so powerful to see the Passion in person. The church was welcoming, and everyone seemed so nice. I wish the Catholic Church was as inviting. After we saw the production play out, we were about to commit to that church, but my father stood fast, "We are not joining that Church." He declared. Normally I would have thought he was being over dramatic, as he has a temper, but this time I was feeling he may be right. Even though I never took part in the Eucherist, I could feel the power. The bread really is Jesus. Not once in The Bible did Jesus say, "Eat this Bread it is a *Symbol* of my Body." He always said it literally. Besides the eucharist, I could feel the power in the Latin Bible quotes, even though I had no idea what they were saying. I could feel the power in the Homolys, and sometimes the music. One major point not to join Uncle Jason's church was simply, the Pastor. The Pastor was Bertha's son from a previous marriage. My parents never mentioned that as a con or the pros and cons, but I felt it. How can he be the son of the devil's mistress and be a Pastor. I know there are such stories where God intervenes this way, but I also know that there are witches that join Christian Churches to infiltrate and take them down from the inside. Either way, I still give my dad the respect for standing strong for Catholicism.

To join a Catholic Church and receive all the Sacraments except Marriage, Holy Orders, and Anointing of the Sick, we could all be in the RCIA class, and get all our Sacraments. RCIA stands for; Right of Christian Initiation of Adults. Anne was the youngest and she was about 13 years old, so we would all be able to get into the same class. We started attending RCIA classes and there were two teachers teaching the same class. Joanne was alright, Marge was very confrontational. While trying to get involved with the program in the first place Marge was rude, dismissive, sarcastic, toxic, negative, and made it seem as though trouble when seeking guidance. "Most people don't finish the class, " She snarled. "Even the people that do finish think they are done, and they only come to Church three times a year. Are you going to be those kind of Catholics?" When she was in the presence of the priest she was so kind, submissive, and praising of him and his work. This spirit of obstinance should never be a part of any ministry, it was nearly enough to break our feeble spirits.

The Non-denominational Church was so welcoming, and that's how it should be. Christians should be welcoming, with open arms, to everyone, to sinners and all who seek God. Some Churches see newcomers and welcome them and their pocket books, as they see money signs. New people to tide the church. Either way, We didn't yet understand what we were attempting to persevere for; the Body and Blood of Jesus Christ made Flesh it the transformation of the bread, also known as; transubstantiation. We always represent our Church, in our actions, we represent our community, state, and country. As people our minds categorize what is good and evil. If I am a sloppy rude person, in another state, or country, the people from that area would form an opinion about me and may generalize that all people from my country, state, community, or church are that way. This drives me to be as Christ-like as possible, and one never knows what someone will generalize in their mind, but a wise man once said, we should view the Church as a hospital for the sick, and not a museum of saints. With this statement in mind it allows us to judge more accurately. I'm not going to go into the cliche; Christians shouldn't judge. Jesus said we shall be measured to the same standard we are judging, as we should, we should never be hypocrites. St. Paul says to judge everything, and one gift of the Holy Spirit is discernment of spirits. Patterns should be recognized to determine if the Church, Pastor, or sermon is of God.

Listening to the instructors of the RCIA program preach, "God isn't going to give you an A on the test, the only way you are going to get an A, is by putting the hard work in." I saw their point, but their statement bothered me. I wanted to know a God that anything was possible. One that could part the Red Sea, and heal the sick, and bring someone back from the dead. I couldn't shake the thought that God wouldn't help in any matter if I called for his intercession. Maybe they should have said, "You shouldn't use God for trivial things that one can attain by hard work." I hate when people put limits on God, as if he can not do anything. The question should be, if it is His Will. We returned home, and had a conversation about the class and decided it wasn't right. I was influential in my family dynamics, and my parents respected what I had to say as if I was an adult, even though I was an adult at this time. This started when I was younger, but it was not to be confused as a controlling measure, just a sound perspective. We didn't return to classes, and a year went by.

The urgency came full force and I knew we had to get into Church regardless of any stumbling blocks in front of us. We entered the RCIA program again and Joanne was teaching the course alone, and it suited her well. As Marge was near her, she was a completely different person and uncorrupt. I could feel her hesitation in our family, she remembered us, and I could feel her doubt in us. We pushed forward and completed the program after a year. At the end of the program there is a weekend retreat and is to be done with fasting. It was so powerful, and important. At one point the Catholic Church would hold these retreats in the mountains. How much more powerful would it have been, but either way It was powerful. God is not restricted from anywhere, and the Holy Spirit was present and palpable. Right before the Easter ceremony when the Sacraments are done, besides the retreat, the people in the program have a pilgrimage, and are obligated to go to a Mass where a Sacrament is being done to a random person. We attended a Baptism at another Church. Watching the Sacrament was interesting, but I didn't think much of it. After returning home that night I was sitting in my room alone. I wasn't watching TV, I was just sitting there in silence, and an overwhelming feeling came over me, I couldn't refrain. I burst into tears, as I knew I was in the presence of God and the Holy Spirit during the Sacrament. The feeling was uncontrollable, and my soul was in Awe, and my body was just there experiencing it.

I had been racking my brain to figure out what I was going to do with my life. I kept feeling the urgency to be a priest. It weighs so heavy on my mind. It was all I could think about. I felt God calling, and it is an undeniable feeling, my heart longed for it. I was sitting in silence in my room praying. In my prayer I let God know that I would not dishonor the position. Did not want to lust after women or commit any acts of licentiousness. I wanted to have children, and raise them. I didn't want to disgrace myself or the position. I felt that there was no way I could be a priest and not dishonor the position. As I attended Church, the feeling of emptiness of family and children subsided as I felt the emptiness disappear. I realized the Church is my family, and the children within the Church would be my spiritual children. Then God gave me a spiritual belt to guard my loins. This sounds preposterous, but let me explain. For more than a month God gave me the ability to not feel any sexual urges. I didn't need anything of that sort. He gave me a way out of that burden. It was peaceful, but it also scared me.

We attended Church, and the Bishop for our Diocese was there Celebrating Mass. As we exited the Church the Bishop met us at the front door, "There wouldn't be anyone thinking of joining the priesthood here, is there?" as he looked at me and my brother. I laughed it off, but inside I was in awe, how did he know? Was this my vocation? Our RCIA class planned a pilgrimage to New Mexico. There is a Sanctuary in Chimayo which has a rich history. It was a Spanish missionary. The Natives occupied the area and believed the were healing properties in the land at Chimayo. The natives there were converted to Christianity for some time. After some time the natives revolted, and took back the land.

Some time after the Spanish returned to the area and reconquered the area. In Guatemala and throughout New Mexico colonial people passed on tradition from the Francisian friars of Our Lord of Esquipulas, which taught that the earth was said to be effective in curing illnesses. In 1810 on Good Friday, a man/penitent Don Bernardo Abeyta saw a bright shining light coming from the ground. He ran over and started digging with his bare hands. From the ground came a life size wooden Crucifix. This Crucifix was immediately associated with Our Lord of Esquipulas. He left the Crucifix there, and he and a group of men went to a local priest to decide what to do. The priest set out for Chymayo and carried it from Chimayo to Santa Cruz. He placed it in the niche of the main altar, the next morning it was gone. It was found back in Chimayo. The process was repeated twice more with the same result, The Crucifix ended up at the same place, Chimayo. Don Bernardo Abeyta was said to have a vision; while plowing his fields the vision directed him to dig under his plow to find great healing that came from the earth. Don petitioned the priest to build a chapel at Chimayo in honor of Our Lord of Esquipulas.

A Chapel was built with the Crucifix in the chapel. Since being built, so many testimonies have been related to the chapel and the earth from that Sanctuary. The earth is collected by pilgrims, and made into a paste, and applied to any ailment, or ingested. The church is full of crutches, wheel chairs, casts, canes, any medical equipment used and the condition was miraculously healed. Any Christian denomination would be quick to say, "It's not honoring God, it's honoring false idols, relics, and all you need is Jesus, not another version of Jesus in the form of a Crucifix." I would say, true, all one needs is Jesus. Honoring his image is not worshiping a false idol, it is Jesus being honored. All the "Weapons and tools" that Catholics have are not necessary for salvation, this is true. But why not have a spiritual weapon is a choice. When walking into a battle, it's wise to arm yourself. If one doesn't know they are in a spiritual battle, they are in denial, a fool, or so out of touch with reality that they are lying to themselves, and why would one not choose to arm themselves.

At one point during the slave trade, people from Africa brought over their religion, voodoo, which has disguised itself under santeria, spiritualism and other spiritual sects. With their religion, they hide their deities/demons in Catholic statues. When a Catholic priest blesses/prays over a relic, it becomes the image of saint depicted, whether it is Jesus, Mary, or an Apostle, but only a Holy Godly spirit. These voodoo practitioners were placing demons in these statues, and the response of certain Christian religions was to not have any statues or relics. They would extinguish the problem, by taking away all statues out of their religion. Anything can be used for good or evil, one can not just take away everything, there will be nothing left, and evil will have all the weapons. For one who denies that the miracles from Chimayo, or the Lady of Guadalupe in Mexico are doing the same thing the Sadducees and Pharisees did in Jesus' time. Denying the Holy Spirit, and the presence of God himself. When Henry the eighth split from the Catholic church nearly six million people left the Catholic Church. Meanwhile, in Central America, due to Spanish conquests, nearly six million people converted to Catholicism. Matthew 3:9 *Don't think to yourself, "We have Abraham for our father,' for I tell you that God is able to raise up children to Abraham from these stones.*There is something to be said for the numbers of people that belong to a Church, it's a sign for the presence of the Holy Spirit.

Chimayo is one of the most visited pilgrimage destinations in America. I have watched two hundred people stand in line to fill up quart ziplock plastic bags from a well of Holy dirt. The well never runs out or gets low. There is nothing feeding the dirt to this well. The chapel is old and built in the 1800's, there is nothing surrounding the church around the well suggesting the well is being fed to the well, that alone is a miracle, despite all the healing miracles that take place.

We were on our way to New Mexico in a van, and it felt like nothing could stop our pilgrimage. I could only focus on one question, "Was I going to become a priest?" The question overwhelmed me, I had to hold back tears as I walked through the Chapel and touched the Crucifix of Our Lord of Esquipulas. There was standing room only as I huddled in a back room with at least fifty people who tried not to knock over the hundreds of crutches clinging to the wall. God's presence was so heavy my legs wanted to fold under the pressure, my knees wanted to fold under the pressure. He said, Philippians 2:10 *Every knee shall bow*. My legs were not known for being weak, two years prior, I squared 585 lbs, this was truly the presence of the Almighty. He asked what I was going to do? I replied, "Yes, I will serve you, but I will not be a priest, I will take a wife." The harshness of my response made my soul cringe. An overwhelming happiness and joy came over me, and my heart bursted with a fire, and my body could not contain the joy as tears came from my eyes. I realized, this was not my happiness, it was God's happiness. That explained why my body couldn't contain it. Wait, what just happened? I could not wrap my brain around what just happened. I agreed to serve The creator of all, but I set the stipulations, and he was still so happy. Was he not upset that I didn't choose the priesthood?

It wasn't until later that I understood what a vocation was. A vocation for God is not an obligation, it's a choice, and we have free will. I was not forced into my vocation, I was offered something precious. God didn't hold it against me, would it have been better for my soul and life to go with priesthood. I do think that God knows what is better for me. Perhaps it may have been the path of least resistance, or maybe I would have been able to focus more attention towards the Church as St. Paul warned. Pleasing the Church, and a wife is one of the most difficult things to do, but maybe that is exactly what God wanted me to do. Having a family will keep one foot planted in the earth, and the other climbing to heaven. I would be a great mediator between the two. Helping people of the earth relate to, and I could help them relate to heaven. God knew what I was going to choose before he asked me. Perhaps that is why he was so overjoyed in my response. Perhaps, he got everything from me he was supposed to get. I was destined for this exact scenario. Years later I would understand exactly what he expected of me, and now looking back, I understand what he was asking, it is definitely a tall order.

Chapter X

Getting my Sacraments was more important than I could ever have imagined. Communion and reconciliation keeps us bound to God. The more we sin we push ourselves away from Him, and leave us vulnerable to the devil. Some Christians say, "One should choose to be baptized in Christ's name." Catholics have an anointing only a few mystics can see. Many years ago The Catholic Church realized baptizing an infant protects the baby from being possessed. It also allows them to be protected by The Holy Spirit until they are confirmed in The Catholic Church, pouring forth the entire gifts of The Holy Spirit. Just because someone doesn't believe in the devil or demons doesn't make them safe from them, in fact, it puts them at a higher risk, because they don't know what they are in a spiritual war. A spiritual war for souls. Conformation expedites the gifts of The Holy Spirit in completion. With this Sacrament, God revealed his plan for me with a prophecy. I've learned patience, It has been eighteen years for them to blossom. He showed me how I would take a wife, and how her love would be proven through struggles and the spirit of poverty. He gave me a prophecy about myself not to be revealed. The gifts of the Holy Spirit are said to not be allowed or by the Catholic Church, as other Churches can be seen speak

105

in tongues, interpretation of tongues, prophecies, discernment of spirits, casting out demons/deliverance, healing, miracles, faith, knowledge, and wisdom. Nothing can be further from the truth. Only speaking in tongues isn't experienced much in the Catholic Church, and casting out demons, which has a lengthy process. The Catholic Church does promote Speaking in tongues, but even in St Paul's time, this was something that needed to be carefully. St Paul said in Corinthians 14:27 *if any man speaks in an unknown tongue, let it be two, or at most by three, and thar by course; let one interpret.* The reason St. Paul wrote even in his time people were speaking in tongues, and it does no good if nobody can interpret, but also that each spirit must be tested, and the devil can also cause a person to speak in tongues, and one must be cautious.

Some people are better Christians than they would be Catholics, and some Catholics are better Catholics then they would be Christians. All Christians create the Body of Christ. How remarkable would it be if all Christians united in Christ's will. It was not his will that we separate and attack each other while the devil runs off scott free to pick us off one by one, and that is what he is doing. Let us unify. The devil knows that if we unify, we could all focus on him, rather than each other. Unity is the devil's stronghold, if we took that, there isn't a place for him to rest. Christians have been wrongly judging people from other churches. This forms opinions of that church that may be false. Nobody is perfect, and we shouldn't make a decision about that Church until we do diligence in our research. It was once said, "The Church is not a museum of saints, but a hospital for the sick."

I was able to move forward with my life. God had healed me from the inside out. I'm not proud of this, but as I said earlier, I literally agreed to continue in my sin so the devil would leave me alone. God forgave me, he is so merciful, no person alive, or that has ever lived except Jesus, will understand the vastness of his mercy. It was time for me to move into the next phase of my life. I was able to get a job and pay off the scholarship money I owed to my previous university, and my parents helped with a portion as well. I applied to a local university, and was accepted. I started college courses, and was thrilled to be back in school. My life was headed in the right direction. I had run into Lanie a couple of times, and remembered what the Lord had told me, I would meet my wife soon, was this a sign I should talk to Lanie. I looked for on campus, but it was like she had disappeared. I ran into her a few times a week, but now that I was looking for her, I never ran into her. It had been a few weeks, and then I realized, maybe she was not meant for me. Shortly after that, I was hanging out with my best friend who had come back from the military, and his cousin came to spend time with him as well. We started talking about the college courses we were in, and one thing led to another, and we started dating. 3 three months later I proposed. I knew we were meant to be with each other, and she was created for me.

I never knew things could be so great. God had created this woman for me, and moved what I thought I wanted, and guided my life in a different direction. She was and is everything I want and need. After thinking about how my life was supposed to go, and what I thought I was going to do, how crazy it ended up. I was definitely good enough to play at a collegiate level, and I say that with complete humility, my stamina, agility, ability to find the ball, and my strength was unmatched. I could and did knock guys on their backside that were three times my size. I didn't have the help I needed at the college level. I didn't have any help from counselors with scholarships, she pointed me to the applications to apply to college, and so I did. I was accepted to every college I applied to. I didn't have any help from my coaches for recruiting, probably because I am of average height, and most athletes are tall, at least in football.

My parents didn't go to college, and didn't know how that process worked, so they were only of little help to me. All the things I was fighting in high school related to football and academics I assumed was bad luck, or maybe the family curse. I was certain it had to do with the curse. I could never understand why God would allow me to suffer from the effects of that curse. All the games I performed well when the coach called my number. I was consistent. I made all American two years in a row, but why during the only two televised games did the coach rarely call my number? Why, when they created a special defense based around me did I roll my ankle? Why was God allowing all these bad things to happen to me? It was at this point in my life that I realized that God allowed me to suffer those things in order to keep me for himself. Sounds egotistical, but it's not. He does this for everyone. He draws us to himself constantly, but either we push him away or cling to our cross and Him.

The curse and devil definitely worked their way back into my life. As blissful as it was at that point. Small things worked their way in very discreetly like they do. The devil knows not to push his way in drastically, it would be too obvious. These days he is blatantly obvious because he is in desperation, he hides in plain sight. He knows when to be subtle, and he was then.

The car my parents bought me for my graduation present was more important to me than Church. I didn't realize how football and my car became false idols. After meeting the woman that would be my wife, I fell so head over heels that it threw me into a tailspin. I loved God and going to church, but I was in such a haze. I don't think she knew how much I was devoted, or loved God. She of course was Christian, and attended Church, but wasn't making it every Sunday. I didn't realize it then, but she became my new Idol. People aren't perfect, and no matter how great they are, they will let you down. However, God is perfect, and He will never let you down. I haven't always known that. I had some very low points in my life, just like most people.

There were points in my life that suicide seemed like an option, as I have said, the devil plays the same hand again and again, and if you resist he stops, but only for a time. He is persistent, and eventually will play the same hand. When I was a child it came off as curiosity. "What would happen if I killed myself? Is there a heaven and a hell? If I believe in Jesus will go to heaven even if I kill myself." Or I would wake up from a dream and feel like I could fly. It made me want to go to the roof and jump off. This is how he toys with a child, and it is enough to convince someone at some point. I have talked to many people that either had a suicide attempt, or they were on the verge of suicide, and the same two demons were mentioned. One was a silhouette of a man with an owl head. The other was a black mule or horse with red eyes. These spirits are certain demons that try to convince people to take their life.

One night I was in a place where circumstance after circumstance went against my favor, and it felt as though nothing went right for me, and God was so far away he couldn't help me. I had a gun in my mouth and as I was about to pull the trigger three demons flew into the room running up the walls and started circling me. They ran up and down the walls, and hovered around me in a frenzy. They were black in appearance, but a little transparent. The one I could focus on the most was about seven feet in length, and had a body like a python, but it had six legs. Its body and legs were skinny. Its head was the shape of a football and had dreadlocks. Its mouth spanned the entire length of his face, and he had sharp narrow teeth. His eyes were a faded glowing red. They were in glee at what I was doing, and that was enough to make me come to my senses. I obviously wasn't thinking logically, but their presence in a sense saved my life. Anytime a demon or the devil wants you to do something, the best thing to do is the opposite, they are a good gauge of what we should be doing.

Life was good for the most part. While in college I was finishing my last course of prerequisites and applied for the nursing program. To my joy, I was accepted. I applied for a part time job at a local auto parts store, and worked hard. I was promoted three times within a year. Things were heading in a good direction. Then, like I said earlier, the devil moved in suddenly. My fiance and I went to a celebration for her college graduation. It was at a local bar and grill.

The night started out fine, and I can't put my finger on it particularly, but we had got into an argument. I couldn't even tell you what it was about now. I wasn't anything remotely substantial. I pushed past it for her night, and of course there were plenty of drinks going around. I was sipping as the night went poorly, and I didn't want to make things worse by doing something in a drunken stupor. One thing happened after another, and another and I kept swallowing the grief down. Her father was joking, making light of the mood, and I have never been able to be ingenuine. I half heartedly laughed at his jokes, "Is everything alright. Am I making too many jokes? I can stop." "No, you're fine, everything is ok." He could tell I was lying, and that me and his daughter were in an argument. Another thing would happen and it became a snowball effect, turning a small snowball into one the size of a boulder that raced down a mountain creating an avalanche.

I couldn't take it anymore. She had both sides of her family there, as her parents had been divorced, and there were plenty of people to take her home. I felt like I was just annoying her by being there, there was no winning. Every time she would come back to the table she would remark how stupid the expression on my face was. I should have told her I'm leaving but I didn't. I called a cab to take me to my parents house. The cab driver was a gem. Knowing where he picked me up from and the time of night, he assumed I was drunk, so he continued to take a long route home to drive up the bill. Turn after turn he took the wrong route. I wanted to get out, but I had heard stories of dirty cab drivers calling the cops on intoxicated people refusing to pay cab drivers. I wasn't drunk, but I was worried I would fail a breathalyzer and the legal amount of alcohol. This clown was driving down every block around my parents house. A perfect ending to the night. Eventually he stopped the car. I tried, but I could hardly sleep. I knew I was going to have to face the music tomorrow. I should have told her I was leaving. At that time I had been sleeping over at her house nearly every night, and she still lived with her parents. I still had a room at my parents house, but I felt like I didn't live there either. It was now the next evening, and I went to her parents house to talk about what happened.

I could feel the anger from her and her family. I could feel it from both sides. I sat on her couch, "Everyone is mad at you, my stepmom said, "How much of a man is he, that he can't have the decency to tell you that he is leaving? It's a good thing my family was there to drive me home. And you are still sitting there with that stupid look on your face. I can't stand it, I hate you, I can't even look at you anymore." She stormed out of the room. There I was sitting there alone in her parent's living room alone. I couldn't go home, I felt like I had already moved out of my parents house. I couldn't stay at her house. She had so much hate for me at that moment, and her entire family was mad at me. I can't stay here. I estranged myself from my family. I estranged myself from God. I had stopped going to Church to hang out with her. I had nobody, and no place to stay. I have nothing. The tears poured, and the thought of taking my life arouse. "You should kill yourself. Your alone, and have no place to go." I layed there on her parents couch crying my eyes tightly clinched shut. I told my self, "I'm not going to kill myself, I'm not going to do that." Even though my eyes closed I saw Mary appear from the dark abyss with stars around her... She looked so, so beautiful, there was never a woman to match her beauty. She floated to me and hugged my heart, and disappeared. Happiness surged through my heart and my soul. Her touch is unexplainable, but I can try. It felt Better than any mother's hug to a child who is hurt. Sweeter than any lover's embrace, but completely platonic with no perversion, just pure love. I opened my eyes, and now the tears of sadness were tears of joy, and I was so joyful I could not contain any of it. Just then my fiance walked into the room, "I'm sorry, I don't know what came over me, I'm so sorry." We hugged and her heart was converted, we didn't even have to have a follow up talk that is necessary after fights to talk about what went wrong and how to avoid fighting over the same situation again. It was wrapped in a gift. How can something so sweet come from such an awful experience? I would reduce those two days over and over just to feel Mary's embrace until the last day of my life.

Out of curiosity I looked up Mary on the internet, and it said she is the patron saint for the desolate. I still can hardly tolerate any image of Mary I see these days. None of them are as beautiful as she is, nobody can capture such beauty. Some are more tolerable than others, but no image on earth does her beauty justice. I started attending Church regularly, and we would alternate between her Church and mine. It's good to hear different perspectives on the same Christ. I can not stand Christians bashing other Christians. As I said before, at the point the Body of Christ is harming the Body of Christ, every part is important. I started watching football again, but If my team was playing at the same time as Church, I chose Church, as I should have.

Chapter XI

Life was getting better, and I had a decision to make. My manager was Russell, and he was offering me another promotion, and a chance to run my own store. I really enjoyed the business, and there was no change in pay from what I would be making after two years of nursing school, only I would be making it now, and I would get quarterly bonuses. It was a salary position, and I was used to the hours, as Russell had been mentoring me. Yes, I was working long hours off the clock, but it helped me learn how to run my own store, and it showed my loyalty to the offer in front of me. I decided to walk away from college, and take the opportunity presented. It seemed as though something good would happen, and then something bad would happen. On the way into work my truck lost power and started to smoke. My engine blew, and I had a wedding to plan, I couldn't afford any expenses. Russell offered to help me rebuild it. In the meantime, I had to get a junk car that can make it to work.

I found a cheap car, the only thing it was lacking was rotors and breaks. They shook violently while coming to a stop. I bought it, and the next day, I was driving back to work from my lunch break. On the interstate where I nearly flipped off the bridge, I was speeding, and switched lanes into the fast lane, and before

I knew it, the car ahead of me was at a dead stop, but its brake lights were not working. I slammed on the brakes, and my tires screeched. I wasn't seatbelted, so I Locked my arms on the steering wheel and locked my knees on the floor to brace myself. As I crashed into the car ahead of me, a SUV simultaneously crashed into me. Me locking up my joints was a bad decision, the force slung my face into the steering wheel, and ricocheted my head into the windshield shattering it upon contact. I felt the warmth of my own blood rush down my face and chest. In a moment my entire shirt was red.

The crash was not the worst part of the ordeal. The Lady I hit was yelling at me for my car insurance information as I attended to my facial wounds. As I answered the paramedics questions she badgered the cops with her side of the story. Even though it was a five car pile up on the interstate, and I was the fourth car in the accident, I could hear her yelling at the police how it was my fault. Like I said, "The worst part was about to come." I was out the money I shelled out for the car and I still didn't have a car. The previous month my mother-in-law invited me to join their car insurance company. They are great people, but I declined as I was still on my parents plan, and it was the only bill I was not paying. In hindsight, I should have offered to start paying it, but I was trying to save up money. After talking to the insurance company, I learned that the account was closed due to no payment. Besides careless driving, I got a ticket for driving without insurance. Long story short the judge granted the lady I hit the right to withhold my driver license. In order to release my license, She needed to sign a waiver, and the guy who rear ended me also needed to sign a waiver. The judge totaled out her car, and the only way I could perceive her signing the waiver was if I took out a loan to pay off her entire totaled value.

Everytime I took two steps forward, I took one step back. The devil tried to take a hold of my wife. We would argue, and it wasn't her I was arguing with. The same for me. I would say things that I really didn't feel, but they were digs, by someone other than myself. We were both hurt, and being used by the devil. One night I saw a vision as my eyes were open. I saw this elephant, but it was standing upright like a man. It was a mixture of the two. He was laughing with his trunk raised in the air and his head tilted back wearing a maroon Shriners hat with a gold tassel hanging down. His clothes were ornate, and expensive. His maroon vest was lined with gold tassels as he was displaying vanity. I recognized this demon. It was a demon of lust, gluttony, and worship of expensive materialism. Trying to fill the void of God with worldly greed and lust of the eye, flesh, and insatiable desire.

My relationship suffered as we pushed forward. Robert spoke that the spirit wants us together. Reivelling, he knew it was fragile. There were times that we were hurt with each other, and I became spiteful. One night I was lying in my room on my belly crying with the lights out. I was home alone as my wife was at work. Thoughts raced through my head of her hurting me, and me retaliating. I lied to myself, "I'm glad I hurt her back." It wasn't true, there was no joy in revenge. I only felt more unsettled and bothered. As soon as I said those words in my head, "I'm glad I hurt her back." My body became paralyzed. My breathing felt like a ventilator was breathing for me. I was numb. A presence entered the room. My eyes were closed, and I couldn't move a muscle or open an eye. At that point I came out of my body. I was hovering over my body looking at the closed door to my room. A yellow smoke billowed from under the doorway and filled the entire room as it rose. I went back into my body, but it was still paralyzed. Then I felt it. It grabbed my ankles and my wrist. One being. All my mind's eye could make out was the devil. He came in the form of a huge dark muscular black shadow, with huge horns. It slowly lifted me as if I weighed nothing. It lifted me, and I couldn't resist. Before I knew it I was completely upside down.

My feet were near the ceiling and my arms were outstretched as if I was nailed to an upside down cross. I thought to myself I can beat this. I'm going to flex my right arm to pull away. With all my might, I flexed my right arm. It worked, I was slowly flexing my right arm. But then I felt something hit my numbed face. Then my arm snapped back to the outstretched position. I told myself to flex my arm again. I did it! Then I felt something hit my numbed eye. I realized I wasn't stronger than it. It was allowing me to poke out my own eye. I cried out to Jesus in my mind. It released me, I drifted back to the bed. Jesus didn't let it just drop me on my head. I floated down to a soft landing. I could breath on my own and open my eyes. The room, once filled with yellow smoke, had vanished. All I could do was cry. I cried with remorse for hurting my spouse. I knew I had to make amends. I called her at work and apologized. She forgave me, but sounded doubtful at the story I told. I hadn't fallen asleep, I was awake. This wasn't a dream or a night terror. I knew at that moment, the thing the devil hates the most is forgiveness. When we don't forgive the people who hurt us, they are bound to that sin, and he can't use that against them, or us. When we don't forgive, we continue to sin, and it's a vicious cycle of sin. When we forgive, the cycle is broken for the forgiver. If the transgressor asks for forgiveness, now they are lost from their sin as well.

The devil would come back to visit me a few more times, as he had a right to me, as I had sinned and pushed myself away from God. The next time was when I was watching TV in bed. I wasn't sleepy or dozing off. I was wide awake. My wife was laying on my right arm, but she had fallen asleep. I was laying on my back. I told myself I'm going to keep my eyes open this time. I was able to, but everything else was paralyzed again. The room filled with yellow smoke, and I felt his presence. This time he grabbed me from the back of my neck and was pulling me into another dimension behind the head board. I was being sucked into nowhere. I called out to Jesus, and he left. Another night was very similar. I was laying on my back watching TV, and my wife was asleep laying on my arm again. This time was very similar. I was able to keep my eyes open as the smoke entered the room and my body became paralyzed. This time he grabbed my toes, and started pulling into a dimension at the foot of the bed. In my head, I called out for Jesus, and he vanished.

Life goes on, even for the outrageous life I was experiencing. It was evident the curse was on me and my vehicle. When My mother-in-law's car broke down I asked Russell if he could help me rebuild the motor. While we worked on her car, I let her borrow my truck. It was telling, maybe there was something to this family curse, and the fact that she was borrowing my truck was evidence I could prove the curse. My mother-in-law is and was a great driver, never speeds, and never gets in car accidents. While she was using my truck, she received a speeding ticket, which doesn't seem like a lot, but she also got in a couple of fender benders as well. They were not her fault, but they were significant enough to leave my passenger side door crushed in as someone backed into her. My curse which involved my vehicle was marked by a spell, even if I was not the one driving it. After getting her car back, her luck had changed. Car accident free and ticketless since.

While working on the car I opened up to Russell about my childhood, and all the crazy stuff that had happened regarding my curse. "Russell, coincidence after coincidence, after coincidence stops being a coincidence. I have a gut feeling that all of this is a curse." "You know Robert, that new guy I hired? He does that sort of stuff? He is from Cuba, he does magic. He was telling me he used to charge five, ten, even fifteen grand for cleansings. Look at all those new vehicles he drives. His wife is in the military, and he works as a part time salesman, how do you think he affords that lifestyle? Maybe he can help you. I'll ask him, if you want?" "I could use all the help I can get." Robert spoke English, but it was very broken. Russell was fluent in Spanish, and came from Mexico, so they were able to communicate better in Spanish, but Cuban Spanish and Mexican Spanish are different, so some things don't cross over. One day Russell says, "Ok, I talked to Robert, and he agreed to help you for free." "Really," "Yeah, but he gave specific instructions that must be followed. You're staying at my house tomorrow night after work, you can't tell anyone you are going, not even your wife."

That night Russell was driving home, he was stopped at a stop light at the intersection of two major streets, one boulevard, and a highway. As he was waiting for the light a SUV sideswiped his SUV, and stepped on the gas to escape. Russell's SUV was badly damaged, but was still drivable. Russell has never been a guy to fight back, so he stomped on the gas to chase him. He pulled his cell phone out and called the cops. As he followed the guy, he shot from the boulevard to the highway. The authorities were reluctant to follow as jurisdiction changed. On the boulevard it was the city police department's jurisdiction, and as he shot up the highway he was the state patrol's, and when he turned down rural areas after the highway, he was the sheriff's jurisdiction. Ultimately, the state patrol had jurisdiction everywhere in the state, but it came down to who wanted to arrest the guy, and who would do the reports I guess. It probably made a difference to the law enforcement agencies, and whom was about to get off shift, but eventually the sheriff made an arrest after the pursuit. The guy was a drunk driver. This whole ordeal made me wonder if Russell and I were still going to continue with our plans we set for the next day, but

Russell was true to his word, and we drove up in my vehicle. I felt terrible not telling my wife what exactly was happening. I explained that I was with Russell, and nothing was wrong with us, but I needed to do something very important. I didn't expect her to understand, how could I?

It was all so overwhelming for everyone involved, even Russell. This curse had levels to prevent me from getting help. If Russell would have been a coward, my help would be foiled. He could have been seriously hurt or killed in the car accident the night before. After mine and Russels work day ended, I told him I needed to stop by my parents house. I didn't know why. I was running off of intuition. I still had a house key and I let myself in, as nobody was home. I started grabbing random things that I felt that I needed to bring to Robert's house. I grabbed a pair of socks from my dad's drawer. Two spools of thread from my moms sewing kit and a couple more items. After putting the items in a bag I headed to Russell's. "Here are some blankets, you can sleep on the couch in the living room." "I don't know how to thank you?" "I got you man, don't be weird…" I layed on Russell's couch wondering where my life was headed. I had waited decades to get to the bottom of this. I had a hard time falling asleep, it was all just so strange. "What has my life become, why can't I just have a normal life? One where a witch doesn't have a vendetta against me and my family?"

Morning arrived, and I didn't feel like I got any sleep. But Russell and I headed to Robert's anyway, nothing was stopping us. When we arrived Russell answered the door wearing what looked like a small purple chef's hat. He welcomed Russell and I in and showed us around. As soon as I entered the living room I saw a statue of a saint. It was about two and a half feet high. It looked like it was a statue of St Jude with a staff and it was shepherding three sheep, but this was not St. Jude. This thing was foreign to me. Its spirit was angry and powerful. It noticed I was there, and I could feel it look at me when I entered the room. This thing was a solid adamant object, but it had a blurry haze that covered it. It looked as if a void in space was covering it. It looked like the movie *Predator.* It had a blurry clear presence, and I knew it was not of an angelic Spirit. It was moving, and I could make out that the statue was made to be St Jude, but it definitely was not.

There was a bamboo mat layed out in the living room with a stool on it. There was a large piece of white chalk sitting on the matt next to the stool. "Have a seat. Turn your palms to the sky, and ask God to let me help you. Let me in, and have an open mind." I did, I prayed so fervently. He covered my palms with white caulk. Then he returned to the room with several things. He had a coconut shell that was cut in half, and it was filled with water. He came back throwing the water all over the room and the mat, and on me. He explained, "The earth was first a giant glob of water, and mother earth called for the land, and it rose. That is why the ocean holds power, and the things from the ocean have power." As he pulled out a collection of black and white sea shells, and a black stone and a white stone. He gave me the stones. He drew a circle on the mat. He told me to close my hands around the stones and mix them up. And hand me only one. I did this, and the black stone continued to be handed to him. "Put them behind your back and do the same thing." The same results. "Now drop them in the circle, if they bounce out, that's ok." Then he gave me the tiny sea shells, roughly 30, half black and half white. "Drop them in the circle, and if they fall out, it's ok." I repeated the direction several times. "Yes you have a lady who has cursed you and your family, you know who she is." This was a relief. It was only Her and not her daughter too. "Your mom suffers greatly, and she wishes her dead, and it pains her that she is still alive as God wants her alive. She can't kill her." Tears filled my eyes, and

I wept. "Russell, can you get him some water? This is natural, a lot of people become emotional." Russell looked at me with shock, as if he didn't know that I loved my mom. "Before I help you, we have to help your sister. She is pregnant and the baby's life is in jeopardy. There was a man who built something beautiful and tall on his property. People came and tore it down every time it was finished. This has been your life, every time you do something great, it disintegrates. I also see another who wants what you have. Your career, your truck, and wife." I knew who he was talking about a coworker that worked under me. He thought he should be running my store, and I knew without a doubt. On the other hand, I was so shocked, I couldn't remember that Maggie had recently told me she was pregnant.

I left with Russell soon after. I was mind-blown, so much confirmed, years of thinking, but not having any proof. I called my mom and told her what had been going on. I need to come over, and Robert needs to do a ceremony. She agreed, and Robert came over. We were standing outside of the house where the doggy door was. I stood by my mom and we were facing away from the house. Robert stood behind us. "Alan, don't turn around, I don't want you to be afraid of what you see. He grabbed the rooster by the talons and threw him forward as the wings spread and they grazed our shoulders. All I could picture in my head was a native medicine man eight feet tall, wearing an eagle on his head, and his skin was pale blue, I could see him doing the ceremony. Then I heard the rooster cackle as the neck snapped. Robert buried the bird. My mom looked at me terrified, with wide eyes, what are you having me do.

Maggie was soon at the hospital, and the baby had the cord around her neck. It was time to see if Robert's ceremony worked. Maggie went to a C-section where she and the baby survived. It was a success. The next time I saw Robert he said, "I will help you, but, it will be a very small chance we will be able to make it happen, less than one in a million." I prayed fervently that it would happen. "Come back to my house in five days. Wear the same under-shirt with your clothes every day and do not wash it. It needs to have your scent. Don't be intimate with your wife, you can't even kiss your wife. You can't even masturbate, all your fluids/ your DNA need to be in your body, you need this for spiritual strength. When you come, bring an entire set of clothes." "OK." I told my wife what the instructions were, and she agreed. The night before I was to go up to Russell's house I accidentally kissed my wife, as it always is a habit when leaving or arriving. "Hey, Robert, I'm so sorry, I accidentally kissed my wife, is that going to mess things up?" "Are you kidding?! We have to start over. I have to do the same thing you are doing too. I can't kiss my wife either. We have to start over, and she has a back up spell, that whoever helps you will be attacked too, so I'm getting a cold. We need to handle this. Remember what I told you. You can wear sunglasses to hide yourself from your enemy, they will not be able to see you. Bring a young rooster, a bag full of brown and green beans. Green like the earth, and plantains, make sure they're green. After you buy these items, put them in a brown paper bag as your enemy can't see what you have."

I made sure to not break any of the rules. As I walked into the house he was wearing a purple hat, it looked like a chef's hat. He was wearing a plain white T-shirt and white pants. He was grading the white part of the coconut with a cheese grater. "The coconut was a healer. He went house to house healing people of their ailments. God gave him this gift. He was originally white. The coconut started only healing who he wanted. He healed pretty girls and became partial. So God placed him in a hard brown covering and made it hard for people to get to the healing part. He took the plantains and wrapped them with thread. I recalled thread was one of the items I took from my moms house when this all started. He too, had white thread wrapping it around the green plantain saying, "The white thread symbolizes purity." Then he took the black wrapping it saying, "The black thread symbolizes death, and the red sacrifice." as he finished wrapping the red thread. "Follow me." I followed him to the basement. It was a concrete basement, and there was a large circle drawn with chalk. Next it was a bottle of rum, and one of his saints. It looked like a tin pail filled with dirt, and it had some items in it. It had the neck of a violin, a horse shoe, and a cigar, that is all I could make out. He took a cigar and lit it. He put it in his mouth backwards and drew smoke into his mouth. As I was kneeling in the circle he blew the cigar smoke over me, then he gulped a mouth full of rum and spit it on me. Then he took the rooster out grabbing it by the talons. He threw it forward so the wings grassed my shoulders, then I felt the warm blood pour over my shoulders. He said, "Take all your clothes off and put them in the plastic box you brought the rooster in. Clean yourself off with this towel and throw it in the box as well, then change into your clean clothes. I did as he instructed, and as I changed into clean clothes and walked away from the box I could see three black silhouettes clawing at the box. They were at least nine feet tall. I could see that they were muscular, bald, and their fingers were long and sharp. All three were non-stop clawing at the contents of the box.

I was in aww, "I'm starving, let's get something to eat, it's on me," Robert smiled. What…How can something like that happen, and he just comes out with, "Let's eat." I felt indebted, so I agreed. As we walked up stairs he said, I can see that you are a good man, and you can do what I do. What… How can I do these things, and why do I have to come to you for this?" It just left me with more questions. We celebrated at of all places, a Chinese Buffet. It wasn't any crazier than anything else that happened. After dinner we returned to his house. He said, "Drive as far as you can, somewhere you never have to drive again, and throw the box on the side of the road. If by some chance you have to pass that place again, look forward, don't look at the side of the road.

On the way home I could see the three figures grappling with the clothes in the box as it bounced around the bed of the truck. I was emotionally drained, it was such a long crazy day. He lived thirty miles from my house, so I drove another thirty minutes east of my house, and then home. After the ceremony I could hear demons cackling outside of my house as if they were looking for me. Since that experience, I realized every image in my head prior was a vision. I could see demons and recognize them. Russell Gave me a necklace that was made of small white beads, "It will give you luck, and ward off evil, before you put it on kiss it. You see I wear one, and you see this yellow and green bracelet? When this bracelet breaks I know I'm going to die, and I can prepare myself."

That week I went to work, and as I was standing there typing at a computer. It was designed like every type of auto parts store design, and all I could do is pray. As Robert had been helping me, I knew there was a battle happening. I could not stop praying, my soul was praying for me. In between answering phones and helping customers, a prayer was on my lips. A coworker came up to me. "What are all those necklaces you're wearing?" I tucked them into the collar of my shirt as I was embarrassed. I was wearing a crucifix on a chain, a Rosary, and the white necklace Robert had given me. "Was it too much?" I asked myself, "And should I be mixing Christ with whatever the santeria Robert practices?" I was so thrown off. Robert talks about God the creator and St. Michael. I know that what he was doing was helping me. "Are you OK?" she asked me. "Yeah, why?" "You are pale white, you look sick." I walked to the bathroom, and was shocked. She was right, I was so pale, all the color had left me, but I felt fine. I attributed it to me being cleansed of my curse.

I was the store manager for that auto parts store. I had been navigating my own management style. It doesn't matter what is being sold, what a manager is doing is managing the people. The logistics can be learned. They are repetitive, and learned, even by a low level employee. I was getting a great idea of what was happening in the store. The manager below me who had outgrown his position and had expected to be the store manager for that store was disgruntled. This was the man Robert spoke of when he told me he wanted everything I had. I was still going to be professional, and I never abused my power. I did have him under my thumb as I was wiser than he thought I was. I had found car parts damaged out that fit his year make and model of his jeep. I knew he was stealing, and he wasn't the only one. The commercial account manager was stealing as well, just not for herself. She was a previous store manager from another store that was implanted and demoted. It was a slap in the face for her, and personal. It hurt her pride, as the district manager that demoted her, was also having an affair with her, as he was with a few of the female managers in his district. She wouldn't steal for herself, but for her commercial accounts. She would always brag that her accounts would only talk to her. There was a reason for that. My store was in tip-top shape. Everything was in order, and I constantly scanned inventory. There were a couple of tricks to the trade. For some reason that branch of stores only carried certain car parts for that demographic of customers. It would carry four lugnuts of a certain type of vehicle. So if a customer needed twenty, they had to drive to four stores all over town for a complete set. The wise store managers would delete their inventory until they had a full set, and then when they sold them, it proved they had twenty in stock. The wise, but corrupt store managers would sell a part that only your store had in stock, but they would sell it at their store, and send the customer to pick it up. It was all the same company, but it skewed the numbers for that store. The district manager would praise the sales numbers, and compare them store to store in that district, and that was how we were given hours to staff our employees. If another manager was selling all the parts of another store, it made their numbers look good, but it was that store that was getting shorted.

I noticed that everytime I would count the expensive car parts next to the commercial office, the commercial manager would redo the inventory the next day. I asked myself as I noticed the pattern. These were all the fuel pump, shocks, power steering pumps, all the expensive car parts. These were the parts the commercial accounts would buy as they are the more difficult car maintenance the average person would not want to, or know how to replace themselves. I started scanning these parts during the weekend when the commercial manager was not there. I corrected the inventory, and was amazed to see that there would be a twenty thousand dollars deficit in inventory. The reason the commercial accounts would only talk to her, was because she was giving them free parts. If she did sell them anything, it was a case of the item of the month, instead of an expensive car part, so they were still getting a bargain. Companies would pay to upsell certain items that month. As we did not work on commission, it was a competitive drive instilled in the employees to sell these products. It was on a comparative flow sheet that compared each store in the district, and the district manager drilled us for numbers. This made her look good, and gave the commercial account a bargain discount for a car part. I called a meeting, and let all the employees know that Loss prevention was monitoring the store, they weren't, so I lied, but I wanted to let them know that everything they were doing was being watched. I let the district manager know there were problems, but he didn't respect anything I had to say. I was a new manager, and green.

There was a problem with all the sales coming out on the weekend. I printed them off again, to put up the new displays. I called a couple of other stores in the district, but they were different. I called the district manager and he didn't answer, so I left him voicemails of the issue. I set up the displays that looked appropriate, and didn't adjust others, due to the inconsistency compared to the other stores in my district.

Monday came and the commercial manager was picking on another employee that was her driver. She and the other driver did not like this girl. They definitely made her life hard, and I could see the pecking order. I put a stop to it, and she picked up the phone to complain to the district manager. I could hear her lies, as she spewed them into her ex-lover's ear. Just then one of my managers walked into the office, "I need to take a seven day vacation next week?" "The schedule is already made, I need more advanced notice than that. If there are a few days I am off, I'll work those for you, but you'll have to find coverage for the others. If you can't find coverage, you'll be responsible for working those days. "Man, this is fucking rediculous, I can't believe you are doing this to me!" As soon as the commercial manager got off the phone with the district manager, he picked up the phone to call him as well. Ten minutes later the district manager calls me. "What is going on down there, can you not run your store?! It sounds like you don't have control of your store. I'll be there tomorrow."

The next day he arrived with two managers from a different store. They apparently had not been clued in as to why they were there. They were told; they were there to help work to fix the store as if it was in shambles. They were clueless, and this is how I know why; They walked the store in amazement. They were amazed how organized it was. Even the back stock room was in order.

Almost all stores have a stock room of things that are outdated, and not in inventory, but you can't sell, or throw any of it away. My store was in order, and they let me and my district manager know in what good shape it was. Complements kept coming my way all day. It didn't save me the two berating I took in the back stockroom. My manager was furious, "Why didn't you let me know that the new sales were corrupt in your system!?" "I did, you didn't answer your cell phone three times, so I left you three voicemails." He didn't like that very much. He stood up yelling and throwing his arms in the air. He got closer and closer to me as his lisp slurred with spit shooting out of his mouth. His entire face was beat red, and he got closer. To me as I sat in a chair. I was waiting for him to punch me, and I wanted him to. I told myself to breathe as I noticed my breaths get shorter and shallow. It finally ended. I could feel my power being stripped away from me. I knew it was coming to an end. I did what I could for that store. I worked so many hours off the clock, in spite of having my own personal life suffer. I felt what Jesus felt having his own people turn on Him. I hired every one in that store except the commercial manager and the manager that felt like it should be his store.

The HR guy was there the next day to sort everything out. I was honest. I wanted to tell him how the district manager was having an affair with the commercial manager and another in another store, but I didn't. I showed integrity and only responded with the truth, and the topic in question. The next Sunday the district manager called me in to have a meeting at my store. I knew what it was about, so I agreed. In reality, I should have said I was off, and I could meet him the next day, but I didn't want to delay it. He was already there with another store manager. Both looked angry, and ready to fight. They called me to the back, and he handed me my last paycheck. I took it gracefully. I guess he thought I was going to fight. I walked back to the office to get my jacket and keys, and he came running in behind me as if I was going to steal or push over displays. It was so irritating, but I held my composure and walked out gracefully. "If this is your Will Lord, so be it." This was the first time I felt a crucifixion. It was not symbolic, but truly following in Jesus Christ's footsteps as his apostles did. I rose to power, and was betrayed by those who supported me, and left alone, cast out. Saint Paul writes, *"I have been crucified with Christ. It is no longer I who live, but Christ who lives in me. And the life I now live in the flesh I live by faith in the Son of God, who loved me and gave himself for me."* Galatians 2:20. It was not figurative, but literally.

I decided to use my time wisely, and write this book. I was scorned by my former store manager peers, but I knew it was what God wanted me to do. We had to be sparingly with our finances, as I had to wait for unemployment to kick in. But I was walking into the fire, as everyone told me not too. My wife was the only one who supported the project. I got to work on this book. I was finally lifted from my curse, and I felt amazing. For the first time things didn't crumble in my hands. I have heard many wise sayings about the adversity of the human spirit, and everything is achievable if one puts their mind to the task. Those people have never been crushed by a curse. Every advancement one makes, gets ripped away. It's not, "Take two steps forward, and one step back." It's more like; you take two steps forward, and three steps back. Your boss berates you, and then your co-workers. You go to the store to pick up dinner so you don't have to cook, and drop it in the driveway while you're bringing it into the house. Then your wife yells at you for dropping the food. Feeling terrible, you make dinner to appease her, and she goes to bed mad anyways. Then you wake up and do it over again. It wears you down, and when it's truly time to fight, you are already exhausted before the fight. The devil never fights fair. He doesn't wait for the bell. And if by some chance you have the upper hand, he pleads with you, and by surprise you let your foot off his throat, and he stabs you in the back. Your work, finances, car, friends, family, and spouse is irritated at you, and it all comes crumbling down. He makes you and your spouse feel as if you are unfaithful to each other.

For the first time in my life since I was eight years old, I was lifted from the curse. Days were great, the world wasn't against me. The clerk at the store wasn't irrationally annoyed at me for no reason. The car next to me would suddenly cut me off and then honk at me as if it was my fault. I got to work on my book. As I wrote, I started to turn on the TV in my office to drown out the silence in the room. For the first and last time in my life a series of sitcoms aligned as never before. For more than seven hours a day all my favorite shows came on, one after another. I realized what a distraction this was becoming. I could but notice that the devil may have had something to do with this distraction. But I chalked it up to maybe a coincidence. My wife also noticed my distraction. I turned off the TV, and weaned myself back to the silence.

The Holy Spirit commanded me to save my work. I didn't understand why, but I did as He instructed. I purchased a jump drive, and saved my manuscript. Suddenly while I was writing on my desktop computer, the tower caught fire, and the screen went black. I unplugged it, and the fire fizzled out. Astonished that I saved my work to a jump drive. I realized, this was no coincidence that I was told to back up my work. I purchased a laptop and a new desktop, and even with money tight, I knew the importance, in order to complete the task at hand. Even living outside of the curse, the devil didn't want this story, my witness, to be told. He knew even if one person was different after reading it, they would be converted. He knew that my entire life of sparing with demons, I would reveal how they operated, and warn people of their traps.

Before I had got fired from my job, My wife and I had planned on having our first child. We discussed if this was going to derail our plans to have a child. We decided that there is never an opportune time to have a child, as we felt like our time was running out. Women problems ran in my wife's family. So we started trying. After a couple of months, I felt at peace. I felt that she would have a baby boy. One day my wife yelled for me, so I ran to her. She was in the bathroom. On the floor was a small pile of blood and tissue. I asked if she was in pain and she said she wasn't, but this fell out. We decided it was time to see a doctor, as we had been trying for several months, until this happened. In the meantime we tried several holistic measures to increase the chance of fertility. We tried acupuncture, anything we could to increase our chances. I went back to Robert to seek help. He sat us down, and said. "You lost a baby boy." And we both wept, and we both knew the small pile of blood and tissue that lay on the bathroom floor was him. Whomever says the fetus is not a baby in the womb is DEAD wrong… Robert gave me an assignment. He told me to find a certain squash. "You will only find this squash at a Mexican meat market." There is medical evidence that the family of squash and pumpkins have many health benefits for the reproductive system of a female, so it was no surprise to me that he recommended this fruit. I drove to a larger town thirty miles away to find this fruit. I drove to over 15 stores. I found only one store that had it, but there was one problem.

There was only one, and this squash was so rare here, that the store sells it in sections. There was a huge chunk cut out of it, as the store allows it to be sold in slices if desired. I asked the store clerk if they would be getting more. He explained that it is rare, but there is no telling when he would get another one. "What exactly do you need this for?" He could see my desperation. I couldn't tell him. That should have been a sign that I wasn't exactly following

God's will. I called Robert, "I don't know if this will work?" "The spirit sees that you have tried so hard to find the right fruit, so get something close to it. When you get home some night, your wife will have to pick up a stone. She will not have to directly look for it. It will make itself known to her. There will be no doubt. Once she finds the stone, she will have to rub the stone all over her body, especially her belly. Do the same with the squash. You will take the stone to the yard where it will not be covered by shade. You will place it on a plate with a white candle. Light the candle, and make sure the stone is outside for an entire day, so that the sun will hit the stone during noon, the time when the sun is at the highest point in the sky. After that day, the candle will have melted away, and you will go to your yard, and she will pick up the stone and throw it, don't keep track of where it lands, just throw it. Then you and her will take the squash to a river, not a lake, or a pond, a river. Water that will carry the squash far away."

One night we came home late after dinner. On our way up to the front door, "Alan look." As she nudged me with her elbow. "Do you see that?" "Yeah, that's crazy." There in river rock that lined our house was a stone, a little bigger than a golf ball. It was glowing green. She picked it up, and the next day we followed his instructions. We were putting all our eggs in one basket. We scheduled appointments with one of the leading fertilization doctors in the state. Robert prayed for the intercession of certain saints. It seemed familiar with the use of candles. It wasn't later that I realized that if something can be used for Holy purposes, they can be used for evil. They can use a candle in the same manner. Have an alter, but use it for evil. Robert kept referring to the spirit. I just assumed he meant the Holy Spirit. Not once did he say Holy. Santeria had four main saints. Except, they weren't saints, but five demons masquerading as saints. Santeria was voodoo disguised as Christian religion. Comfortable as many hispanic, and Central American countries unknowingly embrace black magic and Spiritualism. It became very evident to me that I need to pay attention to what I'm doing. As an exorcist Fr. Dan Reehil says, "When you do the sign of the cross, you invoke the Holy Trinity. Whether the Holy Trinity knows you or not, it doesn't matter, you got its attention. The same goes for the demonic realm, if you do things that invoke the demonic realm, you get its attention." I learned this when Jesse was pregnant with her second child, and had episodes of bleeding during pregnancy. Her doctor was very concerned. She was at risk alone for being older than a woman should be for carrying a baby. I went to a local grocery store for a devotional candle to help with the safety of my niece. While I was there I noticed a candle with Jesus on the Crucifix. The candle is called the Just Judge. There is a skull sitting at the base of the Crucifix, and a rooster perched to the left a fiery background.

I knew at that moment it was a candle used for santeria, as roosters are the sacrifice used in the practice. Not to mention the ominous flames in the background, and skulls that are used in the practice. I chose another candle, and researched the Saint, as I knew Lazarus was a good friend of Jesus in the Bible, and a well known Biblical figure. However, He is used in witchcraft as well. The candle I chose was St. Martin de Porres, a recognized saint by the Catholic Church. I prayed the devotional prayer for days, and near the end when the candle was nearly gone, I heard a voice, "Would you choose to save this baby, even if it meant your team loses the Super Bowl?" I answered, "Yes." That doesn't mean it didn't sting. I was a devout fan. But ultimately, family, and life is more important. When Jesus comes back, is he going to care who won Super Bowl 58? Absolutely not. As a famous quarterback said, "People pray all the time to win, and fans pray for their team. That doesn't mean God won't answer their prayer, but God doesn't care who wins, He cares about the people who play the sport, and the fans that watch, but He doesn't care who wins."

I had a misguided thought about miracles at this point. I felt as though I had to be selective with my prayers. Should I save it for something more important? God does not have a finite number of miracles for anyone, God is limitless. The Holy Spirit taught me to pray all the time, and if God doesn't want to grant the miracle, it's not His will for a reason. It's not me who does the miracle, but God who grants the miracle. That year my team lost severely from the coin toss on. They were favored to win, and nothing went their way. Does that mean that this miracle for one baby cursed the life of the athletes, and teams at her expense? Only God knows. Maybe they were destined to lose anyway, and God was testing me to make sure I wasn't idolizing football again. I have the belief the game went the way it did simply related to all the mistakes made throughout the game, uncanny and so uncharacteristic of everyone involved.

I told Russell all that was going on. "What the hell are you doing Alan? I took you to Robert to figure out who is hurting you and your family so we can confront them. You are treating him like God." I felt ashamed. I was in disgust with myself. He was right. I just couldn't understand why it was so different from Catholicism. "Alan, I went to Roberts one night, I just stopped by without calling him. He was in his ritual garb and covered in blood. He mentioned that he was going to put your spell back on you, he hinted it was attacking him instead. I told him that he better leave you alone if he knows what's best for him." I felt so stupid, and thankful. I was so confused this entire time. I had relied on Robert as if he was God. Hoping and praying that he could help me out. Why would God allow me to do this? It was at this instant that I realized. God wanted me to have this experience and tell people about my experience. How it was wrong.

All these spiritual practices that people think are harmless and self medicating are allowing the demons of the earth to play God. They will control you, and you give them rights to your soul and body by participating in them. This is why God wanted me to write my book. It's not about me. I am a nobody. I'm not famous. Nobody cares to hear about my life. It's not a biography. My story is about God, it glorifies Him. It is simply a testimony...

Soon after. Robert woke one night during the witching hour, and in a state of psychosis, he cut up his wife's face with a box cutter. He ended up going to prison. I felt terrible. Was this my destiny? Did he take one for the team? I noticed Robert saying that he was helping pretty girls, and was doing things spiritually for them. I didn't know if they became inappropriate, but power like that has to be handled carefully. Humans aren't perfect. They are not perfect like God is perfect, and if they are going to play God, they must be perfect. And since we are not, the demons will attack even their servants. They are not to be trusted. They are not loyal. They steam roll even their own if it benefits them. I returned to the true Church. I went to confession. I can still see the horror on the priest's face as I spilled my guts in the confessional. He was so frightened and off put. I spoke of these things as if they were common knowledge, and he looked terrified. I have spoken to many Christians about these concepts, and it astonishes me that they are so oblivious to the spiritual warfare that happens on this planet. They live in their cookie cutter world, and go to Church on Sunday to hear a watered down version of the Bible where everything is hunky dory, and the World is not such a bad place. They are happy in their secular world. Happiness will come if they have a good job, a beautiful spouse, a nice car, and children. There is a reason there are awful events in the Bible, because that is part of life. It's the Truth. There is a devil and demons, and a battle.

We decided to renew our vows. But this time We did it in the Catholic Church. We went to our local priest, and instead of making us go through a lengthy process of going through the Bishop. I explained my wife was Christian, but not Catholic. I asked If we would be able to get married in the Church, and have it be official. He agreed. I only felt comfortable asking him because of what he did for me the year prior.

When we had been married in a Christian Church, I asked him if I could receive Communion with everyone else. Since I was not married in the Catholic Church, and did not receive an official sacrament from them, can I participate in Communion? To most unknowing Christians, even Catholics themselves, the Host is not a Symbol. It really is the Body of Christ. If you don't believe that, ask an exorcist how a possessed person responds to the Holy Eucerist. Many are disgusted that the Catholic Church has so many rules and regulations regarding this, and many other matters. But it is the only Church that was founded by Jesus, practicing the traditions he taught the apostles, passing them down in unbroken succession. Eitherway, I knew I was asking for a lot when I asked if I could participate in mass. His response to me was, "Alan the apostles first started taking communion not because they were perfect, but because they were trying to become better people. The Father blessed our marriage. We were still in pursuit of completing our family with a baby. We had a doctor appointment coming up with the specialist. We had seen him for a previous visit, and I had an overwhelming calmness that we didn't need to go. I explained it to my wife, but she was so disappointed that I wasn't going to budge on the matter. Weeks later, she took a pregnancy test, and she was positive. Try and tell me that getting married in the Catholic Church doesn't matter if you are Catholic, I will never believe otherwise

I was trying to finish my book, and take a college course for a CNA. I had just finished an EMT course the previous month, so I had that to back me up, but nobody was hiring at the moment, so I started working as a CNA after obtaining a certificate. I was working five days a week in a nursing home, going to paramedic school and trying to get this book done all at the same time as trying to care for a pregnant wife. I had a final paper due for class and I had to decide to work on that or finish the book, and I had an overwhelming urge that the book was more important.

I was wrapping up the book. This is the revision to the first book as the first was so rushed, and I have come lightyears spiritually since the original manuscript. I was using my laptop to race to finish the end of the book. As I layed on the couch punching the keys I could hear the walls cracking and crumbling around me. I could hear people running on the ceiling. I could hear hundreds of demons gathering around the house in angst that I was going to reveal their secrets. Finally, I reached the last word, and punched the period key... Then I saved it to the jump drive. All A sudden, the cursor flashed a few times, then began to arrow backward through the book. The cursor flashed backwards as if someone was holding down the left arrow key. It wouldn't stop for anything. I tried pressing the backspace key. I tried the arrow forward key. Nothing worked. I tried the power off button, and the computer wouldn't turn off.

I ripped the battery out with hopes that it would shut down, but that did do anything. It stayed on without the battery, and continued to go through the book backward. I pulled the jump drive out and went to the desktop to upload the document to the computer to send a copy to the publisher. The file couldn't be found on the jump drive. I prayed an Our Father. And finally the document was downloaded to the desktop. But it would not let me send it to the publisher. Meanwhile, the walls were still cracking, and demons were running on the roof. The Holy Spirit told me to pray three Rosaries with my wife, so I did. As soon as we finished the third Rosary the walls stopped cracking, and the demons stopped running on the roof. I ran to the desktop in the office and hit the send button to the publisher, and it worked. The file was sent. I picked up the laptop and the cursor stopped running backward through the book. I was able to turn the laptop off.

That wasn't the last attempt at preventing my story from being shared with others. I had a book signing at a local bookstore. I was sitting at the table greeting anyone who wanted to approach me and talk about the book. A tall slender woman breezed to the table. She was at least six feet six inches tall. That is not uncommon for a tall woman to wear tall heels, and be that tall, but what was uncommon was her presence. She picked up the book and made a comment about witches. She knew what the story was without reading the back, but for a second. She flipped the book back to the table, and made an unimpressed snare as she floated off in dismay. I never saw her leave the store, even staying until closing time. Had the devil made an appearance in her form? Just then a store employee approached me. "I'm so sorry, my co-worker was opening a box of books in the back so we could bring more copies for you to sign, and she cut her finger on the box. There is blood all over several books. We will not be able to sell those, but I'll bring the rest of them."

Chapter XII

We were thrilled to have a baby, and it felt like such a good time, especially since I was curse-less for the first time in decades. I felt what it was like for normal people. Not to have a care in the world, or have the weight of the world collapsing in on me. As I researched things for my book that were evil, in order to explain them. I learned about Aleister Crowley who was an occultist, and created a religion of Thelema, and he died in the early 1900's. He was a self proclaimed prophet. He theorized that people worship in aeons. Where humanity would worship different deities. Egyptian people worshiped Isis. Yes Isis, sound familiar? Then Osiris, then Horus, all Egyptian Gods. And he was right. Then he claimed humanity would move into a phase of self-actualization. Sound familiar? Most People may believe in a creator, or say, "I don't like the idea of organized religion." Neither does the devil, what united force would stand against him. Crowley's axiom was, "Do what thou wilt shall be the whole of the law." "Do what thou wilt," is the devil's matto. God has order, the devil has chaos. Christians follow God's will, but the devil says, follow your own desires. Crowley was a mystic, reporting to have an encounter with another spirit that was powerful, but outside of his body that gave him advice.

He explained it as his spiritual self. He was a practitioner of Yoga. Yoga opens up certain Chakras to demons. Self-actualization is another way of saying self love, or self worship. The occult all ties together, he practiced astrology. All is tied together, and he was right. Society is meshing spiritualism, with self worship. Learn about your spirit guides, your spirit animal. Goes right back into worshiping the bull that the Jews started worshiping in the desert. False idol on top of false idol. Meditate in order to achieve your higher self/self worship. Opening up certain chakras can make one vulnerable to demon influence. The reason Jews wear the yamakas is to fulfill the customary requirement that the head be covered either all the time, or during prayer, but also to prevent evil from entering. Catholics hold to traditions as popes and bishops do the same whether they realize it or not. Native American men were taught not to allow any women to touch their head other than his spouse or his family. To curse someone, or bless someone, the spiritual practitioner touches the head. There are spiritual laws both sides play by. Both witches and Christians fast and pray. Suffering is spiritual currency. While learning about these things I felt the familiar grasp of the devil pulling on my shoulder attempting to suck me into a dimension. All I had to do was ask God to intervene, and he vanished. I realized I should not learn these things just for curiosity's sake. God will allow me to learn these things to teach people to stay away from them, but again, as wise FR. Dan Reehil says, "Curiosity is not a virtue."

The next time a demon attacked me was in broad daylight, which was not uncharacteristic. It happened in the past, but the devil and demons seem to have more power at night. I'm not sure why, but I would speculate that they piggy back on the fear people have from the night. People fear things they can not see. Once fear is in the air they thrive off it. Fear is contagious. It really is, it's a part of our biology to survive. If one is afraid, one questions if they should be afraid as well, or if they don't have time to think, they react to the fear as well. I was sitting on the couch talking to my wife, and mid-sentence, one grabbed me by the throat. I was paralyzed. I couldn't move. I could talk. She stared at me, asking what in the world was happening. I was frozen for at least one minute. It seems to me that being grabbed by the throat could be paralyzing enough, but the demon had powers to paralyze me as well. Finally it released me, I didn't have to call out for Jesus. I had started becoming desensitized. I went on about my day. Months later, when I would turn my head a certain way the cartilage in my throat would pop out of place. It was slightly uncomfortable, but then it would eventually pop back into place. Signs of how hard the demon had wretched onto my throat.

Nothing was going to affect me like it had in the past. I knew the existence of God and the devil, and I could feel God's love for me. In my happiness I was painting my daughter's room before her arrival. As I painted I thought to myself, "If demons are so powerful, imagine how powerful angels are. They threw the devil and the other fallen angels to earth." As I filled the paint roller with paint, I thought, "If Saint Michael was the one who threw the devil down to earth, how powerful is he?" Just then I felt his presence in the room. It was so powerful I felt dwarfed in power and size." I was already kneeling as I was filling the roller, but then I told myself I should be kneeling in his presence. But true to Bible form, a voice said, "Don't keel to me, I'm a fellow servant." Even in all his glory he instructed me not to kneel to anyone but God. When he threw Satan from heaven to the earth showed humility to God by saying, "May God rebuke you." Still giving glory to God. That is when I realized true power is hidden by humility.

His presence entered the room with what felt like a shock wave. It was so intense I begged him to leave as his power scarred me. I wish I could go back to that moment, and learn more from him, but I was just scared. I walked outside to take a break. I was trying to digest what had just happened, and I was staring into the sky to the West. The entire Rocky Mountain range was in view from my front yard. Along the Rocky Mountain range was one gigantic cloud that hovered above the entire Rocky mountains. As I stared into it, it grew and the cloud started rolling towards me. Even though the cloud was over thirty miles away from me, it felt so close. As it rolled, lightning lit up the cloud hundreds of times. Thundered roared. In the thunder I heard God's voice. His voice made me quiver, and amplified the St Michael experience a million times over. The message was simple, He showed me His Power and Might. He showed me why only he is Lord, The Alpha, and the Omega. After my experience I knew what I had to do. I had to name my daughter after St. Michael. Even though it was a boy's name, I didn't care, it could be her middle name. My wife graciously agreed to the name.

I was given the Bible on tape from my wife's grandmother, she had little use, as she read her Bible daily. It was something that came at an important time in my life. Every time I would go to Church I would feel the power of scripture, but it was only a small piece of Scripture, and I thirst for more. Knowing there is something mysterious, but left confused and wanting more. It was like a foreign language I didn't understand. The paramedic program I was in was over forty miles away, and my instructor was very strict. If I was a minute late she would close and lock the door, making my commute pointless. On my way up I listened to the entire set about seven times. It changed my life. It changed how I thought. Saint Jerome says, "Ignorance of Scripture is ignorance of Christ." I learned that Scripture is like a spring of water. One can continually come to the same piece of scripture that acts like a spring or well, and brings something different every time, but nourishes the soul with what is needed at the time. My commute was a perfect opportunity to listen to the Bible. One morning on my commute, I was running late, and I didn't want to be turned away for showing up late. As I sped I prayed, "Dear Lord, please protect me, please keep me from getting a speeding ticket." As I sped down the highway My engine began to cut out. The engine started misfiring. This had never happened before. My prayer changed, pleading with God to prevent my truck from breaking down, but then I would stomp on the gas and continue speeding. Then I would continue praying to avoid getting a ticket, and again my engine would misfire, and I would stomp on the gas to speed and feed the motor gas to not misfire. Four or five times I repeated, then out of nowhere a state patrol car turned his lights on, so I pulled over. "I've been following you for miles. I'm giving you a ticket for speeding." After the patrolman left I pulled back on the highway with hope that I might be able to join in class. I Didn't realize at the time, but God was directly answering my prayer. I was so oblivious to the direct response. He was making my engine cut out. As I drove the highway, My engine never cut out again, from that point on, or the entire time I owned the truck. It was direct intervention.

During the first few weeks of paramedic class, the concepts were all about ethics. For this part of the program a certain instructor joined the class to speak about ethics, theory, right and wrong. He stood in front of the class, and he introduced himself. This is a standard and a professional practice, but his introduction became less and less humble. He explained how he had written a paragraph in the textbook we were required to buy for the class. My mind started trailing off to having to buy a new text book in the school store for such a high price. The book was literally published with only a couple extra paragraphs from the previous edition. Forcing students to buy the new edition, and the curriculum was geared towards being forced to do assignments on certain pages, and was difficult to keep up when you were two three pages from the new edition. I could hear the plug from the instructors who were told to more than encourage students to buy books from the school bookstore bringing money back to the college. Some programs recharge the student for the same text book they already bought the previous semester, such acts should be criminal. After he started into a new subject, it brought my attention back. He began talking about Plato and Aristotle, both were very intriguing to me. This man had spent a career learning about these philosophers and memorizing their work. As I listened to him speak I couldn't help but think of how even these great thinkers are foolish to God, and His Word. It felt so unnecessary and such a waste of time. Earthly knowledge became foolish, and I realized, it didn't serve anyone in the next life. I was consumed by the Bible and my heart led me away from what I was supposed to be doing.

The instructor then posed a question to the class, "Should we live by relativism or absolutism?" Relativism basically, is the doctrine that knowledge, truth, and morality exists in relation to culture, society, or historical context are not absolute. Then he says, "What if your family is starving, is it OK to steal a loaf of bread?" Then he sat back and watched as the class argued. Relativism is a way for the devil to disguise evil. It starts out not so harmless and progresses. It starts as a loaf of bread, then stealing a car to get a loved one to the hospital. Then, stealing a car to get to work, and so on and so forth, until it's not wrong at all. All situations are exempt from the rules or law. Everything led me away from not finishing the paramedic program, I didn't feel like I should be there. I began neglecting the program, and then I failed a test. My time in the program was over. I didn't know where my career was heading, but I was driven by a thrust for knowledge of Christ. Christ says in John 14:12, *"Truly, truely, I say to you, whoever believes in me will also do the works that I do; and greater works than these will he do because I am going to the Father."* Where are these people that supposedly have done works greater than Him? He raised people from the dead. History after Christ should be filled with mystics doing miracles. It turns out it is. It is so downplayed as, but there are documented miracles, one after the other. Most of them have been performed by Catholic saints. I started learning as much as possible about the lives of the saints. They already paved the path to Christ and a Holy life. I started doing the devotions they have done. I began fasting with prayer. I started fasting at least three days a week. It was such a sweet suffering, and I felt myself grow in spiritual strength and understanding. All I could think about was Christ. The love for Christ made every other relationship in my life better, just by putting Him first.

I continued working as a CNA, and I felt fulfilled, I felt like I was helping people. I found a CNA job at a hospital. A couple years passed and our second child was on the way. I knew my wife conceived even before a test would show positive. I knew I had to name my baby after the Virgin Mary. It worried me that the baby might be a boy, but the urge to name her after the Blessed Mother was stronger than the concern of the baby's gender, but it turned out perfectly as the baby was a girl. As I had lived for a couple of years out of my family curse, I felt Jesus ask me if I would accept the curse back? I agreed to accept it back without question. If He was asking me to take it up again, there was a reason. I didn't understand why, but I agreed. Days later I was driving with my wife and we were passing the place where I had thrown my clothes after Robert performed them ritual over me. As we got closer we argued, and as soon as we passed the spot on the road, the curse re-entered my life with a literal punch to my face. It was so fitting. It felt better this way, I didn't want Robert to have to carry the burden of my curse anyway. As I grew closer to Jesus, I felt the devil grasping to pull me away.

As I was reconverting spiritually to a higher understanding that worldly things seemed so foolish. I was also starting to understand that I was being held to a higher standard related to my mission on earth. I wrote earlier about after being confirmed, and I was in a Church, the Lord laid out my mission in 2005, it has been unfolding for the last eighteen years and is still unfolding. He explained major events that would occur, how I would meet my wife, and she would prove her love for me by suffering financially. I have learned patience waiting for all these things to unfold. I thought these events were going to happen instantaneously, but there was much I needed to learn on the way. If God would have done everything for me, I would not have struggled, and all the fruits of suffering and understanding would have been stolen away from me. Most may doubt that I am held to a different standard, but here is a brief example through one of my experiences. I have heard and read many sources about how meditation is good for people. I know that scientifically combined with deep breathing, oxygen saturates the frontal lobe/front part of the brain, which is in control of higher cognitive functions like; personality, critical thinking, memory, emotions, impulse control, social interaction, and motor function. When meditating, cerebrospinal fluid circulates throughout the spinal column and brain cavity. The brain and spinal column are suspended in cerebrospinal fluid, which protects, nourishes, and helps with waste removal for the brain and spinal column. Besides these benefits, I heard that across many cultures have been using meditation for years for spiritual benefit. While praying I have entered into meditation on many occasions, but I had never done it alone. I tried a couple of times, but it was fruitless.

Weeks later I went to a family member's bachelor party. That day I had not eaten thinking there was going to be food, but there wasn't. I had a few drinks to celebrate, but was not over doing it. The few drinks I had without any food in my system hit me hard. I had a few more drinks on top of that, and the night ended up being a terrible night. I did things a drunk would do, on top of it I argued with my wife, nothing completely different than most young adults do. Like I said, I am held to a different standard. The next day as I layed on the couch sobering up, I was thinking of last night and all the foolish things that I did. I was ashamed of myself. I laid there, and the sun was shining on my face through the window. I closed my eyes trying to forget everything, and then my mind was clear. Out of nowhere a vision of a heavy set woman appeared from the neck up. She was very homely looking. She had a short stringy bob hair style with short bangs. Her face was chubby and filled with pot marks. Her nose was bulbous. Her eyes were mostly blacked out, only a small stipe of sclera circled the outer eye. She had a disgusted look on her face as she appeared, I could only see the right side of her face.

Then my mind went blank for a moment and then another vision flashed in my mind. This was a vision of a man. His Hair was long wavy and jet Black, He had a small etched out goatee. His face smiling, and his fair skin and black hair gave me the impressions that he was happy in an ominous way. A smile that an enemy would give his opponent after defeating him. As soon as both of these images flashed in my mind I was relieved. I felt the evil melt away. It was at that moment I realized, drinking too much or living an unholy life can make one vulnerable to demons. It takes the defenses down. I also learned that demons can be cast out by a vision of them. A classic exorcist move is to try to find out the demon's name to be able to control them in order to cast them out. This was the first time I had experienced this technique and understanding that a demon can be controlled by its image.

I learned the three things that sustained me most when having to confront evil. The first is; attending a Catholic mass and partaking in the Eucharist. Second, attending adoration, which is sitting in front of the blessed bread which is the true Body and Blood of Jesus Christ. Third; praying the Rosary has sustained me. I learned that fasting while praying was like dropping a bomb on the devil, especially when praying the Rosary. I started fasting three days a week. My encounters with demons became so frequent. I started seeing them nearly a hundred times a day or more. Sometimes they seemed like a flash out of the corner of my eye. Sometimes they would come in the form of a giant face five or six feet tall, and transparent. Sometimes as silhouettes of animalistic characteristics mixed with human forms. Sometimes as hairy ape-like features with inverted joints and dreadlocks.

One night, I prayed the Rosary with my mom and my family to help with all our struggles. When she got home The entire house was covered in long black coarse hair. The hair was the length of German Shepherd Hair, and it was everywhere. It was on top of the counter, oven, refrigerator, kitchen table, even on top of the upper kitchen cabinets were covered in hair, every inch of the house was covered in hair, as if a demon exploded in her house. I started to question myself, who would believe me. Am I in psychosis? Am I having visual hallucinations? I started to test out my visions. If I could see that other people were affected by the demons, then I would be convinced that it's not just me experiencing these things. My question was answered in the following events.

One night I took my wife and kids to a local restaurant for dinner. It was connected to a gift shop. My kids picked out a couple of toys. My oldest picked out a mechanical dog. It is the type that is battery operated barks and does a backflip. She played with it until it was time for bed. My wife was dozing off, so I offered to put the kids to bed. After tucking them in, I gathered their toys and instead of putting them away, I set them on the dining room table so I could put them away in the morning. The dog was in the pile of toys. I specifically picked it up and made sure the setting was on the off button so the batteries wouldn't be drained. I went to my room for my routine. I knelt by my bed and started to pray. Then I heard a ruckus in the dining room. I ignored it, then I heard it again. I looked at my wife who was half awake, and she said, "I heard it too." So I had to go check it out, I grabbed a bottle of Holy water I keep on my dresser. As I walked past the living room and into the dining room. The dog was standing in the middle of the dining room floor barking at me, and then it did a flip. If this would have happened twenty years ago I would have been scared, but it made me laugh. I walked over and picked it up. I turned it off and returned it back to the table. I walked to the hallway to check on the kids. I poked my head into the youngest's room, and she was fine. I peeked into the oldest's room. There was a black silhouette of a demon standing behind her head board. I cast it out with the Holy water, and it disappeared. I went back to my room. After a few minutes I felt it come back, and it was angry. I grabbed the bottle of Holy water, and pushed her bedroom door open. It grew, it took up half the room. I threw Holy water at it and rebuked it. It vanished, and my daughter looked up at me. "Daddy, I felt something touch my head."

One morning I woke up early and I struggled to go back to sleep. Finally, I drifted back to sleep. I dreamed I appeared in a desert during the middle of the day. I was far from the ground, then I saw a small blue outdated hatchback car. I drew closer to the car from my previous aerial view, and I appeared in the driver seat. I looked to my right and there was someone sitting in the passenger seat. It was a frail skinny old man wearing overalls and a beige jacket. His skin was pale and his eyes were sunken in. The only dark skin I could see was deep back where his eyes finally set. His white hair was parted and draped over his left eye. He looked sick, like death. I hugged him, feeling cold and sadness. My attention shifted to the back seat. There was a small baby lamb laying on its back. It was the size of a baby puppy. I touched its belly and it curled up around my hand. It was soft and I felt so happy and fulfilled. I sat forward and looked at the old man. I knew I had to choose. I realized that the old man was sin, and the baby lamb was Jesus. I could choose death, or Jesus. Then my body was quickly drawn away to a house that was in the desert.

I was inside a house, but I understood it was my house. I was looking out of the window next to the front door, and I could see three men running for the door. I got an eerie feeling from the men. They wanted to kill me and my family, and they all had black eyes. The leader was large and had a goatee. He was wearing a white tank top shirt. He had tattoos all over his face and neck. They ran to the door, and I ran to the door to lock them out. I jammed the door closed with my shoulder, and forced it closed, then they hit the door. They pushed me back and I shoved them back. I reached for the dead bolt lock and there was no lock on the door. What was I going to do? Then the Holy Spirit Spoke, "When you don't keep sin out, there is nothing keeping it from coming back in." As I held the door with all my strength, I was keeping them from coming in. Then I heard something very large fly around the room. As the wings flapped, wind gusted. Then, whatever was flying around the room landed on my left shoulder. I felt claws digging into my skin. I looked to my shoulder and I could see a scally black talon attached to three black claws. Then I woke up and My eyes were blurry, so I couldn't see much. The claws woke me up.

The demon from the dream was still on my shoulder. I felt the presence of the devil enter the room, and my body became paralyzed. Then the winged demon started flying around the room. I asked, "Lord, how many more times am I going to be paralyzed by the devil?" "This is the last time." My youngest child was in a bassinet next to our bed sleeping. As the demon flew around the room, I could hear its over-sized batlike wings flapping, and all I could see was the shadow flying around the room. My baby woke to the commotion and she started to cry. The only part of my body I could control was my right leg. The only motion I could do was rotate my leg. I began to tap my sleeping wife's leg to wake her up, but it was unsuccessful. I don't know what I expected her to do, but I am glad she didn't wake up. While this was happening I realized this was the proof I needed to prove everything I was seeing and experiencing was not a lie. I wasn't in psychosis. I was actually seeing, feeling, and experiencing the reality of the spiritual, in this world. The fact that the baby was sharing this experience was proof. I waited patiently as I knew it would end. Soon after the winged creature flew away, and the evil left the room. It released its grasp on me. As soon as it left, the baby stopped crying. I woke my wife up and explained to her what just happened.

As I said before, I worked as a CNA in a nursing home before I worked in a hospital, and that allowed me to have a few amazing experiences. I had quite a few co-workers who were convinced there wasn't a heaven, or a God. Their logic was; they were able to see a lot of death, and the lack of quality of life the residents experienced. It was the exact opposite for me. For me I saw that people lived a purgatory on earth before death as a lack of reconciling their relationship with God. I met a former priest who was placed in a nursing home as his children placed him there. He left the Church, got married and had children. His wife divorced him, and he was left there alone. All his relationships were basically over, except the remnants of his relationship with God, the one he left for worldly relationships. His spine was an S shape. It may have been a medical condition prior to his admission to the facility that got much worse. I saw the relation to scripture. Matthew 3, *"Prepare ye the way of the Lord, make his paths straight."* Proverbs 3:6 *In all your ways acknowledge Him, And He will make you paths straight."*

One old lady was mute, and I had just changed her before the end of the shift. The next shift would arrive in less than 20 minutes. I could tell she and her family were religious based on her room. Pictures of the blessed Virgin Mary, and her blanket was a mural of Guadelupe. I walked down the hall to wrap up final tasks in order to get out of work on time. The Holy Spirit told me to go back to her room. I really didn't want to. Working in a nursing home is physically and emotionally exhausting. You give a little bit of yourself to each patient and it teaches one great patience. Nursing homes are never staffed appropriately related to state laws that need to change, and there is always high turnover. Sometimes people just stop showing up to work. I fought the urge to go back to her room, and I couldn't ignore the message. I just couldn't understand why, I had just changed her soiled depends. I went back into her room and she was alive, which was a relief, but she had soiled her depends again. I cleaned her up, and helped her get comfortable. Then the Holy Spirit explained, "If you would have helped her, she would have been that way the entire night." Night shift is always an easier shift to work, granted they have their moments too, but generally, they have more down time than day shift. It occurred to me that night shift checks on everybody, and if they need help, they will help them, but if they seem OK, they let them rest during the night. This lady was mute, and could not voice her concerns. Then it hit me, God looks out for his people always, even in the state she was in. Proving my fellow co-workers wrong. There is God, and he does care about every person he created.

As I mentioned before, I was able to get a job at a local hospital. It was a nice upgrade. I met a coworker who was able to mentor me in spiritual matters. I was able to get validation on spiritual discernment. I was able to understand that there are functioning people in society walking around possessed and don't know it. Everyone who is possessed is suffering, and looks very similar to other types of suffering. Being possessed does not mean that they are bad people. Sometimes it's inherited through birth if the parents are possessed. I have mentioned the book written by John Ramirez, a former devil worshiper, and he explains how he passed demons on to people. He explained that the devil would tell him to sleep with a certain girl he met at a nightclub. The act would attach a demon to her. Months later she would attempt suicide. Some demons pass through rape, the innocent victim now having a demon attacking them. How could this be? An innocent person who was a victim is now left possessed. Occurrences of this sort leave the victim questioning, is there a God, and why would He allow it? To believe in a demon proves there is a God, the opposite of the evil in the world. So why would He allow it? All of God's human creation has free will. The evil of this earth is by man not living by God's commandments. God will save us from such situations if we do not sin, and do not sever our relationship with Him. Sin severs our relationship with Him. In some instances the person needs to experience evil, or they will never seek out God in the first place. A life of many sufferings can be a blessing if they seek God. In a spiritual manner, a life of happiness and ease, never needing God is a cursed life. That soul has no need for God.

A whole new world of spiritual warfare was being unveiled to me, then something even crazier happened. All a sudden I felt the devil ask me if I wanted to join his side. I was so aww struck I was speechless. It was hard for me to believe. I needed my spiritual mentor to validate what I was asked, and they did, verbatim. For the second time in my life I was able to experience the bliss of not having everything in life go wrong. Life was easy. I felt no opposition. Along with a life of ease came many offers and temptation. After a few weeks went by my mentor asked why I hadn't made a decision. And I didn't have an answer. It never entered my to switch sides, but it did amaze me that I was a big enough deal to pose a threat that he would consider recruiting me. I am, and always will be God's without a doubt. Logically, how can anyone choose to be the devil's, God created them? I made it official by vocal pledging my life, work, and allegiance to only God. As soon as I chose God, the curse started sinking back in, but the temptation remained.

I learned devotions from the giants in faith, the saints. There is a source of endless knowledge and wisdom on the EWTN network. A devotion came on everyday when I was leaving for work. I could never finish the devotion. It was a devotional to Saint Michael. It started at 6:30 AM and didn't end until after 6:50, but I had to be at work at 6:45. One morning I wanted to finish, so I prayed to be able to finish the devotional, but still not be late to work. That was denying the physics of this planet, it was impossible. I continued the devotion until it ended. I rushed to work, but I didn't speed. When I clocked in, I was two minutes early. I was outside of time. I looked at the clock and it started at 6:30, and I should have been late, but I couldn't explain it. It was unexplainable. It was a miracle. I started to see that in my religion miracles are not exceptional, but common.

It was not the last time something amazing would happen. I started to attend adoration more frequently. As I explained earlier, adoration is sitting in front of the Blessed Bread at Church. This is basically sitting in front of Jesus himself, the creator of the universe. If anyone doubts me, they can spend time researching for miracles of the Eucharist. Even a priest himself doubted as he blessed the Bread and it started to bleed. Science is finally advanced enough to prove this miracle. The Miracle of Lanciano has allowed science to prove it true. The wine that was Consecrated into Blood turned into five clots. All five clots weigh 15.85 grams. When one clot is separated and weighed it weighs 15.85 grams. When two clots are weighed, they weigh 15.85 grams. No matter how many clots are weighed, they weigh the same. The Bread consecrated when the priest doubted started to bleed, and was witnessed by the congregation. The Bread has been turned over to scientists who proved it is actual human cardiac/heart tissue. It showed a blood type of AB and that the person had enzymes released that showed that the person was beaten severely causing liver damage.

As I was saying I was saying. I began to go to adoration in front of the Blessed Bread and spent many hours praying. One day I contemplated why Jesus was crying in the garden before he was turned over. I have heard bishops explain this proved he was half man and half devine. I couldn't wrap my head around it. Jesus knew his purpose on earth since he arrived. I prayed to understand. Then He answered me. He explained that while he was in the garden, he saw all the sins against his Father from the beginning of the world to the end, and saw how all these heinous sins hurt his Father, and began to weep. After the revelation I was instructed to go to the back of the chapel and get a book. I picked up the book that the Holy Spirit led me to, and took it back to my seat. I sat down and opened it. The page I opened it to explained exactly what I experienced. It was how Saint Faustina had an interaction with Jesus. Jesus appeared to her and explained that the reason he was weeping in the garden before he was handed over, was exactly what I just stated. He saw all the sins against his Father in Heaven. It was the validation I needed. He could have sent me to the book first to read it, but he gave me the revelation first, and then sent me to the book. I was amazed, and He never ceases to amaze me. In my excitement I went back to prayer. In my prayer I asked to see God. I immediately received a response. "The reward of faith is lost." Then the scripture came to mind; John 20:29 *Jesus said to him, "Because you have seen me, you have believed. Blessed are those who have not seen, and believed."* I continued to pray to see God, and I explained that I already know God exists.

Weeks later I was at work. I loved my job and the way it serves others. The only problem was, it was about one fourth of what I was used to making, but God gave us everything we needed. I was working on the busiest med surg floor in the hospital. I had a patient who was middle aged, and I took him to the bathroom, then he asked to shower. I helped him shower and changed his bedding. I walked him back to bed and moved onto the rest of my patients. A short time later he called because he wet his bed. I cleaned him up, and changed his bed again. Then he asked if he could have a shave. I agreed graciously, but I was stressed because I had so much to do for all my other patients, and his beard was down to his chest. I went to the stock room and grabbed towels, a basin, and about ten razors. Hospital razors are terrible. I went back into the room, and he asked to leave a goatee. As I shaved him the housekeeper started cleaning his room. She started with small talk.

As I looked at the patient I noticed he had Blue green eyes. They were pure and powerful. Then he looked at me, and without words from his heart and eyes he said, "It's me." Then he looked away. And in my head I said, "No way, this can't be, it's impossible." He looked directly into my eyes again and said, "It's me." Then he looked away." I thought this is crazy, It can't be, can it? Then the housekeeper started in on a story about how her husband is hurt and out of work, and they are struggling. I felt like I should respond to her in between everything else that was going on. Then the patient looked at me again and without words said, "Yes it's me." I wanted to hug him. It took everything in me to not hug him. The joy filled my heart. The housekeeper stayed quiet as she waited for a response. With his mind he said, "This is why you are here, comfort her, and tell her about me." It was odd Jesus was sitting her in the room, why can't he help her? I felt awkward talking about Jesus in the third person, especially since he was in the room. So I gave a generic response that maybe things can turn around and keep your faith. I should have said, "Jesus hears you, He is here now. You have His ear, Ask Him for help."

I finished shaving his beard, so I could rush out of the room to help my other patients. I placed his tray in front of him quickly and his cup fell off due to my haste. I was in a hurry, but I was also nervous, this was Jesus, He only deserves the best. I wanted to only have him as a patient. I wanted to spend all my time in his room. As he watched me pick up his cup and wash it in a hurry he said, "You're excited." It was so true. He didn't say, you're in a hurry, you're clumsy, or slow down. He was exactly correct. It was such a true statement, and simple, but maybe he could see my enthusiasm, but lack of time.

I helped my other patients, and then I went back into his room one final time for my shift. I was running late. I was going to have to stay for an extra hour and a half to catch up, but it was so worth it. As I was ready to leave the patient's father walked in. I know it was the patient's biological earthly father, but in this mystical experience, It was The Alpha, The Omega, The Begging and The End. God the Father was here in the room. His eyes were even more pure and powerful. They were a glazier blue. His skin was tan, and His hair was black. The wrinkles in His eyes were Holy, they permeated complete wisdom. He spoke even fewer words and the words meant even more. I was overwhelmed, almost paralyzed wanting to drop to my knees.

After my recent experience I learned a story of a saint who saw Mother Mary working in a hospital cleaning patients. She was doing the work that today would be done by a nurse or CNA. She saw Mary laboring in a humble way, doing the work that most people despise even these days. The saint walked up to Mary and asked her why she was doing that. Mary replied, "I'm doing the work you refuse to do." Jesus, Mary, and God the Father never appear just to appear, there is always a message. The scripture that came to mind was Matthew 25:31 *"Whatsoever you do the least of my brothers you do unto me."* I learned that anyone in health care knows the challenges of taking care of very difficult patients. Patients who are drug attics, yelling and assaulting the health care provider. This scripture is important to remember as it becomes challenging.

I was still under a curse, so I still had to be mindful that I was under attack constantly. It attacks all relationships, finances, vehicles, electronics, everything. It would affect my alarm from going off, making me late for work. God would counter it with sending his angels to help at times. One morning an angel touched my ear to wake me. It felt like a spark of joy as it poke my ear, and made me laugh from my sleep. When it was not successful in making me late, it made my boss obstinate to me, and made me appear as incompetent. My guardian angel even tapped me on the side of my head to help me out of a sinful situation, and I knew I had to leave.

Every vacation I went on was nothing but a series of bad memories. One vacation we decided to go on, the baby lost it on the flight home. It's common for that sort of thing to happen, but it doesn't mean it's fun, and it was linked to other stressful situations. As the bay was crying, I was about to apologize to the person sitting on my left. He was great about it, and explained that it's perfectly fine, but it seemed to mock the situation even though he was so pleasant. I needed to get milk from the stuartest to help calm the baby down, and it seemed like an opportune time as she pushed the cart next to our row. I raised my hand, "Excuse me, can I get some milk please?" "Sir, I'm serving the three rows up there, unless you can't wait, is that a problem, do you mind if I help them first?" the disdain and resentment dripped from her condescending mouth. I wasn't an impatient jerk that wanted a drink for myself. Ten minutes later she shuffled her way back to the cart. She made sure to help everyone else in my row first making sure that she was kind to them. She made sure to overcompensate her kindness to the guy on my left making sure I saw how nice she was treating him. "Now I can help you, everyone must wait their turn, Is all you want milk?" with an attitude. "Yes please." We filled the baby's bottle and it did the trick.

It seemed like the flight took a lifetime. We were emotionally drained from the trip, and the stressful flight. I was drained from all the bad things on the trip, so we decided to let everyone else unboard the plane, and walk off the plane without fighting our way off the plane. As we sat there while the plane unloaded I stared blankly at the back of the seat in front of me. Then while my eyes were opened a vision slammed down in a square frame right before my eyes. The image slammed down with power. The angel had his arms crossed and was not wearing clothes. All that I could see in the frame was from his waist up There was an orange and yellow glow radiating off of him. His skin was tan, and his hair was dark brown and maroon undertones. He was grinning and I felt his masculine power and feminine compassion. I knew his name, and I didn't understand why I was seeing him. Then the frame lifted from my eyes as I felt like I needed to shake my head and ask myself what happened? The last of the passengers trickled off the plane. And there he was in the form of a chubby little old lady. She was dragging her rolling bag, and as she walked to the front of the plane she turned and looked at me and gave me the same grin from the vision. She turned and shuffled off the plane in her earthy weak body. I realized that the angel gave me encouragement after what should have been a week of happiness and leisure, and a gift for the merit obtained.

Chapter XIII

Many signs came through animals. As I felt an attack I was being attacked by a demon I was thinking of it as I walked to the car carrying the baby in a car seat. I walked around the truck to get in and as I turned the corner I almost stepped on a snake headed in the opposite direction. The snake was about six feet long and blue. I had never seen a garter snake that color, but they do exist. As I turned in amazement of what just happened The snake's head raised and turned toward me; its yellow eye looked like it winked at me. It continued slithering away. Another day I was at work, and feeling an attack from multiple demons, when I received the call from home. I walked outside to the parking lot to talk. My wife called saying there were three large bull snakes on the front porch. Yes it could have been their mating season, but snakes can also be spirit guides. As soon as I told her it was a sign related to the attacks I was feeling, the parking sign right behind my head pinged like a gong was struck. I turned around quickly to see one was around, but there was nobody around.

One night I had a dream that I was outside next to my house. I had a blue five gallon bucket, and there was an upper part of a blue snake in the bucket. I grabbed a putty knife and chopped it to pieces, but even though it was dead water continued to spray out of his mouth. I couldn't stop it from spraying water, eventually it stopped. I woke up that morning wondering what that dream meant. It was late October, and snow had started falling to the ground. I realized I didn't winterize the sprinkler system in my yard. I ran out to the garage, grabbed the key and went to the shut off valve. I started to turn the shut off valve and it snapped. The pvc tube filled with water, and the ground turned to mud. The water started to fill my basement window well. I ran into the basement to turn off the main water valve. The basement was flooding. I quickly turned the main shut off valve. It did nothing as the sprinkler system was connected to the main water supply. I ran outside again dawning my muddy boots in the freezing cold and forced the city water lid off after several minutes of fumbling with it. I turned the water off. I had to make several trips to the hardware store to spend money. I didn't have to fix the shut off valve.

I spent days fighting this, meanwhile we had no running water to the house. Digging up the mud in the freezing cold I prayed the pipes in my house didn't freeze. Finally after working all day I fixed the valve. I looked down at the remnants of the pvc pipe and tools I placed in a blue five gallon plastic bucket. I sat down exhausted as I stared at the bucket and realized the dream was warning me of what was to come. The snake that wouldn't stop spewing water was the sprinkler system. The neighbor across the street was retired, and was always outside with his dog. He was able to see my misfortunes unfold. My truck transmission seized up, then my wife's transmission followed two months after. A septic tank fails only after being eight years old, and having to come up with 25 grand out of nowhere. It was endless, my privacy fence getting blown down twice. One thing after another. One day he approached me and said, "Sometimes I feel bad about life when it gets hard, but all I have to do is look across the street at you, and see that I'm blessed."

Many animals tipped me off about what was happening spiritually. Snakes since the beginning have been an enemy of man since the devil used him in the garden to convince Adam and Eve to sin, then again in the desert with the Isrealites. I noticed as I was driving and praying doves flew over my head, and as I was fighting demons with my prayers hawks flew over my vehicle. When I saw an owl, great change would happen. One night I had a dream of an owl the size of a telephone pole. It was far off in the distance, on a certain side of town, and it was in the middle of the night. I could see the silhouette of the giant owl. It started to flap its wings and lifted from the ground. I knew the meaning of the dream the next morning. The owl was my family curse that was cast against me and my family in that neighborhood, and the flight of the owl was a sign that the curse would lift. Many dreams came to me. I had a recurring dream of being in an Asian country and climbing buildings to get to higher ground. I stopped having that dream after a giant Tsunami hit Asia and killed many.

I had many dreams as a child and even as an adult of a buffalo. This buffalo was sometimes the size of the house. Sometimes it would walk up to me crying. Sometimes it appeared to me on my great grandmother's property and I could see it running in stride. One night I had a dream that I was in an alley of a big city. The alley opened up into a big parking lot. It was dark and I was standing in a circle of about thirty people. We were spaced out about a car length between each person. I had an eerie feeling as we stood there in the dark. Then, from the right side of the alley came a Buffalo. The Buffalo was not alone. He had a host of spiritual I beings around him. I couldn't see their form, but the beings blocked out the background with a transparent blur. The Buffalo walked up to a person and started to talk to them. I couldn't hear anything. The person dropped and died. He moved to the next person and a moment later that one dropped, but he didn't die. His body seized and he went into a coma. The Buffalo made his way around the circle. Then he reached me. I was terrified. What was he going to say? He talked without words. He was using ESP. The Buffalo was Jesus, and the host was his angels. He said, "You're doing well. Keep doing what you are doing." Then he moved onto the next person. I woke up and felt wonderful. He approved of me. I wondered why he chose a buffalo to present Himself. I know that a lot of Native American tribes worship buffalo, as it is used for absolutely everything. The sinue/tendons and ligaments for the bow in the bow and arrow. The bones for weapons and tools, the hide for shelter, clothes. Meat for obvious reasons, and every part had a purpose. The natives believed the buffalo gave himself to the people, so that they may live. It mimics the lamb for Jews and Christians, a self sacrifice. Perhaps Jesus took the form of a buffalo due to my native roots.

One night my mom went into a weird coma. We rushed her to the hospital and she was to be admitted to the ICU. The doctor couldn't really understand what was going on, but she was severe enough to earn a bed in the intensive care unit. She would not arouse by voice, or even pain. Somehow my grandfather Marty and Bertha were notified of my mom's condition. They rushed to my mom's room. I met them at the door. My grandfather seemed concerned, Bertha was there in joy. I could see how excited she was, happy that my mom could be near death. I yelled at both of them to leave, and they did. I thought to myself, should I have sent my grandfather away. I thought about it, but he knew that she was attacking my mom, and he stayed idle. I had no doubt that he loved my mom, I could see it, but not enough to make her stop, or leave her. After a few days my mom returned home. My cousin threatened to kill me for turning away my grandfather, but had nothing to say to me when we saw each other face to face.

My visions of demons never stopped, They harassed me daily. One night I saw the demon that had attacked many people throughout history. It was the demon who possessed Emily Rose, Nero from Rome, and who possessed Caiaphas, the High Priest who had Jesus crucified. I walked out of my bedroom and there he was standing near my front door. He was a transparent blue. He was a very short man, maybe 4'8", 4'9" maybe shorter. He was chubby, and his bone structure was very petite. His hair was cole black just as his eyes were. His beard was long and black, but very thin. I could see his fat white face through the beard very easily. His garments were very lavish and looked like a black velvet with the fringe golden with golden tassels. It was difficult to tell how tall he was because of the crown he wore. The crown was About at least a foot and a half tall. It was made of Gold, but it was not a solid crown. It looked like a ribbon of gold about an inch wide was spiraling upward in a beehive shape supported by various golden rods. At the front of the crown was a large ruby jewel. I eventually cast him out.

I would come into contact with many different demons. I learned the signs of their presence. Some signs of the presence are; choking, hair raises on the back of the neck, bad smells like; (sulfur, rotted meat, dog feces, dirty diaper), itching of the noise, itching under the finger nails, feeling of depression, suicide, and many more. I learned from the movies based on true stories of possession. After watching *Deliver Us from Evil,* I realized why one of my fingernails itches underneath only one nail when a demon is present. The possessed person in the movie scratched his finger tips off because they itched. I'm sure some of it is dramatized, but there are a lot of truths as I can vouch for. I watched *The Conjuring,* and I could not believe the similarities of my family's stories, and their story. I had to talk to my mom about the movie. I called her and we talked for hours about all the similarities.

Soon after I came under attack by that demon. I could see her running at me down the hall. This happened several times. One night me and my wife were putting the kids to bed, and I got a bad headache. The headache got worse and worse. My eyes started watering. The kids were now in bed, and I couldn't get relief. The only thing I could do was get on all fours. I was on the couch. My wife was holding my head, "I don't know what to do?" For some reason I don't know, I said, "Get the Holy water." She did, and handed it to me. I blessed my own head, and out of nowhere I let the longest loudest burp of my life out. It felt like it came from the core of my soul, and the headache was gone. I felt normal. Had I been possessed? Had I exorcized myself? The next day I looked up exorcisms /deliverance on the internet. There were many videos of people being exorcized, and the one thing most of them had in common; the people were burping uncontrollably. I would be attacked by that demon again a couple of years later, causing me to be temperamental with my children, so I casted it out. The demon in that movie caused parents to kill their children. I fought back, sending it away a final time. Watching these movies can be portals, and I learned I have to say a prayer to bind these demons up before watching these movies. These movies are entertaining, but I watched them to learn my enemy. I don't waste my time with scary movies that are not based on true stories anymore. I treat it as a learning experience, so I watch them by myself so nobody else is affected. I learned that if I have a rough night, like I didn't do my devotions, lack of prayer, or I was sinful throughout the day or night, everyone in the house would suffer. I learned that I suffer if I don't help his people. I was able to see how much God loves all the children I am to help serve. Father Dan Reehil told a story related to this concept. He explained how living in a house full of priests, this is the same for them. He explained if one of the guys was having a problem with lust, then they all would suffer.

The next morning they would all say what they experienced, and one guy would apologize for opening that door. It explains the Body of Christ. That is what Saint Paul meant when he was talking about the Body of Christ, the Church. Many Chrisatians talk about a personal relationship with Christ, and they should, it's very important, but it's not all that one should focus on. The reason we should develop that relationship is to serve the Church. The people God loves.

I realized while I was fighting my curse, by attending Mass, Adoration, prayer, devotion, and self sacrifice, any break in these, and I would feel the impact, but not just me. My family would feel the impact, and especially my kids. When a curse is ineffective at hurting the person it's meant for, it can attack those in the house that are spiritually weaker, usually innocent children. I could not bottle up the fire that burned in me. The Holy Spirit is alive in me, and I helped all who would accept it. Some of my coworkers struggled with certain things in life, and I shared my experience with them. All of them opened up. Eventually, some of them asked me if I would bless their house. One coworker in particular asked me to come to his house. This can be a difficult scenario, because sometimes a person is just going through a rough patch in life, and they want a resolution. Sometimes, it is just the rough patch in life they have to suffer. There is also another element to the situation; if it is a demon that is causing chaos in their life, then it requires a lifestyle change, and a blessing of the house is only half of it, and will need to be done routinely. It gets spiritually exhausting having to repeat this task again and again simply because someone does not use the grace God gave them. In one instance I went back to a house two more times, and I was frustrated down to my soul. I did as God instructed me to. Besides casting demons away, God wanted me to emphasize forgiveness to this lady. She had been hurt by her ex severely. I did as He ordered. I became drained, and agitated going back a third time. Similar to Moses when he hit the rock for God's followers the second time. The rock was the symbol of Jesus. The Life giving water to his people in the desert. The rock was struck symbolizing Jesus would be sacrificed. Striking it twice meant sacrificing Christ twice, and that was not necessary, and it was disobedient. God told Moses to speak to the rock, but he struck it in frustration, calling the people rebels, which they were, but Moses was not allowed in the promised land. His lack of patience caused him to strike the rock with his staff in anger. I was trying to avoid this, but it was hard. Soon after she was killed in a car accident. I didn't realize what I was doing, but God did. That is what blind obedience is the highest form of following God's commandments. I was preparing this lady for death, and he continued to encourage forgiveness.

Before blessing a house I would ask the person a series of questions, and if they answered them correctly I would move to the next step which happens simultaneously. While I was speaking to them God would let me know if they have an infestation. Before agreeing to go over, I learned that they should make lifestyle choices. Start attending Church regularly. Pray, read The Bible. If they chose not to, the demon would come back, and probably bring more with them. I would agree to bless the house, but repeat blessings can be prevented. I have not denied anyone a repeat blessing, but at some point it is that person's fault. Choosing sin lets the devil right back in. People aren't perfect, that is why Catholics should constantly reconcile themselves to Christ, which is going to confession. While this conversation was happening, the demon would know I was coming for him. One night, after agreeing to bless a house, I was sitting in my living room with my wife and kids. Something tapped on the window, and then drug its claw across the glass. My wife looked at me with wide eyes, trying not to alert the children. I looked back letting her know I heard it. Then out of pure obligation I walked up to the window to make sure it was a human, but I knew what it was. I suppose most people would have been too afraid to look out and see something terrifying, but I am beyond their games. If I would have been afraid, they have control of me, but they try. Maybe they think it will prevent me from blessing houses.

Back to the story of the coworker's house I went to bless. All the red flags were there. Also, his brother worked with us in the same hospital, and urged me to go bless the house. I went over, and he met me in the front yard. He was living with a woman who he was engaged to, and she had a couple children from a previous relationship. He starts telling me what's going on. "The other night we were in our bedroom watching TV, and all a sudden in the left corner of the room, we saw this black silhouette of someone standing in the corner staring at the wall. The door to the room was open behind it, and it was blocking half its body. It stood there as if it was trying to hide behind the door, and didn't want us to see it. It looked like a short stubby female. It had long knotted black hair. It couldn't have been more than 4'5". We looked at it in horror, and everything went silent. What was going to happen. All of a sudden it leaped onto her shoulders and started to choke her. We fought, but couldn't break its grasp.

We hear strange noises all night. Stuff banging. Things running through the house and up the walls." As we walked through the house he pointed at the ceiling in their bedroom, "Look there are hand prints left after it ran up the wall." Sure enough I could see small chubby hand prints, the grease outlined its hand. As I blessed the house I had to find the root of the infestation. I asked the investigative questions related to someone using occult practices. He explained, "Well her brother is a huge warlock in the four corners area, and they have been on bad terms lately." As soon as he said that, it hit me like lightning, this was the demon of the four corners he was using. He was attacking her, and it was attacking her children, as I could tell from the recent photographs. I blessed the house and offered to bless her and her kids. He explained she was terrified and didn't want anything done. I got the feeling they separated shortly after that. I got the impression that she blamed him for all of this, and probably the dysfunction with her brother. Running from this type of problem just doesn't do anything. The demon follows wherever she goes. If anything he was a strong provider that could only help her situation. Sometimes people rather live with their demons. I fought that demon a few more times since, but once one is recognized, it makes my job easier.

I stayed busy blessing houses, and demonic activity has intensified over the past few years. My sister Anne started having trouble of her own. I felt like I needed to help her. I asked if I could take a couple pizzas over and we could have dinner, and she agreed. When I arrived she looked like something was wrong. We sat and talked for a while. She asked me, "Why did you decide to come over?" "I felt like you needed my help." "I do. Before you got here, I was thinking of taking my life. Everything is falling apart." I blessed her house, and things got a lot better, but some work still needed to be done. I recommended three Rosaries. We started to pray and her four year old became even more rambunctious than before. She tried ripping the Rosary out of Anne's hand. "Stop it, stop it!" Anne pulled it back and continued to pray. We made it to the second Rosary and she stopped trying to take the Rosary out of Anne's hand. She layed on her chest while we prayed. "I don't like that," she whispered. She stared into Annes eyes, and both pupils dilated. Then her eyes started moving independently as if she was a reptile. We finally made it to the third Rosary, and I blessed her. The demon was gone. I never saw that. Normally a person has to agree to the demon to get possessed, or a heinous act has to occur to possess a child, as explained earlier. If a child is born to a mother or father that is possessed, then it can transfer to the child. If the child is sexually assaulted, then they can become possessed. Neither of these happened, it literally hijacked her. This is another reason children should be baptized at a young age. She wasn't baptized allowing the demon to enter her. In Catholic baptism, it's not just a baptism, but an exorcism as well. After the Rosaries and the blessings, they were both back to normal.

The next house I went to bless was another co-worker. I decided to take a friend I worked with. He is a spiritual man, and a warrior for Christ, and I wanted to be able to show him the ropes of blessing houses. The Holy Spirit told me to fast and pray the Rosary. I was working that day and I had brought lunch, and one of its ingredients was meat. Abstaining from meat prior to a spiritual battle gives the spirit strength. Abstaining from all food gives it more strength. Whatever makes the body week during self denial strengthens the spirit. My friend Gabe, who was invited, ended up having a catastrophe at work that nearly stopped him from going. I was meeting resistance as I was only working an eight hour shift that day, and I was trying to get out on time. Then another obstacle, I couldn't find the text message of the co-worker whose house I was supposed to bless. I made a few calls and after some resistance, I was able to obtain her number. We stopped at a convenience store on the way and I bought two bottles of water, and I blessed them. We arrived at her house, and she met us through the open garage door. She welcomed us in. She explained to me earlier that her ex husband might be there, as she thought he may need help.

We entered the living room, and I could see that he was anxious and didn't want us there, but out of the obligation of courtesy, he shook my hand. I could see he was suffering from a demon deep in his soul. I felt like I owed him an explanation of why we were there. He felt pressured by his ex-wife to be there. He reached his hand out to shake Gabes hand. Immediately Gabe backed up and walked back to the garage. I didn't think anything of it. Gabe reported later, "As soon as he shook my hand, a death grip traveled up my arm. The pain was so intense I had to get out of there. I walked a little ways down the driveway, and then as I walked I felt a dark spirit leave me. I couldn't see it directly, but a black figure lifted off me and disappeared into the sky." At that same moment the Holy Spirit instructed me to touch each of their heads at the same time and bestow a blessing. I said basic words that the Holy Spirit instructed me to say. Even though they seemed basic to me, they came directly out of my heart, and the demon that was in him fled, and she felt the joy of God's grace. I blessed the house. Then I instructed Gabe to finish the outside parameter. Things were better, and I left the Holy Spirit instructed me to bless my vehicle. After we finished her ex-husband approached us in the driveway. He tried to ask us where he knew us from. He guessed several places and trades, but explained that we had just met him. It wasn't after that I realized the reason for the sudden amnesia was the demon. It had him so blind, that he was barely seeing with his own mind, or with his own eyes. I have made it an attempt to live in a manner of blind obedience, and it is not easy, but it also makes it difficult to take a step back and see the big picture. Gabe pointed out how blessing the vehicle prevented any evil from following us, and he was right. I learned that when doing these blessings, the practitioner must bind up the demon from retaliation, whatever form it may take, financial, odds with a supervisor, attacking the relationships of a spouse or kids, or their health.

After these two previous blessings I learned a lot about this type of vocation, and about myself. After a week or two the coworker asked me to come back to her house. She said her cat was attacking her, and acting strange, and things felt weird again. I went back and re-blessed the house and set the parameter again. The parameter I had Gabe finish. I blessed her cat that had become possessed, and the rest of her house. I realized I had to return because of that. I didn't realize I had a certain anointing, and others don't. Catholic priests, deacons, bishops, cardinals, ect… have this blessing. Jesus was baptized by John the Baptist for a reason. In Jewish tradition a Levite was the one who had to perform the Baptism. That line of succession has passed down from Jesus, to the disciples, to the bishops they have anointed, all the way down to the current day. While working in the ED I was able to test and grow my skills of spiritual discernment. As I started the IVs on patients the admission representative would walk in the room to question the patient. They always asked questions if they were to be admitted to the hospital. One of the questions was; "If admitted, do you want to be put on a list to be visited by a chaplain, and what religion are you?" I was able to know what religion they were going to say. I realized what I was seeing. All the Catholics, even if not practicing, their religion has given them a special anointing I could see. It is like a glowing white hologram where their third eye is. The third eye connects the person to their Creator, Yahweh. This hologram looks like a 3 dimensional dove. When a person is baptized into the Catholic faith, they are baptized as a Priest, a Prophet, and a King. Gabe has that anointing, but he doesn't have the anointing of Holy orders. Holy orders are blessings when a man becomes a Deacon or a priest. While fighting the devil through exorcisms one needs to be as pure as possible. That means attending confession/reconciliation regularly. Doing exorcisms, one should have an anointing of Holy Orders, or have an anointing by God himself. God anoints many people without having Holy Orders. I realized I should not have taken Gabe there without confession. I realized not everything is just a house blessing, sometimes an exorcism needs to be performed.

Exercisted usually stack the odds in their favor. They work in teams of priests, and work during the daytime when demons are more vulnerable. The work in stages as some possessions take time, and repeated rituals, sometimes taking months to cleanse the soul. It was my fault taking Gabe there, I was excited to show him spiritual warfare in person. The ladies' house we blessed was a good learning experience. I learned that her brother is assigned to a team of exorcists in our diocese. I wondered why she asked me to perform the house clearing rather than her own brother whom she is not estranged from, and this is his own specialty. I didn't pry as I knew it was God's Will for all of us.

I have seen so many miracles, few things seem possible. So many miracles that they have become countless, and this book will never end if I continue to write about them. God has protected me countless times, here is one example. I was making dinner, and as I always do, when I'm at home I wear gym shorts and a T-shirt. This night was no different. I was cooking, and I wasn't even wearing shoes or socks. Somehow a grease fire erupted. The flame touched the vaulted ceiling. I quickly grabbed the pan and tossed it in the sink. Shocked, I looked at the stove, the floor and checked myself. I was unscathed, grease splatters everywhere except on me. There was not one tiny grease splatter on my clothes, legs, or feet. I looked around, and on the floor there was a dry area just where I was standing. Turned around and I saw grease was even splattered behind me. It was as if I was in a protective shell. Just where I was standing grease was repellant. How did the grease get behind me? I was protected by the Holy Spirit, enveloped by His protection without even asking for it. Then as I stood in amazement of the Glory of God and thanksgiving, just at that moment He said, "I did this, but that you may know that I protected you, here this is what you would have suffered over your entire body." Suddenly a small drip of grease popped from the stovetop and landed on my right thumb. The grease seared the tiny section of my posterior thumb and it burned intensely. That little spot on my thumb hurt for a week, but it only brought me joy and amazement at the Glory of God.

I was able to have many spiritual meetings with people in the emergency department, all walks of life stroll through there. I was able to meet plenty of young people suffering from depression. Some of them were able to recall a black horse or mule with red eyes. This was a certain demon that tries to convince people to take their life. I was so surprised that so many people are walking around with demons. Most are unaware that they are possessed, or they may speculate, but go through their day trying to function. So many with black souls, avoiding God and his help.

One morning an ambulance brought in a psych patient as she kicked screamed and fought. She was restrained to the stretcher, which was a good indication that we would need security's help when we moved her to a hospital gurney. She was cursing and thrashing violently. All the staff rushed into the room to transfer to the gurney. We moved her quickly as she fought. She had multiple demons in her. She glared around the room as she prophesied. She glared at each person in the room, "You are a liar, you can't control your temper, you are a womanizer, you…" Aww crap she looked at me, what was she going to say to me? "You're OK." She continued to go around the room telling people their inner darkest selves. I did the bare minimum and got out of the room as fast as possible. I was not afraid one bit. I knew that if I stayed in that room for too long and prayed for her, the rest of my work day was going to be hell. Everything that could go wrong, would go wrong, basically Murphy's law. I hesitated for hours. The Holy Spirit urged me to go back into the room. I fought against it, and he said, "This is why you were put here. Do what you were made to do." I went back into the room and prayed for her. The demons weren't coming out. The Holy Spirit made it clear that these are the demons that have to be prayed out while fasting, just like in the Bible Matthew 17:19 *Then came the disciples to Jesus apart, and said, why could not we cast him out? And Jesus said unto them, Because of your unbelief: for verily I say unto you, if ye have faith the size of a mustard seed, ye shall shall say unto this mountain, Remove hence to yonder place; and it shall remove; and nothing shall be impossible unto you. Howbeit this kind goeth not out but by prayer and fasting.* I prayed for her, and sure enough the rest of my day was hell, but not just the rest of my day. As a punishment for not acting quickly, God allowed me to fight them for two weeks. He explained it would have only been the rest of my work day if I would have done what I was supposed to do.

I noticed a coworker who I considered a friend became possessed by multiple demons after taking a management position. I asked if she wanted help, and she agreed to let me bless her. She instantly felt better. I fought those demons for two weeks as well, but it was very manageable. I shared a little too much with her about the inner workings of spiritual warfare. God instructed me to steady my tongue. He explained that if people realize I take part in their suffering with them, they may feel bad, and reject the blessing, not wanting to burden me. I needed to suffer in silence. Sadly, our friendship would end on a sour note. I wanted to help her cousin with her demon. She also worked in the Emergency Department with us. Even though I continued to look past her jezebel demon, I never confronted it, and eventually I had no other option. My error was waiting to allow sin to seem OK, or seemingly agreeing it was OK. By the time I finally confronted it, it caused a huge rift in our working environment. Jezebel spirits come off as charming and passive, and as soon as your guard is down, it attacks. I took myself away from all their negativity. Someone told them I started a rumor that she was having an affair.

I didn't, I actually defended her. But she made it hard to defend her as she fawned over another coworker. She wouldn't let go of her demon, it gave her the false pretense of comfort. Her cousin now in a manager type role would make me pay. Everyone was afraid of these girls. Everyone in the entire ED was afraid to talk to me. I was isolated, and they tried to make my life hell. It was just high school drama. It was silly, but they held nothing back. Her cousin in a management role was in control of the schedule. She scheduled all my shifts at the other stand alone hospital. I was isolated. I didn't mind, but the schedule changed my hours, I would now get out two hours later which made child care difficult. After eight weeks I was scheduled at the main hospital. She went to HR to try to get me fired. She threatened to make up lies to tell my wife I was cheating on her. I felt like I was going through another crucifixion. I was drained, and I didn't know what to do. Even the males in the department cowered with their tails between their legs. I have heard someone talk about the life of saint Therese and how she lived a short life, but her sisters bullied her. They explained that it was such a small minor affliction, but it's not. Things like this can cause people to commit suicide. I am battle tested now, and would not think twice about this situation, but then I was young and learning. I cried out to God, "You were only crucified once, why am I crucified again and again?" I shouldn't have said that. I said it in weakness. I did feel the crucifixion rule over. No matter what I did, it went against me. They talked to every other employee to turn them against me. Now HR and my boss were involved. They made up lies. I finally asked God what to do in Prayer while I was staring at an image of Jesus in the stained glass of the chapel. He said one word, "Fight!" I was emotionally drained, but now I was invigorated. Things got a lot better and I realized; there is no compromise with demons. They suggest compromise, but they can never hold up to their word, because they are all liars and there is no compromise, only war.

My kids were growing fast and there were no rules for spiritual warfare. Both would be targeted in ways I mention, but I knew the demons wanted blood. I was brushing my youngests teeth for bed as she stood on the toilet. Before I could react, something pushed her off the toilet with such force, her body folded in half, knees touching her face. Her head flying to the bathtub, I could only imagine her head smashing into the tub. Her face was shocked by the ripping force that jerked her off the toilet. Before she hit the tub her guardian angel caught her and set her down. Even though she was a toddler, our eyes met with surprise and astonishment. I organized Rosaries with my family once a week to help with all this craziness.

One night before we started I laid my youngest down for bed. I started to lay my oldest one down, and she suddenly got a migraine. She started screaming and thrashing. I contemplated taking her to the hospital. The Holy Spirit urged me to pray three rosaries. I started the first one, and then the second. Typically one Rosary takes twenty to thirty minutes to pray just one. I prayed the first Rosary in about five minutes. I was flying. I was nearly done with the second and the Holy Spirit told me when I reach the next decade the headache will ease up, and it did. Then I reached the third. When I finished the third she was peacefully sleeping. I walked her to bed and laid her down. When I walked into the living room everyone asked if she was OK. After assuring them she was fine, they explained how the mirror near the front door was waving vigorously as if it was angry waves in an ocean. It was waving so vigorously they expected it to shatter. After I finished the rosaries, it came to a stop.

Even though I won some battles I lost some, and the battles never ended. My motorcycle stopped working. I tried repeatedly to fix it, I drained my wallet to fix it, but no success. It sat in my garage for a year. I couldn't afford to fix it. I was getting ready to go on a hunting trip. I bought groceries and packed the truck with gear, and all the groceries. I got in and turned the key. The truck wouldn't shift into reverse. The transmission went out. I had to cancel my trip. Each vehicle I owned was failing. The next day I pushed the lawnmower to the backyard to mow the lawn. While I started to mow, the lawnmower engine cut out. I pulled the lawnmower start cord, and it ripped. We were down to only my wife's vehicle working. I grew so enraged, I had enough. I grabbed the lawnmower and threw it twenty yards in frustration. I stormed into the house and grabbed a Rosary. I felt the devil tremble. He was terrified. I kneeled down and prayed. As I prayed I saw the demon attacking me. She floated into the dining room.

She was at least nine feet tall. She was made of roots and vines as used in the occult. The roots and vines interweaved to make her body. Her legs were about three feet wide and so were her arms. Her head frayed out to the shape of a broom. Her entire being looked as though someone picked up a pile of sticks and vives and wrapped twine to form a body. The eyes and lips were very feminine, but looked as though made from playdoh and placed on the sticks to form the female being. She was wearing a purple dress. Gray smoke fumed below her as she floated. I understood that she was Mother nature spirit, and the female form of the occult used for witchcraft. I don't know why demons love going into wood, but they constantly flow into trees and bushes. I don't know if it is to disques. Maybe they are attracted to its energy. But It makes sense since the druids, pagans, witches of all sorts go into the woods to worship. As I prayed, I overcame the battle. It's better to act like a mule or a donkey so to speak in the wrath of demons. I have fought and fought to fix things. Sometimes it is better not to panic. If a horse steps in a bad or unsafe ground, it panics or fights and makes things worse by thrashing. A donkey or a mule stops what it is doing, and it doesn't make things worse. The next day I fixed the lawnmower, and mowed the lawn. By watching a couple of videos on the internet I fixed my truck myself. Then I was able to get my motorcycle to the shop to get it fixed.

My love for God grew. While at church I heard a wise priest give a great homily. He said, "How many of you would kneel down to pick up a twenty dollar bill. How many of you would do that even if it was painful, yet how many people sit in their pew's when the bread is transformed into the Body of Christ. Every knee shall bend. A muslim explained to me how irreverent we are. If we truly believe we are in the presence of God, we should not even walk up to the host, but crawl in reverence to the Bread." He was right. From that moment on I chose to never use a kneeler. If one doesn't believe that to be a sacrifice, they should try it. It makes a huge difference. I started showing more reverence when I genuflected right before getting the bread. I laid prostrate, and then stood up to receive the Host. After another priest saw how much time I spent honoring God, maybe an extra ten seconds he called me out in the announcements after mass. He explained that when receiving, bow before you get to the front to not hold anyone up. Is that how we ought to join Communion with God, quickly like moving through a buffet line? I accepted the criticism with honor. If I am to be a modern day Saint Thomas, then so be it, may God Correct me. But I will gladly accept the embarrassment for ten seconds of making people wait. In Africa where Catholicism is spreading like wildfire, the people go to Church and are angry if the Homily is less than three hours. The walk for hours to get to Church. Here in America, we get antsy if the Homily is more than thirty minutes.

When I helped as a Eucharistic minister I didn't realize the gravity of what I was doing. This is an Angels job, distributing the actual body of Christ. I would go out with my friends on Saturday night, and show up to Church tired and barely on time in a hoodie to hand out Communion. I started to realize the people as they came to get the Bread. I felt their love and understanding in what they were doing. As I gave Bread to people I thought their reverence was for me stupidly, but I finally realized it was for the Bread I was giving them. Not all the people. Maybe fifteen out of a hundred which is sad. The number should have been a hundred out of a hundred, or why even go to Church. To escape hell, sadly, that may be true for some. It helped me understand my faith. I realized, not using a kneeler is not enough. I prayed that God would make kneeling harder for me, and I would still kneel for all those who can kneel but don't whether it is hard or not. God granted me my wish. One day I was kneeling down to grab a box from a shelf, and I felt my knee smash down as if something inside it crushed. I needed surgery to cut out most of my meniscus. The first time I knelt after surgery, I was scared. I was scared I would tear up more inside my knee, but it didn't stop me. I haven't used a kneeler since.

Chapter XIV

My children were getting older, and my oldest was now in preschool. We chose a school with a Christian curriculum. The pastor/spiritual director of the school was a female, and invited all the kids and their families to a festival in a local park. We arrived and there was a nice picnic set up. We found seats in a row of chairs organized for a service in the park. It was a great idea. I had never been to a service outside. The ceremony started and the Pastor started mass. They were offering communion. As she blessed the bread and grape juice Many visitors showed up instantaneously. Some knelt down, and some stayed standing. They filled the park, but were focused on the altar, and the pastor as she blessed the bread. Their height was marked by the height of the five story building across the street. They were joining in glee of what was taking place. The demons reveled in the fact that a woman was performing the ceremony. They were gigantic demons. They towered over the one hundred year old trees. My wife looked at me, "Are we going up?" "No, we are not." I prayed why they would even attend such a ceremony. God explained how he is so disturbed and what an abomination it was to see such a thing, and that is why the demons took joy in it. They were gleeful. I have always understood that many people think of the Catholic Church as being chauvinistic. I know that Mary is a woman, and the most powerful person the earth has experienced just after Jesus. I know that there are doctors of the Church that are woman. A doctor of the church is someone whose writings have contributed to what the Church believes. I know that some of these powerful women's presence when they were living sent the devil fleeing. The Church is not mistaken. Women are equal to men, but have a different role. The person chopping down a tree gets credit for the work, but he had to use the ax. The ax is what was used to actually cut the tree down. Both man and ax worked in union for the result, both are important and equal in the chore.

I have heard, even today, God is a female. God was here on earth, His name was and is Jesus. He was verified and documented as a male, and repeatedly referred to his Father in Heaven. I don't know how many times he stated his Father in the Bible, but it was a lot. God is Spirit, but if He takes a form, He is a Man. Jesus is the Glory of God, Man is the glory of Jesus, woman is the glory of man. Jesus chose to come down and be subject to a Woman. As Father Blunt says, "If Jesus is the King of the universe, Mary would have to be the Queen, that is the only way He can be King." Science shows most men have X and Y chromosomes, and most women have X and X chromosomes. Men have complete DNA, women only have part as Eve has been pulled from part of Adam. I believe that men can be strong and courageous, and also sensitive. Women can be both as well, but the majority of men will always be stronger. Females can be more nurturing, as is their nature. I can talk about these as I have a medical degree, and I have heard a lot of foolish people say, "Are you a doctor? Then you can talk about it!" That is the most ridiculous thing I have heard. Can I not cook myself dinner, do I need to be a chef to cook my dinner? Do I have to be a janitor to clean my house? God gave us a brain to learn and do what we need to do using logic and reasoning.

It doesn't take a mystic or a theologian to see the blatant evil persisting in the world, as the devil and demons scramble desperately for the times we're in. The urgency is that of a team in the fourth quarter attempting to achieve a comeback. Much suffering has been necessary, even to the point of me blaspheming. That I'm not proud of, I just mention it to show the severity I suffer. I have suffered more than most eighty year olds, in several lifetimes. When mentioning this to Russell, he said, "Jesus already died for us. Why would God need you to suffer too?" What he didn't understand was that God loves his people so much, and most will never know how much. Most will take advantage, even if they are devout, they will continue to offend, and take their relationship for granted. I entered into the dark night of the soul. When researching what that is, almost all sources have it wrong. It's labeled as depression, and even though depression seems like it can't be worse, the dark night of the soul is a million times worse.

The only sources that have understood this concept are the saints of the Catholic Church, and Saint John of the Cross in particular. I didn't really think much of the saint when watching a brief documentary, but after experiencing the dark night, I have so much admiration for the saint, I have only started reading a book he wrote on the matter. The dark night of the soul is a way to love God more perfectly. This is what it feels like; I know God exists, and I know he loves me, I feel no joy or happiness. I know I love my family, and I know they can feel my love, but I don't experience the joy. Even just sharing God with someone for the first time, I would feel the joy of the Holy Spirit, or feel the power radiating off a blessed statue of Jesus or Mary. I would feel warmth and tingly. Now I feel nothing, but The Holy Spirit tells me the statue is Holy. I feel like a bastard separated from my Father. When I pray, I know He hears me, but I feel like I am Ignored. I know I'm not, as I see the fruits of prayer come to fruition right before my eyes, just as the people see before their eyes that God helps them, through me. It feels like I'm in a dark room, filled with snakes. God is on the outside of the room watching. He can hear me, but does not respond to me. The snakes can bite me, and they do, but the attacks are not fatal. Only annoyances as they attack. I'm allowed to spar with demons without taking a fatal blow, but they are allowed to cause me pain and constant strife. The only relief I can experience is after Adoration, or after receiving Communion. If I do both, I get great relief, and by relief to either I mean that I can feel sadness, and the numbness goes away for a short time. I am extra sensitive, and the sadness takes over. If I see a sad movie, or hear a sad story, it can bring tears to my eyes. God's mercy for me is more than I deserve. Here is how I went into the dark night of the soul.

I entered it during the story that started the book. I will finish the story. Before I went to Russell's house he had a dream. A week before Russell told me, "I had a dream last night. In the dream something drastic happened, and then you became so sad at what you did, You became unconsolable. I told you that I forgive you, whatever it was, but that didn't change anything. So I want you to know that I forgive you." The night I went to Russell's House, I was fasting for a few days. I went to Russell's and blessed his house. The house became infested after Robert spent some time there. It wasn't his presence, but what he brought with him. Robert brought his "saints." They were actually demons in statues, and items filled with earth, as explained before. Robert was fighting with his wife and he needed a place to stay while he worked things out. While Robert was going to stay a few nights, he brought his "saints." Alonzo, Russell's brother, was helping bring stuff inside. While carrying in a "saint," Alonzo dropped it. This "saint," was in a glass container with a lid, and it shattered in the garage. Earlier I wrote; *It wasn't until several years later that I realized where it came from. I didn't think to question, all I knew was what I had to do, to help him out. That was the first house I cleared. Looking back, I know exactly where the demon came from. Russell's brother, Alonzo was 22 years old. He lived in his basement. He tells a story of vivid nightmares he was having that week. He said, " I was laying on my bed in the basement where my room is, and as I was sleeping. I could see myself rise out of my body. There was a giant hand I was laying on, not my bed. The hand head had sharp nails and was so powerful. I could feel it trying to squish me, and I woke up in a cold sweat. The Source finally dawned on me, I knew exactly where it came from. I'm getting ahead of myself… let me start from the beginning, back where it all started.* The demon squeezing Alonzo in his hand was the demon in the "saint," that Alonzo dropped in the garage. That is where the infestation started. It wasn't the worst "saint," Robert brought over. One of them was so evil Russell didn't allow it in the house. It was a three foot tall stump attached to the roots. There were three faces carved into each side. Russell was telling me about it. "That thing was evil bro. I could feel it's evil. It was alive. Robert said that was the saint that he used to attack his enemies. I didn't let him bring that thing in my house or garage. In fact, I told him to take it to the edge of my property, you know, I have an acre. At night that thing would glow bro. It was glowing green, blinking green as if it had a heart beat."

Witch craft, magic, voodoo, all the occult, use plants and roots. To break the spell/curse, one must get to the root, and uproot it to spiritually reverse the curse. However, that was the source of Russell's house being infested, the dropped demon. After casting out the demon I was on a spiritual high. I wanted to help Russell in another way. Years prior Russell was a young man who was in spectacular shape. He was a golden gloves boxer in California. At the peak of his physical health he was hanging out with a group of friends. They were hanging out in the driveway, one of his buddies had a BB gun. There was a black cat walking by. Russell grabbed the BB gun, "Let me see that," he shot at the cat. The cat flailed on the ground, he shot out the cat's left eye. "Dude, no it's just going to suffer. We need to finish him off." Russell shot him a few more times, but he didn't die. They tried stomping him to death, but he didn't die. One twenty year old man should be able to stomp him out, much less five of them stomping him out. People have been murdered with less force. They lit a fire in a small metal dumpster, then they threw the cat in the dumpster. The cat ran off, he seemed indestructible, and they were unable to kill the cat. A few days later, Russell was leaving his house on the way to the gym, and he fell down. The left side of his body wasn't working. He dragged himself to his car, and pulled himself into the driverseat. He drove to a nearby hospital. Russell had a stroke, and he lost vision in his left eye. His left eye would cause him pain for the rest of his life, and it was his left eye. Telling the story, "I know I deserved it for trying to kill that innocent cat, but I'm not so sure it was an ordinary innocent cat. We were not able to kill that cat. I think a witch was in that cat at that moment, possessing its body, that's why we weren't able to kill it."

Russell told me his story as we talked in the garage. "Thanks for coming over, I know it's late and a huge inconvenience." I responded with what actually happened, and I was not wise about spiritual warfare. I'm not saying I should have lied about the stress it put on my marriage, but it wasn't doing God's Will that put the stress on my marriage, but the devil trying to prevent me from trying doing God's Will. One rule for doing this type of work is to have quite humility, that would have been sufficient. Knowing the strife and suffering one goes through to help cast evil out can make the person feel guilty and the gift will be denied and returned to the person trying to mediate God's miracle.

Since the Holy Spirit was in full strength that night, I laid my hands on Russell to heal his eye. I felt the gift return to me. Russell turned down the gift of healing. As I drove home, I wondered if my wife was going to be home? I arrived at home and she was completely converted. She was happy to see me. The devil let go of his hold on her. The next day, my parents were moving out of their house, so I went over to help them move. As I helped them move I wondered why God did not allow Russell to be healed. It bothered me, and the devil constantly rubbed it in my face. "You can not heal anybody. You are not as powerful as you thought you were." I went home to an empty house as my wife was at work. I'm not perfect, and not proud to say it, but that someone else may benefit from my humiliation. I willingly entered into sin, but it was during a fast, and just after a miraculous battle. Just then I saw a black figure run through the front door and disappeared. It was my height and I was not able to see through it, it was not transparent.

It disappeared and ran through the kitchen, and disappeared. I felt the presence of Saint Micheal, the being wasn't evil. Then it ran at me. From a standing position I crumbled in half. My entire body cramped. My legs folded under me, and I folded in half laying on my folded legs under me. My entire body was in pain. I had no control over anything. I knew Saint Michael came to punish me. After fifteen minutes of an entire body spasm, The Holy Spirit instructed me to crawl to the dining room to the candle of the Guadalupe I had previously lit days ago. I dragged my half spasming body in front of the candle. On my belly, which I was not worthy of being in the presence of Mary, The Holy Spirit instructed me to pray three Rosaries. My heart was resentful, but I followed The Holy Spirit's instructions. After the first two rosaries were completed my hardened heart started to soften. As I finished the last Rosary I saw the Virgin Mary's face. It has been said that Mary never turns anyone away, and that may be mostly true, but in my experience, as I saw her face, it turned away from me in dismay. I realized that I had the gift that Judas had. The ability to heal, and cast out demons, and I chose sin. My soul was pierced forever, and I was unconsolable. Russell's prophecy came true. A prophecy only happens one way, even the prophet doesn't understand it, and it can't be prevented. I entered the dark night of the soul, as its main purpose of the dark night of the soul is to love God more perfectly, as one should love Him, as because of His Omnipotence, deserves to be loved. I wish I could take it back, but my life will be forever changed by my actions. Sorrow for my own soul, and sorrow for not being able to heal Russsull's eye ate at me, and the devil used this against me. After years of prayer Jesus has revealed to me, "It's not that you couldn't have healed his eye, I didn't allow it for his eternal well being. If I would have healed him through you, he would have spent eternity in hell." A piece of scripture shot through my head, Matthew 18:9, *"And if your eye causes you to stumble, gouge it out and throw it away. It is better for you to enter life with one eye than to have two eyes and be thrown into the fire of hell."*

I spent years in the dark night of the soul with hope that I will be able to step out of it come Easter, but I remained. Then my soul hoped, "Maybe by Pentecost I will be released from this prison of the soul?" But I remain. Then I thought to myself, maybe at a landmark year I will be able to be released from my suffering, my soul hoped at year ten I would be released, but my hope faded, I could hope no more. Then one Easter I asked God if I would be released, hope had come back, and he asked me if I can do one more year, and I replied, "Yes Lord." The year came and went so fast. Easter was here again, and my soul rejoiced in the Lord as I asked Him if I will be released, and the Lord asked me, "Will you spend a lifetime in the dark night of the soul?" I replied, "Yes

Lord." Jesus assured me, just before my death, I will be released from my suffering. It has not been easy. Just as my Spiritual Father has made me feel like a bastard, so too, my earthly father has followed in his footsteps. One day I was walking into a hardware store. My earthly father was driving by me, close enough to touch and his window down. We made eye contact, and I raised my head to say hi, but he stared blankly at me. He did wave, say hi, or flip me off. He just coasted away. The devil has been allowed to harm every relationship I have, from my boss, all the way down to my children.

The curse was blatantly obvious how it would strike me constantly, and One night I felt that the witch who cursed me was so frustrated that most of her attempts to harm me would fail. When she would curse me to die, I would roll my ankle. When she cursed me to get in a fatal car accident, I would get a fender bender. I ran into her in public a couple of times. My guardian angel warned me, and I would look up. There she would be. A few moments later the devil would warn her that I was there. Both times she stopped in her tracks, not entering the building, waiting until I left far off in the distance. I could see her, but she couldn't see me, but she knew I was there. One time she returned to her car. That time she nearly walked in front of my car. I was surprised how close she got to me before she was warned, but I realized I had my sunglasses on which believe it or not, can disguise the soul. The eyes truly are the window to the soul. The darker the iris, the more that can be hidden. These are my teachings, but science is close behind proving similar things related to health. A lot can be determined by assessing the eye. Every fall, and winter, the season of witchcraft, I was attacked more severely. I simply held devotions, prayer, fasting, and attending church, and all her attempts barely left a scratch. I had many dreams related to my spiritual attacks.

It was night time and I was in a large building that had many rooms compartmentalized. The rooms were cement and had metal guard rails that looked similar to a warehouse. It led to a large arena with wood shavings in the center ring, and in the rings was over twenty large metal cages. The cages were stacked two to three cages tall and were not directly stacked on each other. They were somewhat in a line as if a child was playing with blocks. They were stacked with the front cage doors turned facing each other, and others adjacent. Then I appeared standing on the cage on the top left. I peered into the cages, and inside the cages were large full grown tigers. Then one by one, the cages started opening. They leaped at me, roaring and blood thirsty. I slammed the door closed even though it didn't latch, and it swiped at me. Then I jumped to the next cage to avoid my hands from being scratched as my fingers wrapped around the bars, leaving them exposed. I jumped to another, and across from me a cage door opened and a tiger leaped out. I jumped to another, and then climbed to the top. I continued to escape their clutches miraculously. I don't know how I avoided their grasp. I scampered to the ground and ran out of the arena. I made my way into a room, which led to a staircase on the left side of the room. I made my way down the staircase, and there I met a few family members and my kids. I walked in front of them shielding them from danger. As we reached the bottom of the stairs we were met by a lady. She was walking a huge tiger to the arena by a leash. As we walked by them, I shielded my family with my body and outstretched arms. Just then it leaped at us. It transformed from a huge tiger to a cub, and as I blocked it from biting my family, it bit me. But it was so bearable.

My next tiger dream involved a setting in a town, and it was overrun by adult tigers. I entered the dream as if it was halfway through. I was on the landing of a walkway of an apartment complex. I was injured, sitting and leaning against the outside wall of an apartment. As I sat there, a tiger on the prowl leaped at me. I looked down, and saw a shard of a pipe next to me. I quickly picked it up and as the tiger reached me, I drove the pipe into his neck and into his chest. He fell over dead, and I pushed him off my lap. I was drained, exhausted from injuries and continually fighting. My clothes were drenched with sweat, dirt, and blood. I stood to my feet, and another tiger was stalking me. He was crawling low to the ground shielding its body from sight using cover from dead bodies of tigers and humans. I ran as fast as I could and as I ran it followed. I ran down a flight of stairs, and made it to a patch of grass that met a curb then a street. As I turned to see where the tiger was, it was in my face, mouth open, claws wides spread, and out of nowhere I pulled a handheld sawed off shotgun. I squeezed the trigger, Boom! It dropped at my feet. I turned and another tiger leaped at me as I turned. I improvised as if assisted by a mysterious force, surprising even myself as I fought.

Each dream has so much meaning and has layers of meaning. The tigers symbolized Bertha, her prowess, and strength. Her attempts to kill me and my family, as I improvised, striking down the attempts. Even if the tiger does harm me, it changed from a full grown tiger to a baby tiger, making the attack bearable, and frustrating my opponent. After so many dreams and miracles in my life, it is hard to put them all in the book, and even remembering everything, but what I could say is that God never ceases to amaze me. The dreams gave me encouragement, as I revealed the fight I was in, and was winning.

A dream I had gave me knowledge, and a way to tread on serpents in a snake pit. It started with me in a rainforest. I was in a swampy river floating down stream, the water was gently flowing. As I drifted down the river with crocodiles. They were big and small, and I panicked. I held on to the shell of bark from a tree as it kept me buoyant. It was important that I not swim too much, as the thrashing would draw attention to me. I arched my back to navigate away from the crocodiles. As I panicked we washed up to land. As I panicked to get away from all the crocodiles, I heard a voice saying, "Evil takes care of evil." Just then a gigantic crocodile ate a smaller crocodile. They continued eating each other. The dream taught me to avoid getting in every little squirmish, let evil destroy evil. Stay still, calm and navigate not making a commotion, and I'll survive. It came at a time when work was a hostile environment.

Bertha was so frustrated that I continued to shatter her attacks through God's help, so she sent a special attack. I had a dream of a vision of the entity she sent my way. This being came in the form of a black stick figure. It looked as though it crawled off of a mens restroom sign. The figure had no fingers on the hands, nor feet. It looked just like the body of the man symbol. It appeared to me as lounging, the left leg laid straight, and the right leg bent at the knee, foot resting on the floor supporting the leg. Its left elbow propped up its torso, and the right arm relaxed on his belly. The head was round, but it had a set of horns that resemble the Texas longhorn bull. The head caulked back for a moment with a shill mocking laugh directed at me. Then God completely put his attack down. I didn't have to do anything. I woke up feeling good about it, it was so easy, I didn't think twice about it.

Roughly a month later, I was talking about the dream with Victor. It helps to talk about a spiritual dream. The dream is always very memorable as it elicits an emotion, which relates to the memory. While talking about it, it brings the feelings back, but it also helps interpret the dream, even if the dreamer is the interpreter. While I was telling him about the dreamland I realized it was Baal and Moloch. The devil disguised himself as the two different personas, but it is the devil. The reason he wanted people to think they were different, is to trick people into believing a different deity. People were sacrificing babies to them. It's the same as all the different types of paganism. The devil dresses it up differently, but it's the same thing. They all have brutal sacrifice, and sacrificing of the innocent, babies. The symbol of Oden is actual sacred geometry which is a symbol to invoke a certain demon. I realized the symbol of Baal/Moloch was actually the devil sent to attack me, but he was wiped out in a blink by God. He fell so easily, his attack didn't even mount a small suffering, I was so impressed. When I had the dream, it seemed so easy, I didn't bother investigating the meaning. I'm sorry Lord, and Thank you…

I think it is very important to have a personal relationship with Crist as many other Christians do, but what is neglected is how Jesus spoke of the Body of Christ, the Church. It can only do well if all parts work together. This is why work is so important, it's not for me, but the Body of Christ. It seems more important than our personal relationship with Cgrist in some ways. How can one help the Body of Christ if they haven't established a personal relationship with Christ? Both are just as important. During the early Church, Catholics did things a lot differently. If someone committed a sin they would confess it to the congregation. How humiliating. Then they would go to church, and stand outside in shame, possibly wearing sackcloth and ashes. As people gathered for church they stood at the front as people walked by, and they would ask the passers to pray for them. They would attend the church service, but they were not allowed to have the Bread/Host/Communion especially if it was a mortal sin. Based on the severity of the sin, they were allowed back to fully participate in mass fully, usually around Easter, and welcomed back into the congregation. One had to earn their way into the Church. Things have changed so much. So many graces that are left unopened by so many.

Contemplating my experience of my personal relationship with Christ while I was driving home from work one day, "Jesus, tell me something about yourself?" I didn't get a response. Days later I had a dream. I was on the shore line of a mountain range. It reminded me of Alaska, as the shoreline met the sea. The sea stretched out in front of me. Across the vast distance was another mountain range that jetted up out of the sea. Beautiful green trees reaching to the edge of the land. In front of me dressed in white was Jesus. He resembled the character from the movie *The Shack* that was based on the novel. He resembled the young Character in that movie. His skin was dark. His hair was relatively short, wavy and dark. His eyes were kind and touched my soul. As I walked toward Him, He continued to stare into my eyes. In the background more than two hundred yards out, a creature came flying up out of the ocean. This creature was at least twenty times bigger than the biggest species of whales. I was aww inspired by its creation, power, size, and magnificence. If God can create this, how much greater is God than his creation? It looked like it was related to the whale. It was part black and white like the orca, and bluish gray like the sperm whale. It had fins that could make it fly or swim.

I Looked at it in amazement, then I looked back at Jesus, and he was staring at me with direct eye contact. Then, off in the distance above the shore line of the land across the sea were two creatures flying. They resembled the flying creatures from *Avatar*, but they had different heads. It looked like they had dragon heads. There were some differences though. They had long bodies, almost like a large serpent. They had four wings, two up front, and two in the middle. The bellies were white and as their bellies met their back, they changed into a blue color. As I looked off in amazement, Jesus said, "Stop being amazed at my creations, Keep your eyes focused on me." John 2:15 *Love not the world, neither the things that are in the world, the love of the Father is not in him. For all that is in the world, the lust of the flesh, and the lust of the eyes, and the pride of life, is not of the Father, but is of the world and the world passeth away, and the lust thereof: but he that doeth the will of God abideth forever.* As I said before, Jesus, Yawwhe, or the Holy Spirit never just appear to say Hi, there is always a purpose and a meaning. At that time I was so focussed on the material things of the world in order to have a better life for me and my family. I need to not be greedy and focus on that. That is secularism, which teaches; if I have a good job, money, a beautiful car, a beautiful spouse, beautiful children, then I will be happy. Although those things can bring temporary and intermittent joy, the only thing that can fill that void in life is God.

Chapter XV

Years ago when I received Holy Communion and my confirmation through RCIA, I received many prophecies which have and are coming to fruition now. It has taught me to be patient, since it has been eighteen years since those sacraments. God continued to test me. Abraham's test was incredible. I have listened to a bishop explain that Abraham knew God would resurrect his son, but I don't believe that. That is an example of a work that proved his faith, and it proved that works combined with faith do merit. There was no guarantee that God would resurrect his son, and God didn't say He would resurrect him. As I drive down the highway and listen to my phone give me a direction to take the off ramp, and if I'm trying to make it to my destination on time, I am leery of trusting the navigation, my faith in it is tested. This scenario seems like such a huge deal, taking your child's life would make one doubt everything, especially a God who is supposed to be good telling you to do something unthinkable to a miracle child you waited over a hundred years for.

Driving down the street, I sometimes have faith that the oncoming drivers are going to stay in their lane. I shouldn't have faith in them, they may be drunk. Calling 911 I have faith someone will answer my call. Why do we have faith in these things? That is putting faith in human beings, how much greater will God respond if we give him faith. When Abraham was told to sacrifice his son, even though he was deeply sad, he was loyal. He proved his utter and complete fidelity to God. I too was tested in the same manner, but I wasn't the one holding the knife. God explained the heinous crimes, and I was going to be blamed for all of them. God knows that after Him, they are the most important part of my life, and even though it would have destroyed me, I agreed. After a year of Him confirming what would happen, everything He said would happen did, and the next part was set to happen. That day I waited with anticipation, and just like Abraham, God revealed it was a test, and with it He gave me a prophecy to reveal at a certain time. Then He confirmed it a week later with a sign that happened three times to the Holy papacy, and gave me precise directives with the prophecy.

There were several books taken out of the Bible in the early church, and I definitely understand why. The pope wanted people to only know that there is only heaven and hell as a final destination, and a temporary destination in purgatory, which always leaves to heaven. Saint Peter had part of his work extracted from the Bible. The part that was taken out explained that in some, very limited circumstances, there is a loophole to where very few people will be able to get another chance to prove their love for God. If people are aware of this, then they may not try as hard to earn heaven, and may end up in hell for eternity. Just to be clear the next story is my experience and not a teaching of the Catholic Church, and the reason is; reincarnation poses an issue when Jesus returns people are resurrected in their bodies. If someone is reincarnated, which body is resurrected. The Catholic Church does acknowledge one reincarnation; Jesus teaches his disciples that Elijah was reincarnated into John the Baptist. They ask Jesus why the pharisees say that Elijah will come before the

Messiah. Jesus explains in Matthew 11:13 *For all the prophets and the Law prophesied until John. And if you are willing to accept it, he is Elijah who has come.* This is the only part of the Bible mentioning reincarnation. It challenges the traditional Eastern religions that teach reincarnation. The first difference is that The Bible teaches Elijah was in heaven for years, then his spirit was placed in John the Baptist body to announce the Savior's arrival. Eastern reincarnation teaches, the person's spirit moves into another human body with no time gap. Also some teachings say that if the person's karma is bad, then they may be reincarnated as another species, animal, or even insects. This teaching is incorrect. A person with logic, understanding and reason, and a conscience could never be transformed into a lesser being, the human soul is made in the image of God. A spirit made in His image is too grand to be put in an insect. The spirit is energy, energy can not be created or destroyed once God has created it, it can only be transformed. The second conflict with reincarnation is that it disagrees with what Jesus explains as the final judgment and are bodies raised as His was. If every single person is reincarnated in several bodies, time and time again, what body will be raised after judgment day? This is different from God re-using Elijah's spirit again in John The Baptist's body, centuries separating his reincarnation. The possibility is possible if God wills it, God can do anything He pleases, He is Almighty, and All Powerful. I'm not saying there is no reincarnation, as it's a mystery that few will accurately understand. If one knows the exact in and outs of reincarnation, then it can be used to lead many down the wrong path as the devil already perverts everything. He perverts the Bible as it is, any mystery revealed will be dangerous to many vulnerable souls. What I will reveal has been approved by Jesus himself, and for many years I have guarded the revelation. Now is the time I am to reveal it. Before I do, here are the pitfalls that are dangerous.

The devil loves the idea of reincarnation for several reasons. If people are continually reincarnated, then there is no hell. If people don't know about hell, then they won't know to avoid it. If one does not believe in hell, it does not mean they will be exempt from hell. They will be held accountable for every action. The devil also loves hindu teachings of a world of artificial reality. This is a dangerous teaching. An individual seems to not be completely held responsible for their actions, but indeed they will be. The devil also loves the idea of aliens. I am not saying there aren't aliens. The devil uses the idea for his advantage. He invokes the idea that aliens created the human race, and placed the idea of God and religion in our heads to comply with their will. Religion is used as a weapon against God. It is already being taught in many universities that religion was created to create order and peace. This is also an idea the devil placed in the minds of many. I prayed long and hard about the existence of aliens. There seems to be so much proof throughout history. This is my understanding, I'm not speaking for Christians or the Catholic Church. I figured that if I want to know the truth, then I should go to the creator of all. In prayer I received this; Aliens are guardians to the human race. They have freewill. They can do good and evil just like angels and human beings. I got the feeling not all are for us but some are.

I have had a recurring dream for many years. It starts during the middle of the night. I look up into the night sky at the stars. Then they start flying. Shooting from one side of the sky to the other. One star shoots at another and it explodes. Then another star shoots another star. The sky breaks out in war. Then I realize, they aren't stars, they are alien space crafts. The crafts are of different shapes, and the fear of them being so close to earth terrifies me. How can we defend ourselves if they come into our atmosphere? I feel that some are defending us, and some want us obliterated out of existence. There are so many reasons writing about aliens is taboo. I have thought long and hard about even writing about this topic, but I am obligated. Everything I have written is true, this is the only speculation in this book, but if it is nonsense then so be it. I don't know if it helps anyone, or if anything good can come of it. But it was given to me to share. If humiliation comes to me, so be it. I will suffer humiliation for God's sake. I will follow God with blind obedience. Blind obedience, humility, and piety are the way in which God's warriors become so powerful. There is no way in which one can honor God more faithfully, except blind obedience into death. Blind obedience is the reward of Abraham, and proves ultimate faith. There are many pitfalls in believing in aliens. Many of the miracles throughout all of creation will be attributed to aliens, and many may worship them instead of God. Why is it logical that a superior race with far superior technology has so many crashes on this Earth, and possibly on other planets. The only logic one should ponder is; maybe they didn't crash, maybe they were shot down? These are taboo topics, but people are becoming aware of so many concepts lately. There are so many spiritual dangers with aliens and reincarnation.

This is only one of my experiences with reincarnation which just like the rest, is a true story; A friend of mine, who I went to highschool with, and played football with was caught up partying just like many people do. His name was Matthew. This guy was pretty tough. He was a big guy. On three separate occasions he was jumped at a party, and two of the three, he won the fight. He enjoyed getting into street fights, and he was good at it. Overall he was a good guy. A great friend, and always willing to lend a hand. I never really knew if he believed in Jesus, but among many of our times together, I know he believed there was a God. The Holy Spirit urged me to talk to him. I was to tell him there was more to life than fighting, and that there is something more. Just like everyone does, I ignored my intuition. Time came and went.

A month later he died at a young age, and I felt so guilty I didn't make more of an effort. Lord forgive me. My uncle was reading a book about purgatory, and I became fascinated with it, as I wanted to find answers for my friend.

One night I prayed that I learn what happened to Matthew. When I went to bed I had a vivid dream. I turned into Matthew. In the dream a group of friends and myself were at a local bar and grill. A group of guys from the other table started getting rowdy, so I took it upon myself to physically handle the situation. We all walked outside. Me and someone from their party squared off, and right when I threw the punch I fell backwards out of my body, and started to descend into the middle of the earth. Once I reached an extremely dark pit where no light could reach, my body stopped falling and turned upright as if I was standing, but I wasn't standing, I was suspended and not using my legs. I was beyond depressed, and without God. I had no hope. My soul was in agony. Then in a vision a foot above my head, a face appeared, it was transparent and it was praying for me. It was my face, not Matthew's face, but I was praying for him. As I prayed for Matthew he rose steady and fast, the more I prayed the faster he rose. As fast as he was going, if he was alive, he would have that feeling deep in the pit of his stomach if he would have had one.

Then I came to a stop. I was in space. I could see black, and stars everywhere. To the bottom right I could see a small cluster of stars and planets. It was a galaxy, and it looked like it was spun out in shape. It made a shape with four legs. I thought to myself, it looks like a swastika. The galaxy was the size of a golf ball. I looked up, and an angel told me to seal up what I am about to see until the appointed time. The appointed time is now as this happened over thirteen years ago. I looked up and I saw a blue planet, and it looked like earth, and I entered it.

I woke up with my mind blown. If I wouldn't have experienced it for myself, I would have a hard time believing it for myself. I was looking up a word in the dictionary, and ran across a picture of the milky way. It looked like the spiral galaxy I saw, but it wasn't the same, either it was farther away from the pictures I have seen, or it was a different galaxy. Then I looked up a swastika, as all I knew was that it was a symbol the nazi's used. I learned that the Nazis adopted it as it was a Hindu symbol first, that meant reincarnation. Thirteen years later I was praying and meditating on that experience, and God told me that the place where Matthew went was another planet like earth, where he will get another chance to prove his love for God, and earn heaven. There is no guarantee that people will gain this chance, and it is so slight, that it is risky, many people earn hell. I would die again, and again defending the beliefs of the Catholic Church for it is the wholeness of truth, and I am not speaking against it, but there are certain things that were hidden from people because of the people's fragileness.

The devil gives a few truths to certain people in order to start a religion. People seek God, and if a religion gives them a small amount of comfort, they believe. If there was no truth, the religion wouldn't last, it would crumble. But the way the devil sees it, is that he would rather have a particle of a religion, rather than one that teaches the entire truth, Jesus Christ. He might even accept Jesus in a religion to draw people away from the true religion, but he prevents Jesus to be known as the Messiah, the living God sent to earth. He will let him be considered to be an angel, or a prophet, which is not the complete truth.

In my personal life I wanted to learn about psych, and its relation to possession, as they seemed completely linked. I took a job at a psychiatric hospital. I learned many things. I learned that the psyche and intelligence are completely separate. I've seen people who have scored as a genius on the IQ score, that had trouble functioning due to their mental illness. I realized people with mental illness are like someone who was born with a medical illness, some are genetic, and some are induced by drugs. Meth is one of the worst drugs for initiating mental illness. Some of the signs for being possessed by a demon overlap with mental illness. Suicidal, and depression, obsessive compulsive disorder, hearing voices, and seeing hallucinations are related to mental illness and possession. Sometimes, someone is mentally ill and possessed. I never advocated for psych meds until I was able to experience it first hand. In most cases, once a mentally ill person is chemically balanced in their brain, then the demon can be addressed. The mental illness will sometimes remain, and sometimes all symptoms resolve.

While learning about psych and mental illness, I learned about cultures all over the world, and learned from people all over the world about their cultures. I learned a lot about eastern spirituality. I learned about stones, crystals, meditation, and self actualization. All are controversial topics to Christians and Catholics alike. Knowing what I know now I would recommend doing a lot of research. If in doubt, and not knowing what you are dealing with, don't even bother, stay away. Most Catholics and Christians say to stay away, and this is good advice. When exploring these, I always followed bread crumbs back to my home, Jesus, and scripture. Stones and crystals hold onto energy. Energy is spirit. We are spiritual beings. As explained the heart beats due to an electrical impulse that travels down the heart. To move a muscle, an electrical signal comes from the brain, travels down the spinal cord, then travels through the nerves to the muscle, and the muscle moves. The stones exposed to the moon, and sun, and elements constantly charge and clear negative energy. That is why people who use them set them out to recharge during a full moon.

Energy is expelled during this time, and energy on earth changes at this time. If not recharged, demons will occupy them. When hung and used as a pendulum, the demon is in control of the stone. They can tell the truth, but lie when they want to for their benefit. I tried this once, with God's permission. He explained to me it is the same as using a ouija board, which is never OK. While trying the pendulum I got a vision of the demon standing behind me. He was tall Gray, and looked like he was made of stone. While asking it if it was a good spirit, or of God. The stone stopped moving, and didn't answer.

I immediately blessed the stone to rid the demon, and got rid of the stone. I tried using stones in bracelets, and they worked, but there are downsides. Each stone is designated with a certain function. They do help with stress, protection, healing, and many other things. They are of value, but should only be used with God's permission. Whoever uses these things are getting God's benefits through his creation without going through Jesus. It is like one showing up to a thanksgiving feast without being invited, and taking the seat of honor, and pigging out. Only God should be giving the permission, and not everyone should be using them. Only Healers should be using them, and people who have merited on their own, or people who are strong enough to close the doors they open. The problem is, most people don't discover they can't close the door, and it's too late, then they may need an exorcist's help.

Since the beginning of time people have abused God's natural gifts. There are natural laws that he created and the same for spiritual laws. Many have learned these ways without going through Jesus. Many Buddhist monks have channeled these. They have learned self denial and self sacrifice that act as spiritual currency. Pagans have learned about blood sacrifice for spiritual currency, similar to Jewish sacrifices. These things work but can draw demons and can be regulated by demons. If I wear stones that help give me patience, then I never earn the virtue, it is given to me. It's robbing me of the chance to prove myself. There is a stone to help be loyal in a relationship, this prevents the chance to gain chastity, or prove the love of the relationship. While wearing a stone to calm, I was in a daze while demons attacked me. It was as though I was drunk while an intruder snuck into my house to attack, and I was slow to know, or to react. If someone has a urinary tract infection, they take medication to help with pain. The pain will subside for a short time. Then, it will progress to a kidney infection, and then death. Treating the pain masks the need for antibiotics. Self actualization and meditation can heal the body and soul. Knowing oneself can help learning who God is once one knows themselves. Knowing your spirit guides, and spirit animals can be beneficial in some ways, but meditation when not meditating on Jesus leads to self worship, along with worshiping animals and angels in God's place. All can become false idols. This is why most urge people to steer clear of these tools. The very small number of people who have the blessing from God to use his tools don't really need them as they have earned virtue, been tested in the fire, and they know Jesus is the only need. Through Jesus, all is possible once one truly believes it. The kingdom of heaven is written about in Revelations. The streets were made of twelve layers of stone. The devil, before falling, was adorned with precious stones around his neck. Stones are placed in crowns for kings and queens. They have a purpose, but God who created all, should give permission for use.

While meeting many different people around the world all channeled through the psych hospital I met a unique nurse. I could see many demons in her, and I tread with caution the entire time I was around her. She was a great person and I could see the image of God inside her. I was able to draw her in by what I learned from Eastern spirituality and teach her about the truth, Jesus. She explained to me a vision she had. She was in a dark cave holding a large glowing egg. It was beautiful and she wanted to protect it. A moment later, a gigantic black snake appeared. It cornered her, but she saw the snake's beauty and allure. Letting her guard down, he swallowed her while she was protecting the egg. She was terrified and when she was swallowed she began to fuse with the inside of the snake's digestive organs. She started to feel comforted by the snake. She felt it protected her, and hid behind its strength. The snake slithered around the world. Literally around the globe as if it was the same size.

The snake symbolizes the devil of course. The egg symbolizes a new beginning of her soul that was robbed by the snake. She became so comforted by the devil, but only went where he went. It completely took over her life, and he became part of her, and she of him. I offered her a blessing, and much to my surprise, she accepted. She also allowed me to bless her house. We were at work, and as soon as I laid my hands on her the devil was ferreous, he had her so rooted in, he took it personally. Instantly, I was attacked by a psych patient that has always been harmless, and never had a history of violence. The next day I got covid, and it hit me hard. I had covid the year before, but this was different, it hit me hard even with the previous exposure and two covid vaccines. When I returned to work, I was severely attacked by another patient, but it was all worth it. The curse I was under was constantly keeping me at battle, and with this act, I was in a war. I had no rest. The devil never fights fair. He will fight you after you are exhausted, or with a group of demons. He will only fight if he has an advantage. He might test a person before. If they show weakness, fear, or both, he persists.

Everyone struggles to do the right thing, even if one has a great deal of knowledge. It's a struggle for everyone. I had a friend who was having a really hard time in life. He was trying to get out of a dangerous stressful career, he recently was separated from his wife. His family owned a house that was recently vacated after his grandparents passed away, so we all went over to help get everything out of the house. I wandered upstairs and found a bedroom. The bed was still there and a few pieces of furniture. I layed on the bed to take a break. As I laid on my back I glanced at the doorway I entered as I heard a creak from the old house. This house was built in the early 1900's. As I laid on the bed staring at the wall I noticed an old doll. Its body was a blanket, and the doll's upper torso was sewn into the blanket. It made sense. A little girl could hold the doll well going to bed and have the comfort of a blanket which also served a purpose.

As I layed there staring at this doll I got an ominous feeling, I felt like it was alive and staring at me. I closed my eyes and let my mind rest for a moment. As soon as I got comfortable and let the stress melt away I had a vision. A female demon floated in the room as if it was made of cloth but moved as if it was smoke. Her color was gray and white. It floated with an elegance, but just enough to let your guard down and attack. Her face was seamless with the rest of her body, and looked like a skull. It floated into the room, her gown acted like arms as it pulled herself into the room resting in the doll. I opened my eyes and the doll was smiling at me. Its little stitched face had a mocking grin. My instinct was to cast out the demon with Holy water, and bless the house. That's what I do. I stood up and started to question myself. Not about what had just happened. I have done this long enough to trust my instincts. I knew the doll had a demon inside of it. My doubt stemmed from the doubt of my friend's family. I had shared with them some of my experiences, and I could feel their doubt in things I would talk about, even their adversity from their spirit, even though I love them like family, and they love me like family.

I had known them for over twenty years. My thought was they don't believe in what I see, and do, and it would be rude of me to bless a house without consent.

I walked downstairs to inquire about the doll. I asked if it was sentimental, and let them know it may not be good to keep it, but I didn't want to let them know the entire vision, as I didn't want to scare the kids in the room, and I didn't want to argue or deal with their doubt. They gave permission to throw it away. Just then the kids in the room shared a couple of experiences they had with the doll. "We were in that room jumping on the bed, and the doll started smiling at us," the children said. They all confirmed what they saw. Then I saw the doubt set in, as it settled in the room like a fog. The adults in the room smirked and laughed. Just then I decided to leave the situation alone, I didn't want to offend anyone. Even if I blessed the doll and threw it away, the house needed a blessing. I decided to leave well enough alone.

Months later my friend moved into the vacant house until he and his wife worked out his problems. They had a child together that adored him, and it broke his heart every time he left. The little boy would cry so hard when he would have to go home with his mom. He was dealing with a lot of stress, stress from everywhere. He tried to numb his pain with alcohol, and one night he took his life. I should have blessed that house, did the demon in the house influence him, I'm sure it did? It definitely didn't help the problems. Was it the main cause? Of course not, but he was so fragile that he didn't need much influence. I should have had more spiritual courage. If I would have just blessed the house, I could have changed the trajectory of the situation. I should have suffered the doubt. People don't always know what's best. They reason with the reason of this world, and it is foolish in the eyes of the Lord. I learned a lesson, and I don't care how foolish I look, I vowed to always do what I ought to. If it worked that I cast out the demon, and he wouldn't have taken his life, nobody would have realized what I had done through God, except for me. I am the type of person the devil hates most. People who don't want fame or fortune, they just want to do God's will, and nobody will know the contribution we make.

As for my friend, I worried about his soul. The Bible is very clear about what happens to people who take their own life. It says they go to hell. Matthew 10:38 *And he that taketh not his cross, and followeth after me, is not worthy of me.* I immediately prayed for his soul. He was always such a good guy. He would attend church three times a week at times. He knew God. Did God have mercy on someone in his situation with everything wrong, and influence from the demon? I prayed for his soul, and the prayers started working. He was moving up from purgatory where his soul was paying its debt. But where would he go? Would he go to heaven, would he go to another earth like my former friend. I was at work, and I took a break. As I went into prayer, the Rosary, I went into ecstasy, as I have before. God allowed him into heaven. My soul rejoiced, and I was on a high. Despite me being in the dark soul of the night, I felt joy. Then I didn't know how to handle the joy. Joking around with a coworker I joined in a lowbrow conversation, and my joy was taken away. God calls us always to be Holy as He is, but the miserable soul that I can be, abused His gift. Why is it when everything is going right, people want to celebrate? Celebrate with booze, or whatever the joys of this world we seek? These joys are only temporary, and as soon as it's over, we want more. They are all temporary highs. But I'm encouraged that my friend is now in heaven. God judges the entire soul over a lifetime, and has mercy. It is up to us to maintain our souls. We maintain our houses, our cars, how much do we reconcile with God to maintain our souls?

Chapter XVI

Most of my life I have lived under a curse, I entered it aproximately at five years of age. For years I prayed for it to be lifted. After about twenty years I questioned the power of God. Why is he allowing me and my family to suffer, why allow the devil to prevail? Many years later, I learned I could fight back. Being cursed allowed me to know my enemy, it allowed me to spar with demons constantly. I realized my cross, which I saw in a vision years ago. It was not just to just bear my own cross, but to help people carry their cross as well, just like the apostles. I would follow Jesus' example and carry it for humankind, and Simon who helped Jesus carry it the rest of the way to Calvary. I know Jesus could have finished carrying it himself. He endured so much, I know He had the strength, but Jesus allowed Himself to become weak out of humility in order to set an example for us. When our cross seems too heavy, He will send a helper to help us bear it. It may come in the form of the Holy Spirit, a friend, or a stranger. I was to forgive Bertha from the bottom of my heart. My mother tried years ago but Bertha's daughter who also was into Witchcraft mocked her at a family gathering. "See, isn't it better to forgive?" she said in a mocking voice and an ominous grin.

I decided to forgive everyone who hurt me and my family. I forgave them wholeheartedly and genuinely. Then, I made it a point to not cease praying for them to ask forgiveness for the sins against me and my family, and convert to the Sacred Heart of Jesus. After months of praying before The Holy Eucharist, I felt a battle won. It was working! After eight or nine months of prayer, Bertha was converting to Christianity! I felt good about the situation. I returned to prayers for other intentions. I had learned to pray for the souls in purgatory, and for the conversion of sinners, both are important, so I returned to those intentions. Then, one day at Adoration, in front of The Holy Eucharist, I knew Bertha returned to the devil. I prayed for her to be converted, and she didn't budge. Her soul returned to the devil. I made a vow to not pray for anything else in the world. Not for the souls in purgatory like I had, the conversion of sinners, I would designate every prayer to her conversion. I asked saints on their feast day to help with her conversion, but all I got from them is, "This is your cross, you must bear it." I prayed without stopping, every Rosary designated to her Conversion. She only gripped onto the devil tighter.

I had noticed once, and so had Victor, While praying during spiritual battle I would see shooting stars, they could have been meteors. While praying and feeling the power leave me, these shooting stars would pass by the earth when praying the Rosary when I prayed it outside day or night. There would be nights I would awake to demons disturbing me. I realized, it's time to battle. I'm being called to fight evil. Around two or three in the morning, I would awaken to them attacking me, or not letting me fall asleep in the first place. This was the battle call. I awoke and Slothfully prayed a couple Rosaries in bed as I tossed and turned. At most, I would only get an hour of sleep. I have done it on many occasions, and I would spend the next day at work exhausted. Other times, I would get up out of bed, and go to another room and pray. I would feel great. I would go back to bed after, and even if I only got an hour or two of sleep, I would feel well rested. On other occasions, while praying the Rosary I would relax and go into ecstasy, and I looked forward to the blissful rest of ecstasy. On this occasion, God instructed me, "This is not for joy or to feel good. When praying for conversion of sinners, or to convert Bertha, this is war!" He explained. "When you are praying in spiritual battles, You must kneel and pray fervently and focused." He then gave me a symbol to meditate on. It was two transparent arrows that moved to the right, it skipped to the right with each prayer. I prayed for months without resolve. I realized on some of these restless nights, that many obstacles prevented me from being intimate with my wife, and I realized it was God allowing the devil to attack me. I should be abstaining and chaste at times of spiritual war, just as King David and the Israelite warriors did during battle.

I realized that James and John the disciples asked Jesus in Luke 9:54 *When James and John, followers of Jesus, saw this, they said, "Lord, do you want us to call fire down from heaven and destroy those people?" But Jesus turned and scolded them.* The disciples knew they could do these miracles. Jesus didn't say they couldn't do these miracles, but that they shouldn't do this miracle. I realized when I awoke to the battle cry, and got out of bed, and treated it seriously, things went very smoothly. If I fasted when the Lord instructed me, and prayed for what he instructed me to pray, I would return to bed much sooner, and even if I got one hour of sleep before I had to wake up for work, I was so well rested, as if I had slept all night. Nothing was happening with Bertha's conversion though.

Sixty plus years of allegiance to the devil is not an easy thing to change. I know he began attacking her when she converted, and he treated her as a traitor. So she returned to his side. I went back to prayer in front of the Eucharist, and felt her refuse to budge.

Month after month went by. Was this hopeless? "Lord, she is afraid to leave him. She is afraid of what he will do to her and her loved ones. She is gripping onto him tighter than before?" "Keep praying." My mortal body and my soul were exhausted. One day a friend sent me a youtube Video of a testimony. It was of a pastor who fought against Anton Lavey, the leader of the satanic church. It's a powerful testimony, and can be found under the Link *Top Satanist Attacks Believers, Instantly Regrets It.* In this video they talk about how Solomen mentions cutting someone's silver cord. Which means, God ends their life when their cord is cut. It almost sounds like the Greek mythology of the three deities. One spun the thread of human fate, one dispensed it, and one cut it at the moment of death. But Sololomon mentioned in Ecclesiastes *12:6 "Before the silver cord snaps.* Meaning before death. When someone astral projects, people have mentioned seeing a silver cord that attaches their soul to the human body's belly button. When their soul leaves their body, it's tethered to their body in order to return after astral projecting. Stay clear of astral projection, it makes one vulnerable to demons, influence from them is never for your benefit. It is always a way to corrupt the soul so that it is directed away from God. I tried it with an open mind several times, and woke up with the feeling of a hangover. Sometimes an open mind means you take off your spiritual armor. I have tested everything Through God, Jesus, and the Holy Spirit. But we should not test these things, experimenting in the occult is very dangerous. Opening a door to the demonic is extremely dangerous, one may not be strong enough spiritually to close the door that was opened. God is peace, joy, happiness, and order. Astral projection is the opposite, so it is obviously from the evil one. After hearing the story of the pasture fighting against Anton L., it became part of my prayer. I thought to myself, this is a last ditch effort, should I use this? My prayered changed to; "Lord, If she will not be converted, then cut her silver cord?" I was instantly scolded. I was told not to pray that. God wanted her for himself. There is no greater insult to the devil, than to have one of his own spiritual children taken from him. One day, an evil person died, and I said, "Good, they are in hell." Instantly God made me feel his remorse, each soul is his creation. A soul can not be sold to the devil. He doesn't own it. Our souls are not ours to sell. It's God's soul, for it's his creation. Each soul lost to hell grieves God to his core.

I changed my prayer, "Lord forgive me. Let Bertha be converted to your sacred heart." I prayed for her conversion with hope. I asked Victor to help, and he did. He was in another state. He was called to battle in the middle of the night. He walked outside of the house he was in. He was visiting his in-laws, in Arizona. He was going through a spiritual resurrection of his own. He literally spent forty days in the desert. God is the same as He ever was, and Will Be. Victor started praying his Rosary, and as he stood outside and prayed, shooting stars passed through the heavens, as all spiritual battles start in the heavens. The patio furniture behind him started to slam and rattle. He heard the sound of a beast behind him roaring. Then he walked to the inground swimming pool, and God told him to bless the water. So he did. God told him to enter the pool and face the moon which was full. Then he felt compelled to ask the moon for help, but he knew that pagans pray to the moon, and he didn't want to offend God. So he asked permission from God, and He allowed it, and encouraged him. He prayed to the moon for help, and the beast making a ruckus vanished. Then God instructed him to face another direction and pray another Rosary. Soon after the sun rose. On the Horizon was a mighty warrior angel displaying the Power of God. He was kneeling in reverence to God, in humility. The rest of the summer he swam with his kids in that pool. And it was a blessed time. Victor had a spiritual resurrection. One of his inlaws asked him in the morning, "Did you hear that thing in the back yard last night? It sounded like a wild animal, like a bear growling and knocking stuff around?"

For years I wondered what day of the year is Jesus' actual birthday. I knew it was either in the summer or fall. All the recordings of Jesus, and nobody documented His birthday? He was the most important Human to ever be born, why wasn't it recorded? God must have a reason, since He showed the signs in heaven to the Wise men, but for certain reasons it fell out Christian tradition. Years ago pagans would gather during the winter solstice, the shortest day of the year, when the sun shines the fewest hours of the day. This falls on December 25th. Pagans would party for two weeks. They would partake in debauchery, get drunk, have orgies, and do sacrifices. The Catholic Church wanted to stop this behavior, so they moved the coming of the Lord, Emanuel, God is with us. They moved His Birthday to December 25th, Christmas. It worked. Many pagans converted, and joined the Church. Most of those rituals stopped for many years in that region of the world. I prayed to know Jesus' birthday, and this was important to me. I had wondered for years, but then it became part of my prayers time to time during Adoration.

While trying to convert Bertha, I met with Victor to pray, and the devil caused rifts in our immediate families to prevent us from converting/praying together, so the date was pushed back, and back. Then, finally, the day came that Victor and I could meet. The devil attacked me and my family. I had to be perfect, and I'm not, so I had to suffer some attacks. Just like Peter who loved Jesus, so do I. And just like Peter, who constantly stuck his foot in his own mouth, so do I. His denial of Christ, and mistakes are talked about so much, and some take those parts of the Gospel to say the first Pope has fallen. But he is inspirational, because he rose to the most powerful of the Apostles, even after saying things that got him in trouble. What made him the most powerful is that he served the rest of the Apostles and Jesus' flock/Church. He had the most zeal. He loved Jesus the most. Sometimes that part of scripture is used in a negative way. It helps people feel better about sinning and betraying God, and makes them feel better about sinning, downplaying their grievous acts. What most people don't talk about is how he is the only disciple in the garden to take up arms, and defend Jesus in the garden. Fighting valiantly to protect Jesus, until Jesus stopped him. Saints earn their stripes, and suffer more in one year than many will ever suffer in their entire life. Peter, like most disciples, had a family, and a job, and responsibilities to take care of his family. And one day a man says follow me. He left his life behind, his livelihood. Yes, Peter still had to take care of his family. How many of us could do this? How many of our wifes would stay with us? Most men would be afraid to even tell their wives, much less actually follow Jesus. One should never downplay any of the saint's accomplishments. What if Jesus asked you to leave your career, leave everything to follow him, your family responsibilities? How many of us can do this? John Vienny was physically dragged around a room by the devil himself. Many saints have heroic feats through The Holy Spirit. They earned the Title Saint. How many people would end up in an asylum after being touched by the devil?

All the saints have many experiences with the devil and demons, and it is a sign related to the threat the saint poses to the devil and his kingdom. Most people would not recover from an actual encounter with a low level demon. Peter loved Christ more than all the other disciples. They earn their place in heaven, and their thrones of honor. On August 28th Victor and I met outside of a church in order to pray for Bertha's conversion. The Adoration Chapel was strangely closed. It was a weekday, and not a Holy day of obligation, what is going on? My soul was outraged, we need to get this done, I'm tired of all these obstacles he throws at us, I thought to myself. Just then, I felt the peace of Christ. Just accept it, I thought. I learned; during a spiritual battle, don't be guided by feelings that are not in my control, but God's will… I dropped the ideas of my will, and accepted whatever Jesus' will is. He is the king of all the universes, and I felt the peace of Christ with us. We got ready to pray three Rosaries outside the chapel sitting in my truck. I was showing Victor the *Youtube* video with Anton Lavey that I had watched, and explained to him my mistake, Because Jesus instructed me to teach him my error. Just then I heard a voice, and I recognized it. It was the devil, and it spoke in my left ear. He pleaded with me, "Please come to my side?" His voice sounded like it could have been an upright being. Before I could deny him, Jesus said in my right ear, "If you don't pray for her conversion, I will raise up someone in your place instantaneously who can." I told Victor what just happened. It was just like the cliche; The devil was literally on my left hand shoulder and Jesus was on my right, who says God doesn't have a sense of humor? "Victor, the devil literally asked me to convert to his side, and then Jesus said, "I'll raise somebody up in your place."" "He is trying a last ditch effort to prevent us from praying for her conversion." "Oh yeah, I'm so stupid. I should have realized we were stepping on his throat, and he is not ashamed to plead for mercy, we need to deliver the final blow."

Jesus instructed me where to go. He instructed me to take off my shoes and socks as it was Holy ground, and make an example for Victor, but don't ask Victor to give reverence to Him. He wants people to give Him reverence without asking for it. We walked to a bench outside of the Church and I got to my knees, and Victor sat on the cement bench. God instructed me to take my shoes off, and I realized it also allows energy conduction to the earth besides honoring The Almighty. Victor took his shoes off, and he followed my example. I knelt, and we prayed three Rosaries. When we reached the end of the third, Jesus told me, "Pray for the conversion of her daughter and granddaughter to follow in her footsteps." So I did. Then Jesus said, "This is my Birthday…, and I'm going to give you a gift on my birthday. You are released from your curse." It was August 28th.

One night I had a dream; I saw the demon that detached from Bertha. It was a female demon. It looked like a small child was drawing an evil spirit. The drawing looks like scribbles that formed a woman with jet black hair. The hair was long and went past the shoulders. The bangs were short, and allowed the black and red eyes to pierce a soul. The teeth were very square, gapped, and some were missing, some were short, and others were long. This was the demon identity Bertha was transfigured into when serving the devil. In the dream I prayed for the conversion of Bertha's daughter, and she accepted after seeing her mom's conversion and Holiness. Bertha's granddaughter was more reluctant and obstinate. I woke up in amazement. I have heard it said, "We are assigned one demon, and a guardian angel at our creation in our mother's womb." The demon to attack us and lead us away from God throughout life, and the angel to help, protect and be drawn to God. Whether we grow in virtue or evilness, we unite with one of these spirits. It is written; Our final destination, whether it be heaven or hell, our guardian angel will suffer or rejoice with us there.

Recently, God has made it known to me, that when someone practices living a Holy life, one will unite with their guardian angel, and be transfigured, Just as Jesus was transfigured to Yahweh on the mountain. The angel and the human soul will intertwine so that they become one, and when one is so united with Christ, they become a living Christ on earth, when the soul reaches perfection. Not all will become united with their guardian angel in such a way, or with Christ, but this is God's will. Yet we have free will, and it is our choice. When one has reached ultimate spiritual merit, the two spirits become one. This is my understanding, not the Churches, and may be disputed, but even the truth can be disputed.

Life became easier, and everyone in the family felt the release of the curse. I went from seeing hundreds of demons a day, to only seeing a few. The devil took it so personally, he came for my children, my brother's children, our parents, our nieces and nephews, as me and my brother stole his spiritual child, he would come for ours. The children started doubting God's existence, believing in atheism. Ailments flourished throughout the family. Children started cutting to deal with stress. All of this spiritual warfare increased as Halloween approached. His power increased as Halloween is to the devil, as Good Friday is to Jesus. The devil warned me he would take the children on Halloween. The Holy Spirit instructed me of the rituals to rid the attacks. I had the child say the prayer Father Blount said in one of his youtube videos. "Most precious precious blood of Jesus Christ, save us and the whole world." We said that prayer fifty times, and it weakened the devil's grasp. I didn't realize that cutting is a non-verbal contract with the devil as it creates an unknown blood covenant. To reverse it, I had the child write the Apostle's Creed in their own handwriting. Then, we pricked the finger tip with a lancet from a blood sugar tester. The child signed their name in blood, and the evil covenant was broken.

Maggie started feeling the evil attacking her in New Mexico, and texted me, "Call me." I was at work, but it seemed serious. I called her back. "Alan, Damian came back from Ursula's. He had a bag of clothes that he brought back from her house! I set the bag down in our closet, and I heard it fall down after I walked away! I kept walking away and it sounded like two cats were fighting and screeching, so I walked back to the bag to look through it! I saw weird symbols on the bag, and got a weird feeling! Then I saw a human eye looking at me. I dropped the bag and ran downstairs! It felt like I floated through the air as I ran down the stairs to the living room. It's Ursula, I know it, she's a witch!" Damian was Maggie's fiance, and his ex-girlfriend is Ursula. Damian was a manipulator, he never shut up, continually lying narcissistic and a typical antisocial. Damian and Ursula had a kid together, he is in his twenties. Damian had convinced Maggie that he had to pay Ursula's mortgage as they had a child together, and even though he doesn't owe her alimony, he promised her that he would pay her mortgage to keep a roof over their son's head. It was a strange situation. Even stranger, he would spend all day at Urcila's house while Maggie was working, and go home after. He could never keep a job himself, as he was a terrible employee and was caught stealing. Maggie had self esteem issues as she didn't love herself enough to put a stop to it. The family would try to tell her, but all it did was push her into his arms even more.

I instructed Maggie what to do. "You need to burn all the contents of that bag and the bag itself. Everything she had sent to her house over the years needs to be burned. You need to choose, because if he continues to go back and forth, the portal will remain open. If he is sleeping with her, she is transferring demons into him, and he can transfer them to you." "Should I break up with him? I love him." "That's only for you to decide, I can't make that decision. Only you can, but definitely pray about it. If you stay together, he can never go back to her." She prayed about it, and decided to stay with him. "So what do I need to do, I think she has him under a love spell?" "If you love him, love defeats all evil as Jesus' love conquered evil for us. You need to bury a pair of his shoes in the backyard." This will prevent him from going back and forth from her house to yours. The Holy Spirit instructed me, so I instructed her without trying to interpret it with my human logic. She did as the Holy Spirit instructed. "Alan, I lost my engagement ring. I love that ring so much. I must have lost it burning his shoes. I tore the house apart for days. I loved that ring so much, what should I do?" "Let it be, if you find it, then your relationship is meant to be with that ring. If you don't, then it is a sign that your relationship begins in a new way, the old way is to be left behind." She stopped looking for it, and her mind was settled. The months crept by so slowly, and I yearned for January to come. It couldn't come fast enough. Each week brought more confusion and strife. Maggie and I kept in constant contact. I instructed her, mom and dad, and the rest of the family to pray three Rosaries daily. Attend Mass, and get the house blessed. I felt so helpless as I was in another state five and a half hours away. I was working two full time jobs working seventy two to eighty four hours a week. I couldn't understand all the power Ursula had over Maggie, it baffled me. I sized her up in my mind's eye. Her spiritual strength was only a three or a four on a scale from 1-10. "Things don't stop Alan, Noises, toilets flushing at night, stuff pounding, cupboards slamming. Ann says she is having things going on at her house."

She was right, Ann had asked me to go bless her house. It was following her to work at four in the morning. She was the only one at work. It would pound on the doors at work setting off the alarms. One day she was in her basement, and her boyfriend was at work while her kids were at school. Ann heard the front door slam open as it sounded like three large men wearing boots running around her house, opening the cabinets and drawers in the kitchen, moving the dining room chairs. She ran to the basement window to escape. It sounded like they were robbing her. She ran to the window to escape. The window was jammed, and all she could do was try to pry it open, not making too much noise. She didn't want them to know she was in the house, as the worst images passed through her head. Finally, she pried the window open. She called her boyfriend, and he called 911. She planned her escape to a neighbor's house, and it seemed to take forever. The deputies responded quickly, guns drawn just as she made her way from the basement window to the side of her house. She worried they would think she was the perpetrator. They entered the house, so she mustered the courage to meet one of them in the front yard. "Well Ann," the deputy said "They ransacked the house, things were thrown everywhere. Cupboards all open, stuff thrown from the drawers onto the floor. It's very weird though, they left your purse on the counter, and money was laying in plain sight, but they must have run off when we arrived. It must have been some stupid teenage punks." "That's impossible, I heard them above me as I crawled out of the basement window, and you showed up right after. They were still in the house. "Well I don't know, we cleared the entire property, your house, garage, and your backyard. Somebody was definitely in there, things were out of place as if they were looking for something. Maybe it was ghosts. It wouldn't be the first time." He said with a straight face, no smile or smirk. He was dead serious.

I went to Ann's house, and blessed it. There were a lot of demons in the plants as well as in her bedroom, directly above the basement window she crawled out of. For some reason, demons love to hide in trees and plants. Maybe it has to do with the exchange of oxygen with carbon dioxide. If the number of man is six. Oxygen on the periodic table is the number six. When God created Adam, he breathed the Holy Spirit into him with His breath. Life is oxygen, without breath or oxygen, we die. If life is oxygen, then trees take our waste, our carbon dioxide/death and return life/oxygen. Death is exchanged for life, and death transforms to life, like a Christian baptism. We die to ourselves, and are reborn as the children of God. God uses the ways of the devil to give life back, after death. Death As Adam and Eve ate from the tree of knowledge of good and evil, caused death. God gave us life back, as He allowed His only begotten Son to die on a tree, to give us everlasting life. I'm not saying trees and plants are evil. They are God's creation, and have many healing properties, but the devil and his demons can hide in them. Just like water can hold a blessing, it can also be cursed, just like wood or trees/plants. Druids and many pagan religions worship trees, and witchcraft religions do rituals in the woods, but all will return to God, as He created it all. Ann's house was now blessed after I left, and all the activity came to stop at her house.

I couldn't understand how everyone in the family was suffering, we were all in a daze. "Alan, I don't know how she is so strong?" "Maggie, she is not that strong. Now that we are released from Bertha's curse, we can defeat her so easily. Get your house blessed soon." "Damian chose to be with me, but things are so hard. Sometimes nobody wants to pray, mom and dad want to turn to their vices." "They need to, I'll fast and pray down here. All of you do the same until the house is blessed." "Damian can't go back to Ursula's, should I have him stay in a hotel since mom and dad can't stand him, and they haven't forgiven him? He refuses to be in the same house as them, and they refuse to be in the same house as him?" "Yes, a hotel would be fine, but he needs to cut off all contact with her." "What about all his clothes and belongings over there? She keeps calling his phone, she won't leave him alone?" "All the clothes need to stay there, it's a new life, don't bring anything from the old, into the new. She can feel him slipping away, and try anything to keep him from you, even if they don't end up with him, she just wants to keep him from you." "Alan, everything is bad. I don't have money to pay for my house, I'm going to lose it?" "I'm so sorry, I'm struggling too, I wish I could afford to send you something. I don't have that kind of money, but

I can offer you a blessing. Is there any way someone can loan you the money?" "I'm trying to come up with the money. The priest canceled to bless my house because everyone who has lived here from our family hasn't gone to confession." "It's very important. Get Jesse and her family to confession, and do three Rosaries a day with everyone." Maggie picked up as much overtime as she could, and by some miracle, was able to keep her house. Christmas approached fast, and she was so relieved that she was going to keep her house. She started decorating her house for Christmas with such Christmas joy.

Maggie texted me, "Can you call me?" "Hey, what's up?" "Alan, it's getting bad. Last night Alliah had a really bad meltdown," Alliah is Maggie's three year old daughter. "We were praying the three Rosaries that you told us to pray, and I was kneeling on my knees while we were praying. Alliah went hysterical. She started running around and jumping on me. She wouldn't listen to anyone, so I ignored her. I didn't want to play into behavior, it was just a tantrum. Then her eyes turned black, there was no white in her eyes. I let her climb on me just to get the prayer done, but she was trying to rip the Rosary out of my hand as she climbed up my arm. Mom yelled, "Maggie why are you letting her do that?" Then Alliah ran to mom and bit her thigh, and left a huge bruise on her inner thigh. We held her down and finished the Rosary then she was normal again, she was possessed. Damian was trying to leave, saying he had to go to work. I said he can quit, this is too important, and if he loves me, he will stay and finish praying." "Wow, Ok, I'll do some things down here. Take courage, she is a low level witch, everything is going to be Ok. We need to get that house blessed, and get her baptized soon." "Well, we have been blessing it ourselves with Holy water and dirt from Santuario de Chimyo." "Ok, I know you are scared, but don't submit to it. Demons only gain power by fear. Once it fragments your mind, then it gains power. Everyday, pray three Rosaries with everyone in the household until that house is blessed by a priest, and I'll do the same here. Fast, don't eat meat, and I'll do the same." "OK, The deacon that I have been talking to knows Damian and his family, but he is the one that will come as soon as everyone finishes their confessions the priest passed it onto him. He doesn't seem too concerned about it, he said she has no power." "Ok, the deacon is still ordained by God and has Holy Orders, that should be good enough."

That day was my only day off in weeks, and my daughter had a volleyball tournament in Colorado Springs, thirty minutes away. The tournament was all day long. We left town in the morning and went through a fastfood restaurant on the way out of town. I ate as we drove to the tournament. As soon as I finished my meal, I realized I had just eaten two cheese burgers, and I was supposed to abstain from meat. I felt like I was in a daze and not in control of anything. We arrived at the tournament and I prayed a Rosary. It took me hours to finish it. It should take no longer than twenty minutes, but I was distracted with the tournament, but I also felt like I was in a fog. As I was praying, I was hoping for our team to win as I prayed for Maggie and our family, but my hope was in my daughter's team winning, as if that was more important. I had taught my family how to pray the Rosary, but it's not an easy devotion if one doesn't do it all the time. When they were praying it, they had to turn on youtube and follow along with the prayer. While they were praying the Rosary, my dad was surprised that he could hear me pray with them. "How is Alan's voice on the TV?" He asked, Maggie replied, "Alan wasn't praying with us, that was youtube." "No it was his voice, I could hear it loud and clear." "No dad, that wasn't him." "Oh, I swore it was Alan."

The tournament finally ended, and I had only cranked out two Rosaries. I felt like I was still in a daze, I felt like I wasn't in control of what was happening around me. Everyone was tired and wanted to eat, and go home. While we sat down to eat at a restaurant, everything was off. One of the employees kept coming by our table to yell things to her fellow staff member. Loud and obnoxious, as they were gossiping. The smell of the cleansers stung my nose as I was trying to eat and choke down my food. It was near closing time, and they were cleaning to close up shop. We left the tournament on a bad note, as they barely lost a game they should have won. I sat at the table eating with an earbud in, listening to my favorite Football team play. They were losing by a lot. I should have been enjoying time with my family I thought, and I needed to pray another Rosary anyway. I took my earbud out, and tried to salvage the rest of the meal. Then I snapped at my wife and daughter for some small ridiculous reason. We all felt terrible, but I felt like a jerk, as I deserved to feel awful. Then I finished my plate and I realized I had just eaten a full portion of meat. I never ended up fasting. We drove home and I passed out in stress and embarrassment for acting like a fool. I never got around to the third Rosary. I had a special Rosary to pray, inflicting minor pain to myself. Demons and the devil can't stand to be in the sight of someone suffering as Jesus did. It reminds them of the day Jesus destroyed the devil's plan forever. It reminds him of the day he and the demons Beat Christ into pulp, and then Jesus died Resurrected and destroyed the devils plans forever. I get so upset fighting the devil in every menial aspect of my life. Only receiving communion, sitting in adoration, or three Rosaries chases the devil from my day, but I can't imagine how awful it is for the devil. I don't feel one remorse or compassion for the devil. If it were up to him, every human would suffer a death as bad or worse than Christ. He works for centuries to turn the Church and people to rubble, but God uses it to punish him. If a person says yes to God, as Mary did, God uses the attacks from the devil against him. The devil attempts to destroy God and His creation. He will meticulously plan attacks for centuries. Plans of destruction, and anything to cause God and God's creation/ us sorrow. God builds masterpieces out of the devil's rubble, if a person completely submits themselves to God, even through Blind Obedience. Everything the devil worked for is demolished and turns against him, Glory To God!

A few days passed and Maggie called me at work, "Hey Alan." "Hey, what's up?" "Damian is in a hotel now, and feeling crappy, he is not feeling sick, but he is pale. His color is so pale. All our phones aren't working. I try to call you, or text mom, and it doesn't work. I went to the hotel to meet Damian, and to make sure he is ok, because his phone wasn't working, and mom thinks he went back to Ursula, or that we are meeting to hook up in a hotel. His phone has pictures on it of me and the kids, and I think Ursula has been getting his phone while he is over there. The pictures have weird things in them, it's hard to explain. Should I get rid of the phone, and should he go back and get his clothes from her?" "It's ok, Get rid of the phone after you bless it, and leave the clothes behind. His paleness is the curse leaving his body, get those confessions done, the house blessed, and do your three Rosaries." "Yeah, it's just hard, mom was frustrated that I didn't let Lizzy eat meat sauce with her spaghetti." Lizzy is Maggie's teenager. "All the Rosaries are breaking except for the one you made Hayden. Hayden is Maggie's boy, he is a few years younger than Lizzy. They are all taking a hit. I'm freaking out. I'm finding symbols on stuff Ursula has sent over to my house over the years. Hayden was playing his video game with the headphones she gave him, and while he was playing, he heard chanting coming through the speakers. The other night while Haden, Lizzy, and I were laying in bed, we saw a black silhouette. It was skinny and looked like an oversized lizard. It had a long body, and his arms were human-like, but skinny with no shoulders. It crawled slowly off the bed so we could take notice, and then it crawled out of the room. Hayden has been helping me gather all the stuff with symbols. He can see the evil. Should I burn all that stuff?" Yes, burn everything." They stayed up until four in the morning burning everything in the fire pit in the backyard. "Alan, there is one more thing... Lizzy told me Damian molested her, and made her touch him. I don't know what to do. Mom and dad know, and they hate Damian. I don't know if I should stay with him, I love him, and it happened when we had been drinking, and he was in a daze. I know you and I have been working to get the family together for Christmas. I don't know if he is welcome in your house. Especially since Damian has made advances at Ann." "You need to decide if you want to stay with him. Nobody can decide that except for you. You need to protect Lizzy, and let her know that it is never going to happen again, and give her love. Pray about your relationship, and I'll support you either way. As far as him coming to my home, I accept everyone, and forgive everyone just as Jesus has taught me. You have to work that out with Ann. I don't want any fights. But he needs to apologize to Lizzy and everyone else.

Every single person needs to pray for forgiveness. Otherwise our sins won't be forgiven, and we help hammer the stakes into Jesus' hands ourselves. Damian is still made in the image of God himself, and no matter how heinous the offense, God still loves him, and gives him the chance to ask forgiveness until his last breath. I can go get Lizzy right now and bring here, so she can feel safe." Maggie said, "I told the deacon, and he said we need to stay here, and get her back into church because she is doubting God's existence. The only friend she has is into the occult stuff." "Ok, I can respect that. But every single person needs to go to confession and pray for forgiveness. The devil thrives on unforgiveness, and uses it to spur more sins against each other, which prevents our sins from being forgiven. If you stay with Damian or not, you need to forgive him as well." "Damian needs to go to confession to ask forgiveness for everything he has done..." "He went to confession, I could hear the priest yell at him twice from the confession box. The entire church could hear it. Damian doesn't feel good. He said he had a dream that he went to Colorado for Christmas, and he was killed in Colorado. Here, he is right here, talk to him." "Hello," he said in a whiny voice. As if I should show him mercy, or feel sorry for him, but I restrained myself, and treated him gently, as God has done for me so many times I didn't deserve it. "Hey." "Well, I guess Maggie told you, but just so you know, I don't remember anything. We had been drinking that night and in the middle of the night Lizzy had come into the room and crawled in between us, and that is when it happened, I don't remember anything." "Whether you remember it or not, or whether you were under demonic influence or not, you still need to say sorry for it, and confess it. God knows all, and He knows that if you were under demonic influence. You may not be the only one to blame, but at some point you were weak and let the devil into your life, and that gives him access to you. You have to confess and take responsibility. Once you let the devil in, you will be held accountable for all the sins you do under their influence as well, because you let them in, in the first place." "I know, I just don't remember any of it." "Just because you don't, doesn't mean it didn't happen, but God is merciful, and will forgive more than we will ever understand." "Ok."

I texted Victor, "Hey bro. Pray for Maggie and them down there in New Mexico, they are struggling." "Ok." A couple of days later, Victor sent me a picture of a Rosary I had made him. It is made from 550 paracord and stone beads. A couple of beads snapped in his hand while praying the Rosary. No force exerted by him. One would have a hard time snapping one of those beads if he was using a pair of pliers. I was now December twentieth and I couldn't wait until the winter solstice was over, and I yearned for Lent to arrive as the devil is weaker. The solstice is when the devil and his demons are most powerful, save Halloween. Maggie called me around 10:30 AM, "Hey Alan, sorry did I wake you?" "No, I have been up for a little bit, getting ready to go back to work, What's up?" "Things are good, I can eat meat tonight, the deacon is going to come over and bless the house. Everyone has been to confession. Jesse and her husband came over and prayed three Rosaries with me. I started getting the food prepared to bring Christmas cookies and Candies over to your house. This is going to be the best Christmas ever. I prayed about being with Damian. We're going to get married in the Catholic Church and get the kids Baptized. Will you baptize Alliah? I want you and Jesse to be her Godparents?" "Yeah of course, I would be honored." "My bills are getting squared away, and I only have three more semesters until I finish nursing school. Jesse bought me a computer for school, Moms nurse is showing me things, I'm meant to be a nurse! Everything is working out, I was promoted to that transport job at the prison, It has made going to school manageable. I want to be like you, have a perfect life, and family! I know I'm going on, but things are getting better!" "I'm far from perfect, I am very blessed, but only because it has come from God, it's all His. I have been going through two crucifixions and both of my jobs, but God has made it a breeze as I have learned from the first three. You can do it, you are too smart, and I'll help you with whatever you need." "I'm just so happy, we will have a good Christmas! I'm sorry, I know I'm going on and on, I'm just excited!" "I can't wait. Everything sounds good. Damian came back to the house last night, he apologized to mom and dad, and mom and dad apologized to him. Alright while I better go, Jesse and I are going to Church tonight, and I'm sewing an angel costume for her little one. Everyone is going to church tonight. I love you!" "I love you too, let me know what happens after the deacon gets done blessing the house." "Ok, bye." "Bye."

After Maggie got off the phone with me, my dad asked Maggie, "Hey, are you doing laundry today, or can I do my laundry?" "No, dad, you can do laundry." At 2:30 PM, my phone rings, and my mom's number is flashing. "Alan, Maggie has been shot! She was in the garage, They think she shot herself! I'm going over there now!" I sat there in shock, and told my wife. I couldn't believe it. How could things take a one hundred and eighty degree turn in hours. Ann calls, "Alan, it isn't true! Tell me it's not true! Alan! It's not true! Please tell me it's not true!" "I'm so sorry. I'm sorry…" I'm in shock, how could this happen, she was so happy, she couldn't have taken her own life? What happened? I went to Adoration to ask Jesus what happened. On the way over the radio was playing. I have had the habit of listening to Catholic radio. I love music more than most people. It is a universal language. There is music for every emotion and stage of life. I just could never turn the station. My soul is nourished, and everytime I think of changing the station, The Holy Spirit instructs me to turn it back at times as a program comes on to talk about something I had been praying about. The sound of talking about God put a bad sound in my ear and left a bad taste in my mouth, and I knew it was from the devil. So I forced myself to listen in spite of what just happened, and I prayed to not let me doubt God's plan or his power. While sitting in front of the Eucharist Jesus ordered me Seven rosaries, so I prayed them. I felt a voice say, "She killed herself," but I didn't recognize the voice. Did Jesus order me seven Rosaries because she killed herself, or to break the devil's grasp? Is the devil deceiving me?

My dad left the house to pick the kids up from school at 2:00. Maggie was home with Damian and two kids. Maggie was bathing Alliah and Jesse's kid, Cole. Both kids can barely speak full sentences. When my dad was at the house Maggie was kneeling on the bath mat upstairs in the bathroom bathing the kids. In the thirty minutes it took my dad to get the kids from school and get back to the house. My dad, Lizzy, and Haden enter the house. The first thing they see are the two toddlers standing at the top of the stairs naked crying hysterically. The deacon walks up to my dad, and says to Lizzy,"Help me with the kids?" He helped wrap them in towels, and asked Lizzy to bring them down and sit on the couch with them. The deacon pulls my dad to the side, "Her blood was already coagulated when we found her. Damian came to the church in a panic, screaming. I was sitting at a late lunch with the two parish priests, and the other deacon, and he ran up the Church pounding on all the doors. The priest told me to take care of it, so I followed Damian to the house. Damian pulled up to the driveway, he put it in park and ran into the house screaming for Maggie and crying, so I followed him inside.

He ran upstairs, "See she went crazy, she started breaking stuff, going crazy, scratching crosses into everything, and repeating herself, she was so unstable, I don't know what medications she was on, her parents know, but I don't know I think she was possessed." Daminan ran down the stairs and out to the back yard screaming, "Maggie!" and bursting into tears. I didn't know what to expect, I didn't know if she left. I followed him, and he opened the door to the garage, and screamed, "She shot herself!" He wouldn't fully enter the garage door. I ran in and knelt down to feel for a pulse. She was dead, there was coagulated blood on the top of her skull. He said she shot herself, but I didn't see a gun." My dad ran to her body. She was in the corner of the garage on her back. Her right leg folded under her outstretched left leg, gun tucked her right shine. The gun was issued to her for her transport job at the prison. She kept it in a lock box in the trunk of her car.

The cops arrive, and then Jesse and her boyfriend Andre. Andre runs at Damian, and the cops separate them. Damian, guarded by the cops, puffs his chest at Andre. Jesse runs to Cole, He is hysterical, "No mommy, don't go into that house, don't go in there! He hurt her hands!" My mom gets there and runs up to the cops, "Are you going to arrest him, are you going to test him? My dad yells, test him for powder burns?" The cop replies, "That won't hold up in court, if he was even in the same room, he can have powder on him." My mom, dad, Jesse and her family stood in the front yard in the rain as the cops walked through the house talking to Damian. My mom and dad could hear him pleading his case to the cops. "She went crazy, she was bathing the kids. She turned on the water to the tub, and I kept going into the bathroom to turn the water off, so the kids wouldn't drown. Then she started breaking everything. She packed a bag to leave, and took my wallet and put it in her suitcase. She Kept walking up to me, repeating herself, do you love me? Do you love me? Then she ran all over the house scratching crosses into the furniture. She kept telling me to take a shower so I can go to work. I kept telling her, I'm off today, but I took a shower real quick to get her off my case. She threw herself on the car in the garage, and then locked me in the garage. I showered, jumped in the car, drove to the gas station, put gas, and drove to the church to get the deacon to bless the house. She was going crazy, I think she was possessed. The other night she held down our daughter because she said she was possessed. I told her, "Stop holding her, you're hurting her. Leave her alone."" Not once did the cops ask, "If she was going crazy, kids in a bathtub, why would you leave her alone with two toddlers in a bathtub full of water? She could have drowned them? If she was scratching crosses into the furniture with a sharp object if she was mentally unstable? Why didn't you call the cops when she was going crazy, especially if you were worried for your daughter? Why would you shower if you didn't have to go to work, just to appease her? Why would you feed into her delusions?"

Finally the cops left, and Damian asked the cops to give him a ride to Ursula's house. My mom and dad walked through the house. "Look at all this," she pointed to the bed, "How could a five foot zero, one hundred and twenty pound girl break the back bed frame to that king size bed? The mattresses are on the floor. That mirror is shattered." My dad replied, "look, the mat she was kneeling on is in the washer with towels that are still folded. She told me she wasn't doing laundry today, and it looks like he grabbed handfuls of clean laundry and threw in the load to make it look like it's a normal load of laundry, and washed the evidence away." My mom and dad walked into the garage. "Look," my mom said. "My rosary. It was the one she was wearing. It broke into all those pieces. If they weren't fighting, why would she rip the rosary off of her own neck?"

I called off of work to get my head together, How did this little witch muster up all this spiritual power? The devil mocked me, He was speaking to me directly. "You took my daughter, and I took yours. You're weak, you could have saved her." He played the event in my head over and over again. Years earlier. I was eight years old, Jesse was eleven, Maggie was five, Victor was three, and Anne was two. When I turned eight I was finally able to physically defend myself from Jesse when she would beat me and my younger siblings. I was able to start defending them as well. One day Jesse realized she couldn't pick on them anymore, so she threw an offer out there. "Help me pick on the little ones." I stood there in silence not knowing what to say or think. Hesitation is the worst thing to do when trying to discern morality. Maggie stared at me with tears in her eyes and yelled, "Alan you are the only one that can protect us! Now you're going to stop!" She was right, that was my job, to protect them. The conviction set in, and

I vowed to never let anyone hurt them again. The devil watched this years prior, and used it against me, and replayed it in my head over and over. Maggie was my sister, but she was also my spiritual daughter, I felt like my child was taken from me. I went back to work in order to have enough bereavement time for the funeral in New Mexico, and the funeral in Colorado. I didn't show any weakness, nobody needs to know my business. That day God sent an old friend to my unit to minister. "You know I'm a healer of the healers, and your light usually shines so bright, but you are so dim now." I had to fess up. I can't lie about any of this. I spilled my guts, even though I knew the devil was digging his finger into my wounds. The thought kept passing through my head; If I could have just called off work, went and blessed the house, this never would have happened. I shouldn't have trusted other servants to take care of my family business. "You know Alan, you do God's work, and you do great things, but you are not God." That was just what I needed to hear. Maggie left the world with her soul prepared. She fasted for four days. She returned to the Church, went to confession. Prayed three Rosaries that day, her soul pure. My mom said her face looked like an angel when she kissed her lifeless body. Maggie told me that day, "I want a perfect life like yours." I don't think she wanted a perfect life. I think she just wanted to be loved. She didn't love herself enough in this life or know her worth. The devil used her love against her, as he does. I was astonished at the power the devil had. For decades I have tread on serpents, and walked away unscathed. His power astonished me. I had been so intrigued with everything related to religion, demonology, and the occult, and even though I knew I should not confront the devil head on, I knew that God has and always will have more power. A human being lowly beings we are, but united with Christ sends the devil fleeing away. He took losing Bertha personally, and stole my spiritual daughter. He fought this book, every word takes the will of God to type. My goal was to finish this book by Christmas. I finished it a few days prior to Maggie's death. I had to re-edit in order to add this event in. He doesn't want me sharing my testimony, as it exposes him, and if God's Will be done, it will draw many to Jesus Christ!

We went to New Mexico for her funeral down there. She had so many friends from work, five times the amount of family. The priest did the mass with a black aura. He preached a wonderful Homally. The black wasn't from evil, but shame for not taking my sister's concerns seriously, and having to face my family face to face. He is God's servant, and I have no ill feelings toward him, we're on the same team. My plan was to go to bless the house after the ceremony. The night before my wife grabbed me in tears, "I don't want you going into that house. It's awful." I loved that she cared enough about me to ask me not to go, but I was not going to allow my wife to be used against me. This wouldn't be the first time. He tries to instill fear, and it eats away courage. On one hand I was grieving my sister's death, and on the other, I knew he had provoked the wrong guy. Maybe this was God's way of allowing me to know the devil's power, but also be the kindling of the fire in me for the rest of this life! Victor agreed to go with me, and so did my nephew Chris, and I felt excited that he wanted to go. I felt like we were off to battle on a heroic adventure. Looking back, One nurse, one steel worker, and one plummer were going into a battle that the church should have fought. I realized we are the Church, The Body of Christ is not just the Pope, Cardinals, Bishops, and Priests, but the majority of The Body of Christ is laity. The devil first attacked the family in the Garden of Eden, and now, it is the time for the family to attack back. In our current culture the family is under attack with abortion, transgender, homosexuality, adultery, polyamorous relationships, and communism/welfare state where families are rewarded for not having married parents. A nurse, a steel worker, and a plummer are going to battle. Lord Byron's Don Juan (1823), "Tis strange–but true; for truth is always strange; Stranger than fiction; if it could be told, How much would novels gain by the exchange!" After the ceremony we gathered at the hall. All our spouses were terrified of us going into the house. Jesse said, it is so evil, and heavy in there. Deacon Johnny, the Deacon who went to the house with Damian met me outside of the Church. He has a good soul, I could see he was a true man of God. I told him what we were about to do, and I noticed he didn't offer to go, but this is my battle not his. Victor, Chris and I gathered bottles of water. We kissed our spouses and left. It was a strange feeling, anticipation was welling up, and there was a sense of unspeakable hope. Victor, Chris, and I were on our way. The directions from our phone gave us trouble, preventing us from getting there easily. As we got closer and closer the heaviness started setting in. I could feel the fear attempting to lure us in. We were a block away. A Huge crow sat perched on a lamp post as we drove under. I had never seen a crow so disheveled and mangy. The feathers around his neck frayed out as if he was a vulture. Victor said, "Do you see that?" "Yeah, I used to hate animals like that, all ominous, but now I appreciate their warnings." We reached the house. I felt like the whole neighborhood saw us arrive, and was staring at us. I felt hundreds of eyes on us. It wasn't until after, I realized it was demons waiting with anticipation, not to attack, but to watch and see what was going to happen to us.

I kneeled down and kissed the pavement in front of the door, and blessed the bottles of water in my hands. I blessed us, and we approached the front door. I put the key in the key hole. The door creaked open, greeting us with the heaviest black presence, powerful enough to consume the most faithful. The living room was so evil. I could see the afternoon sunlight as it spilled through the venison blinds from the dining room at the back of the house.

We walked through the front room, and passed the door to the garage on the right, entering the kitchen on the left. Chris looked up the staircase to the right. I took a left avoiding the long countertop island that stretched the entire length of the kitchen. I strolled through the kitchen looking at the dining room and the sliding glass door ahead of me. Glanced to the right where the large living room was. I saw a transparent face as he was walking away from me looking over his right shoulder. He was at least eight feet tall. His face, blue and white. Bright yellow eyes of pure hatred, that can pierce a soul. His white hair shining and a silver glare glistened as the shoulder length hair trailed him. He spoke to me, and only me. Victor and Chris didn't hear a thing. "What did you come here for? To smell the inside of your sister's rotting vagina?" He dissipated into thin air. I knew this was not an ordinary demon. I have done a couple exorcisms, and cleared many houses. Sometimes with multiple high ranking demons, and never have they talked to me in a spirit form. Yes maybe in a person possessed, but, never has a spirit talked to me that wasn't Jesus. This is not a run of the mill demon. Then he appeared in front of me. His sharp teeth open to bite me, yellow eyes with pure hate. All his teeth were longer than a mountain lion's K-9 teeth. He jumped at me and disappeared. I didn't flinch, which angered him. I didn't say a word, I turned to the right to head back into the entree living room. Just then another image flashed before. It was about eight feet long. It was black and white, and transparent. This was a dragon. It appeared as black smoke and sulfur. It was weaving through the air as a winged serpent from the entree living room. it jumped at me, jaws open. I squeezed the plastic water bottle throwing the Holy water in its face, the smokey body vanished. It was time to fight! I went through the house throwing Holy water in the sign of the cross. "I cast you out in the Father Son, and Holy Spirit!" I cast you out in the Blood of

Jesus Christ from Calvary!" Victor and Chris followed my lead. We went through the house blessing everything, making the sign of the cross on the windows and mirrors. We went through the entire first level in the matter of minutes. We walked the staircase next to the garage door. I felt the presents at the top of the staircase looking down at us. I threw water up the stairs preventing any attacks waiting up there for us. Chris said three times, "He is up there leaning on the staircase, with one arm on the banister. He is enticing us, and his body language is saying, "What are you waiting for, I'm up here waiting for you?" I wondered Why Chris repeated that three times, and it hit me like a ton of bricks.

This was the devil. How he spoke to me, so disgusting, and unclean. I had seen him before. The old man in the bathtub I used to see as a toddler sitting in the bathtub looking at me with such hate, One arm leaning on the tub with cocky arrogance, prideful. As I have said, pride leads to all sins. I saw him every time I passed that bathroom. When I layed in the bathtub to let my mom bathe me, he wanted to drown me. Months earlier when I went to Chris' house to bless it, I cut corners though. To cleanse a room, I have to put a part of my body in each room and throw Holy water in the shape of a cross. This casts out the evil spirit. In cabinets I can not stand inside, so I place a hand or part of my body like my foot, and throw holy water inside. That day I blessed his condo, I stuck a finger in the crawl space and threw Holy water down in the crawl space. Then I moved on. I went through the rest of his house. Months later he asked me to come back as they were moving out of that condo, and into a new house, they didn't want anything following them. When someone asks to re-bless a house, that is not a good sign. Something was missed by me, our they are not living a Holy life, and allowing the devil back in. I went back and blessed everything again. I saved the crawl space for last. "Maybe I should actually go down there this time," I said to Chris. "Yeah when I was moving stuff out of there, something was staring at me, and it moved around quickly." I opened up the crawl space. I stepped down the latter, and instantly got an image in my head of my ankle snapping. It wanted not just to break my ankle, but obliterate it. I stepped down carefully, almost spilling the plastic cup full of water. I got down into the crawl space and saw a black and white eight foot transparent creature. It had a mane, it didn't look like a lion, it was too skinny. Its body was long and slender, it shot around the crawl space with angst, and unrest. It was a dragon. There is a reason St John called the devil a dragon, and many others refer to the devil as the dragon. It was the devil!

God mentions to Job a creature called leviathan. Its tail could knock over the biggest of trees. An elephant can't do that. Was it a dinosaur God was referring to? God mentions scales that were impenetrable. Still sounds like a dinosaur, except He mentions a creature from Job 19-20 *flames stream from its mouth; sparks of fire shoot out. Smoke pours from its nostrils.* I think there is a good possibility Dragons were real, but whether they were real or not, the devil takes on the form of any powerful beast to instill fear into us. One more image came to mind after Chris mentioned an arm pridefully resting on the banister. While Victor and I were praying for Bertha's conversion, right before she converted to Christianity, a demon was sent my way. He looked like a black male figure from a bathroom sign on a public restroom. Except he wasn't standing up. He was lying on his back. Left leg bent, and right leg laying flat against the floor. His left arm was laying on his belly relaxed, and the right arm propping up his head with an arrogant swag. On his head was a set of horns that looked like it came from a Texas longhorn's bull. I realized this was not a demon, but Baal, people worshiped him. People sacrificed babies to an idol of a bull. He has so many names, but it's the devil masquerading as another deity. He continually recreates deities for pagan worship, he just slaps a different label on it. I saw the dragon crawling on the walls when I nearly took my own life years prior, they were all the devil. He knew me from the beginning.

Victor walked through the house saying, "Something is under something, and I see Maggie's work shirt in my head." Weeks later they found Maggie's engagement ring under the mattress in her bedroom. As we walked through the house I could see images of Maggie fighting for her life trying to escape. All the curtains were ripped from the walls in the loft, and in her bedroom. Next to the broken bed was a hamper, and a large window. The curtains were ripped from the wall. There were so many hand prints smeared on the window. As I walked through the house I got images of her trying to escape, fighting and running as he chased her. I saw her trying to jump out of the two story window to freedom. How could the cops not see the struggle? There was a shattered mirror lying on the ground at the top of the stairs, right outside the master bedroom. The room was destroyed, the only thing not out of place was a collectors item. It was a nun doll that came from our grandmother Verna's house. She was standing on her night stand like a tiny little voyeur. She watched everything that happened the day of Maggie's death. Her presence was of mockery, like she watched the terror with glee, and refusal to restrain the evil.

The neighbors living in the house next to her bedroom told my parents, "The evil in that house is so bad, it's spreading to ours. Our kid's bedrooms are next to her bedroom. We don't let them sleep in those bedrooms anymore." The evil was so intoxicating it spilled over to the house next door. We blessed the entire upstairs and I saw a vanity set new and still in a bow. Maggie had bought Lizzy the vanity for her Birthday. She was going to put it together for her, but never got around to it. The devil knows it was the last thing Maggie bought for her, making it so important to Lizzy, but he attached himself to it, and it will constantly be a portal to the family. Something like that will constantly need to be blessed. I ordered it to be thrown out. As I walked through the loft the devil whispered in my ear, "I hate you, I'm going to kill you." In my head I replied, "If it's God's will so be it, no greater way to die than doing God's will." He couldn't stand that answer, and fled. God is with me, and can't touch me without God's permission. I genuinely feel that way. There is no greater way to die than to be killed doing God's Will. I know the Apostles died painful gruesome deaths, we could be so lucky. There is a special place in heaven for martyrs. As we walked down the stairs to bless the garage. I had an image that Maggie made it to the front living room, and where the dragon jumped at me, is where Damian caught Maggie for the last time, he dragged her into the garage and used her gun to shoot her.

We blessed the garage, and we were done, so we locked the house. We got on the road and were talking about everything that happened as we drove. I suddenly had a feeling that we were going to rearend the car in front of us. We weren't even close. I felt like it was so real. Victor and I were just telling Chris how it is important to trust the instincts we are feeling. The plan was to meet at the mortuary to make arrangements for Maggie's body. Our parents were to meet us at the mortuary in Maggie's SUV. Ann had a feeling like she felt like she was going to get in a car accident too. We pulled into the parking lot. I saw Jesse, and pulled in. Jesse asked what happened, and I quickly filled her in, censoring certain things that I didn't have time to explain. Just then Jesse got a call from mom, "Ok, ok, are you guys ok? Ok love you bye." "Mom and dad were on their way over her, and they were sitting at a light, and a drunk driver T-boned them." The truck hit the center frame of the SUV. If it would have been a foot toward the front of the car, my mom would have been crushed. The SUV spun around three times, and they were heading for a telephone pole. My dad cried out for God, and they barely missed it. The devil wasn't done, he wanted more blood. We left New Mexico that night, and after we tried to coordinate our exit we were four hours behind schedule. Alliah was in our car, and she was hit with a stomach bug. We had to stop three times before we left the state, and she ended up having an accident in the car, but we pushed forward. We didn't stop, we just wanted to stay on the road. Everyone contracted covid, or RSV after making it home. The devil was still in my ear, constantly trying to make me wish bad things upon myself or family. It doesn't matter how stupid that sounds. Even if it is totally ridiculous. If someone tells you something day in and day out, it might break you down, and you may accept the ridiculous offer. I prayed three Rosaries, went to mass, and Adoration. These three things halted him, but he was still there.

Weeks after we realized that a few months earlier, Maggie changed her life insurance policy. She took our mom and her kids off it. Maggie joked with her friend at work, "If something happens to me, you know who did it." I realized Maggie gave Damian an ultimatum, and he and Ursula realized the gravy train was over. We lost a spiritual soldier in the battle. Maggie was taken from us. She followed in Jesus' footsteps. She became a spiritual sacrifice, as she absorbed the devil arrows, and she died so others may live. May God rest her soul as we will never forget her. He took it personally that we stole his daughter for God. I too take it personal, as he will regret the day he took her from us! She was decorating her house for Christmas saying, "This is going to be the best Christmas ever!" For us, it was the worst, but for her, it was the best. She spent her Christmas with Jesus in Heaven, and finally really felt what it was like to be truly loved.

I called Deacon Johnny to fill him in on what was happening, and I felt compelled by the Holy Spirit. We talked for an hour and a half. He is a good man. He explained, "My church is the

Church that deals with all the possessions in New Mexico. We have a Father who performs exorcisms, but his health is very poor, so I assist him, and I have been put in control of triaging all the possible possessions. What I have been taught in my ministry is to never engage the devil, he is more powerful than us, and is smarter. I don't know why I have no fear when I do what I do, or if it is good that I don't fear demons? I do what I can down here, I wish we can work together. You could be a great help down here. Do you have any advice?" I explained to him all the things I have learned. After our conversation, I felt he was such a good soul, but I was also astonished at how out of gunned they were down there. New Mexico has Holy places, but just like the San Luis Valley that runs into Colorado, witchcraft is rampant. I realized that If I could go down there and face the devil with Holy water that I blessed as a lay person, and walk away, God is with me. It's not me the devil is afraid of, but Christ that is in me. That is why we are to unite ourselves with Christ. The Catholic Church has outlined the remedy from the beginning from the Apostles, then the early Church Fathers passed down through Catholic tradition. Through the sacraments, and sacramentals. The first people to ever exorcize a possessed person was Jewish, they have been doing it longer. However, Catholics use the power of Christ, so they are the ultimate power, for they have been doing it the longest with the power of Christ. I explained to Deacon Johnny, I didn't want to raise any scandal of my family tragedy, as they are always under the microscope, and a scandal like this prevents people from getting help from the Church. The Church can retract help, and the Body of Christ suffers/the people of Christ. The devil loves these types of scandals as he uses them to prevent the Church from performing exorcisms. I will only preach The Gospel a and bring people to the true Church, The Catholic Church.

Maggie's funeral in Pueblo was beautiful. It was poetic. My grandfather Ron and Bertha were there. Bertha's soul was in such a good state, and she was now a Christian. After Maggie was laid to rest in the cemetery, I had a vision of her. She was a pure transparent baby blue, dancing in the sky with the angels. Our battle down her was not over. Days after the funeral the devil stayed with me. I returned to live as normal, and the devil tempted me, and I got caught in sin, and asked for forgiveness and prayed. I returned home from work at 3:30 AM, and I got ready for bed. Thirty minutes later My youngest ran into my bedroom in tears, "I was asleep, something grabbed my leg three times, there is something in my room!" The devil's presence was in there, I blessed the room and knew the devil was attacking her because of me. I needed to get to confession.

My mom and dad spent the next month trying to get custody of Maggie's children, get the life insurance money for the kids and a place for them to live. There was an obstacle for every task. They drove from Colorado to New Mexico, back and forth every week. Everything required a death certificate, and most places denied due to a pending status on the certificate. The realtor argued with my parents for an hour, and left in frustration and defeat. I prayed a couple of Rosaries for them and their obstacles. The next day my dad searched for paperwork, and finally found what he needed. They met with the realtor again, and he completely converted into a helpful agent. He granted my parents the house for the children as Maggie and Damian were never married. Days later the realtor went to the house to take photos of the house to put on the market. Jesse met him there and started to show him around. He asked questions about the house and why they were selling it? She answered him honestly. As they walked through the house they walked by the staircase that led upstairs. Jesse saw a dark figure flash from the Loft into the master bedroom. She shook it off and continued showing him the house. They passed the staircase again and she looked to the top of the staircase and saw a huge silhouette walk from the bedroom to the loft. There was no mistaking what she saw. She didn't say anything to him. "Okay, I'm going to start taking photos of the house." "Ok." He started on the first level and then went upstairs. Minutes later he ran down the stairs, and out of the house.

Days later he met my mom and dad. "I can't be involved with the sale of the house. I met with my Pastor, and explained to him what happened. He advised me, "Have nothing to do with that house."" "What exactly happened?" asked my mom. "Well I was up stairs I started taking pictures and in the loft I saw a pair of red eyes. They were so full of evil and hate. I ignored it, and went into the bedroom to start taking pictures. I am a converted Christian, but before that I was into a bad scene. I was into partying. My girlfriend and I were into that stuff, and she ended up dying. When I was in that room my dead girlfriend appeared to me and she looked dead. Her skin was pale. I couldn't believe what I was seeing. She walked up to me. She turned into the devil and said, "I almost had you, now you're mine!" I've been a realtor for many years. I've sold houses that were two hundred years old all throughout Sante Fe. I've seen evil houses where people did evil things in them. I've seen a lot of evil in the houses I sold, but I have never seen the evil you have in that House. I have never seen the devil himself!"

My mom and dad went to the house with a plan to move everything out. They wanted to just get rid of the house. They figured they would start packing, and moving the furniture out. It started getting late, so they decided to sleep there. They chose to sleep in the bedroom on the first floor. It's right below the master bedroom. They were lying in bed, when they heard a pound above them. There was nobody in the house. They tried to get some sleep. They ignored the sound. Then something fell in the room above them, and rolled. "We need to go back to the Church for help. We need to get the house blessed again," my mom said. They went back to the Church to meet with Deacon Johnny. They told him what was going on. He replied, "Well, I don't think it's over. You all need to be careful. You are all under attack." "Do you have a bathroom?" "Yes, it's right down the hall."

That morning I was at work. Someone brought in donuts, and I was hungry. I opened the box. I really wanted the chocolate one in the front of the box. Just then The Holy Spirit told me, "Hold on, do not eat the donut," I listened, instead I ate some cereal for breakfast. Hours later I opened the box to see if the donut was still in there. I was torturing myself. It was in there, nobody ate it. There were a few missing, but the one I wanted was still there, and it was facing the front of the box inviting me to see the entire top of the donut. It was the only one facing that direction. I remembered what The Holy Spirit said, and closed the box. I wondered what a skeptic, or an unbeliever would say, "You are too superstitious, do you really believe God doesn't want you to have a donut?" The day went on, and soon it was time for my lunch break. I was looking forward to the tamales I had brought. I took them out of the refrigerator and started walking down to the breakroom. The Holy Spirit said, "Don't eat those." I questioned myself and put the container in the microwave, pushed the timer, and the start button. I wondered what was going on, why was The Holy Spirit directing me not to eat my food. He told me not to eat anything I wanted, including the donut from earlier. The timer buzzed. I retrieved my food from the microwave and sat down at the table. I put the tupperware lid back on, "OK, I'll eat it later." I pondered why the Holy Spirit was having me deprive myself of these joys. It must be something big, but I better listen with blind obedience.

Just then Deacon Johnny texted me. "When you get a chance can you give me a call about your parents house and what's going on there?" I called him. "Hey Deacon Johnny," "Hi Alan. Your parents came to me today. They said the realtor refuses to help them with the house. He will not go back into it, or even drive by it." Just then I heard screams coming from the background. Jesse screamed, "Somebody help! Mom said something grabbed her by the throat, and couldn't breath, then she went unconscious!" The deacon ran to her, "Don't touch her, let her stay there until the paramedics get here." "Alan, I need to call 9-11, I'm going to set the phone down." "Ok, thank you." I heard him explaining what happened, and gave them the address to the Church. He picked up the phone Alan, we can talk later about all of this, can you call me back later, and I'll keep you updated about what's going on?" "Sure, that would be great. Thank you." I threw my tamales in the trash, even the tupperware it was in. I called my dad for an update. Later deacon Johnny texted, "Your mom is stable and breathing better. They did transport her. Her blood sugar was a little high. When you get things worked out give me a call or a text so I can make some time. And if you need to call later, in fact, it might be good to talk with you this evening or whenever for a bit." "Ok. Thank you for everything. I'll call you when I get out of work."

I worked the rest of my shift, what am I going to do? I have to go down there. I was told to enter this fast. I can't eat until I take care of this. I'm going to have to go down there and take care of this myself. I called my dad for an update, "Hey dad." "Hey," "What's going on with mom?" "Her sugar was a little bit high, but not that high. They gave her a nebulizer to help her breathing, and something grabbed her leg. She was awake, in the middle of the ER something grabbed her leg, and started convulsing. She started screaming, and her heart rate and blood pressure shot up. The doctor can't give us any explanation, but said they are going to keep her for a while." I realized the connection. The devil grabbed my mom's leg exactly the same way he grabbed my daughter's leg. "Ok dad keep me updated, I'm going to figure some stuff out down here." "Ok, I love you." "I love you too." I called Deacon back. "Hello," "Hey Deacon Johnny, this is Alan" "Hi, so it sounds like they're going to keep your mom for a while. What are you thinking?" "Well, This is the devil, She was in God's house in the middle of the day, far away from the house, and it choked her out. This is powerful." "Yeah, they said her blood sugar was a little high." "Yeah, it wasn't high enough to make her go into Diabetic Ketoacidosis. There are a lot of warning signs before that happens. Rapid deep breathing, sweating, and it can eventually put you into a coma, but it doesn't cause a fainting spell, and then coming back to consciousness that quickly. It would be really strange if she had a spasm in her trachea at the same time. Her sugar wasn't high enough. I know the devil grabbed her by the throat for trying to get help from you." "Yeah I believe that too. All of this has bothered me since it happened. It wakes me up at three in the morning. So what's your plan?" "Well, I was thinking I should call off and head down there. If I leave first thing in the morning, I can make it down there by twelve." The Holy Spirit directed me that I should be there after 12:00 PM. "Well, what do you need, I have Holy water, oil, Salt Crucifixes, what do you need?" This was great, I wanted him to meet me there and we could do battle together. I can show him how I do things and give him tools for his future battles. "Yeah bring all that stuff, I'm going to call off work tomorrow and head up there. Do you think you can meet me there around twelve, and we can bless the house together?" "Um, well let me see what I can do with my schedule, see if I can move some stuff around. I definitely have wondered why I'm not afraid of these things, perhaps it's not a good thing. Let me talk to my wife, and I'll let you know." He looked young for his age, but he definitely looked to be at the age of retirement, and I hoped we could do this together. "It's good that you're not afraid of these things, that's why you're in this line of work, you're made for it. The devil uses fear against people, that is how he has control. I'll let you know when I get there tomorrow." I drove home from work, and a great darkness had fallen over me. I knew that the devil was preventing me from going down there.

Just before I got to my house, Deacon Johnny texted me, "I'm gonna have to pray about being directly involved with you tomorrow, but I do have blessed salt, oil, and Holy water specifically blessed to fight evil. That I can bring, but my issue is that the Holy Spirit is warning, my wife to not let me be directly involved. It's a pretty strong feeling." The wind was taken out of my sale. A thought went through my head, why would I want the sacramentals he was offering. They were blessed by cowards who couldn't defend their own territory. Not even just him, he is a deacon. Where is the priest? He should have more courage. I felt that the priest was cowering behind him, and saw that this was powerful, and didn't want to get involved either. A leader of spiritual battle should have stepped in when things got bad, but he was afraid too. He pushed this off to the Deacon when he thought it was nothing, and left it that way due to fear. I felt disappointed in the Deacon, but this was my battle. I felt like the warriors to my left and right were falling. I need to work this out. I replied to the Deacon, "It's Ok, I understand, It's not your battle. But thank you for everything. I appreciate everything…God bless you!" "Do you want me to meet you if you need any of the salt oil, ect. We want to hold a prayer vigil in the adoration chapel while you're in the house so we need to know when you're going to be there." "Ok. It's ok. I have everything I need. I really appreciate everything, and the prayer vigil. I couldn't ask for more. Thank you!"

I pulled up in my driveway. I need to bless my house if I'm doing this. It is going to attack my family. The devil knew I didn't want to leave my family here, and go over to fight him in New Mexico, he could strike my house while I was away. That was the only thing I was afraid of, I was worried for my wife and kids. My wife was at work that night, and would have to work the following night. I went into the house and started blessing it. I needed to hurry as my mother-in-law was on her way home with my kids. I didn't want her knowing everything that was going on. She believes in God, but she doesn't believe me when I talk about these sorts of things, and the last thing I need is doubt. Doubt prevents faith from flourishing. *A prophet is not without honor, but in his own country, and in his own kin, and in his own house.* Mark 6:4 This is one of the reasons Jesus asks if the person believes before he heals them. Jesus can heal anyone, but faith is necessary when in order for the miracle to take place. I went through the house in a furry. I asked St. Michael to watch over my house while I was away, and consecrated it to the Blessed Virgin Mary, and the Sacred Heart of Jesus. I finished the house and was on my way to the garage when my mother-in-law and my kids walked in, I said hi and finished the blessing. They all looked at me puzzled, and I had to confess what I was doing.

I printed up a Psalm that spoke of blessing a house and keeping evil out. I placed a copy under the doormat at my front door, and my back door. It was similar to what Jews have been doing for centuries. I called Victor, but he didn't answer. I decided to pray a Rosary with my kids for their protection. Victor called back, and I told him what was going on, and asked if he wanted to go. He said he would go, and felt what I did, worried about leaving his family behind, and like he is missing out on a day off with his family at the end of a busy week. He agreed to go, and I was thrilled. I told him not to eat meat until after we finished blessing

Maggie's house. I called my dad, "Hey," "Hey, what's going on?" "Victor and I are going to head over to Maggies tomorrow to bless the house. The deacon backed out on me. He said he felt it wasn't a good idea to go back into that house." "Well, maybe you guys shouldn't go back into that house either." "I have to close this up, it will never go away. We will be OK." "Ok, be careful. I love you." "I love you." I put the kids to bed and I wanted to get to bed and get an early start on the next day. I turned out the light and laid down. I looked to the right and there was the devil in his demonic form. By that I mean, not human, not in the form of a dragon, or bull, but blue and white skin with white hair, and angry yellow eyes. He was crouching down by the side of my bed glaring at me. I made the sign of the cross with my right hand and told him to leave, but it didn't work. I tossed and turned. I turned around and looked at him, and there he was, he was still there glaring at me. I waved him away again, but he didn't budge. I should have blessed water and cast him out, but I didn't. I finally got tired of him staring at me, so I turned away from him, and went to sleep.

I woke up early and drove over to Victor's and gave him two copies of the Psalms to place at his front door and his back door. And we were off. On our drive up there I told Victor our agenda. A snow storm hit Colorado and New Mexico. There were three times I lost control that we should have wrecked, and Victor felt it too. We prayed three Rosaries. Meanwhile, different revelations came to us as we contemplated the Gospel while we prayed the Rosary. We prayed the Seven Sorrows of Mary. We prayed fifty prayers of Saint Gertrude the Great. Each prayer releases a thousand souls from purgatory for each prayer prayed. Once the soul is in heaven, it can pray for you. I was taking an army with me. We then prayed 500 Precious Blood Prayers. We stopped to put gas and as I looked around a flock of crows was nearby. I remembered the crow the day we went to the house the first time. We pulled into town at 12:06 PM and I texted Deacon Johnny, that we had made it. He replied, "We are in the Adoration Chapel now supporting you. Call if you need anything." "Ok. Thank you. I appreciate everything."

We approached the neighborhood and a car cut us off after I allowed him to pass. The Holy Spirit told me to make the sign of the cross. So I did, and the guy pulled away. I couldn't be harboring any ill feelings for what I was about to do. Victor said, "Did you see that, as soon as you did that, the guy dropped the attitude and drove away." I didn't realize until Victor pointed it out. I simply followed the Holy Spirit with blind obedience. We pulled up to the house, and I remembered all the eyes on us last time. It felt like the whole neighborhood was watching with anticipation. I realized all those that were watching were demons. An audience to see what the devil was going to do to us. Last time he brought his army, this time I brought mine. Last time they saw their master fail three mortal men accompanied by the Holy Spirit. This time there were less eyes on us. I walked up to the lock box as the realtor had left the key in there. As we approached the lock box, The wind picked up with a swirling frigid breeze. I opened the lock box and retrieved the key. We walked to the front door, and I knelt down and blessed the water and kissed the ground. I unlocked the door, and peered in. there was a bad presence, but it wasn't as bad as it was before. We started blessing the house. I learned from Father Blount to leave blessed medals of Saint Benedict in certain places. I ordered Victor to place one under the carpet in each corner of every room. I placed one on each window seal and over every doorway.

We went through the house and I gathered some stuffed animals the devil left his spirit in to attack the children. Victor was able to pick a few out without me instructing him. I watched him bless the house. I didn't have to go over his work. I have never blessed a house with someone that I didn't worry about pulling their weight. As we reached the dining room Victor looked up at a 3D picture of The Last Supper that hung above the dining room table. It was a really cool piece, but when he looked up at the piece, over Thomas' face a transparent face appeared over Thomas' face. It made a frowning face as if he was sad. His face was mocking our sadness. Victor blessed it, and it disappeared. I was proud of Victor, while blessing houses or fighting spiritual battles my spirit enters into other dimensions and I start seeing with spiritual eyes. One can still see in the dimension he lives in, but he sees past it, in a blurry focus. I can feel when I enter this state as I feel my brain start firing in places that aren't normally activated. There are times I have done this at other houses and a dog runs at me barking. I can see a spirit that is wanting to attack me and it angers me, as I see a spirit trying to attack me, I have to snap out of the spirit realm. At times I have done this at my house, and my wife and kids have jumped out trying to scare me, and I see a spirit rushing me. I nearly punched them. Victor has leveled up and is seeing what I see.

We ran out of Saint Benedict medals and I used small crucifixes, and Rosary Rings with a crucifix on it to finish the house. We reached the garage and I pushed the button to turn on the light switch, but it flickered and went out. I pushed again, and nothing. I pushed it a couple more times, and felt panic as the devil was trying to leave us in the dark. "Maggie, help us." I pushed it again, and the light instantly turned on. Victor smiled at me. There were four items I felt the evil attached to, but left them in place. I was dodging the traps set for us, but I also needed to talk to my mom, to see what she wanted to do about them as they would need to be blessed routinely, or the evil would come back through the item. Three of them were created to be Holy items. My mom and dad met us down there. We went through the house with them. Without me instructing her. She picked out three of the four items. One of the items was the nun that came from her mom I previously mentioned sat on Maggie's night stand. One was a broken tiny broken saint of the last supper that was on a stand in the loft. One was a Bible that had the false prophets picture on it. We burned them in a fire pit in the backyard. We left for Jesse's house. Jesse was worried it could have followed her over there. We blessed her house, but there was nothing evil there, but a blessing doesn't hurt. I remembered to tell my mom and dad that the broken mirror at the top of the stairs needs to be thrown out, so they did.

"Alan the house is so peaceful now. It's bright, the light actually enters it now. I feel good there. I'm glad you two were able to fix this. I tried calling several Churches to see if a priest can meet you guys at Maggie's this morning, and most didn't answer. Another parish explained that the Church that had been helping us, has two ordained Priests and two Deacons. They should be able to help us. One Church I called, the Father answered the phone. He asked why I wanted him to meet you guys, while you bless the house. I explained to him everything that happened, in a terrified voice he said, "I can't help you," and hung up the phone. "All is well, God is good! Victor and I ate the meal my mom prepared, and then we headed back to Pueblo Colorado. We hit snow on our way back, and had three dicey episodes, but made it home without an accident. Victor asked me, "Do you think I should keep that 3D Last Supper mom gave me. Should I keep it in my garage? I don't know, I can't get that image out of my head. Will I have to re-bless it every now and then?" "I don't know, I don't want it at my house, I wouldn't take it into my house. Just throw it out I guess. I just wouldn't want to make mom sad." "Yeah, I guess I will, I'll just tell her, she will understand." We walked to his dumpster and threw them in. I had explained to my mom that she was going to have to leave some of the things behind. Like Samuel and the Israelites conquered the Philistines, God ordered them through the Prophet Nathan, to kill everything, even the life stock, instead of collecting the spoils of war. My mom had a hard time as Maggie bought everything in the house. She said, "Even the TV? The last thing we watched on it was The Holy Rosary?" "Mom, the last thing I saw on that TV was the devil's reflection in it as he mocked Maggie's death." "Ok." "I'll Get you a new one." "Ok."

When I returned home that night my youngest, my eleven year old, asked me, "Why were you blessing the house last night, what's going on?" I explained, "I had to bless aunt Maggie's house, the devil was there." Normally, I would think every eleven year old is too young to hear that, but she is spiritually advanced, and has many interactions with evil herself. "Daddy, before we prayed the Rosary last night, I went to my bathroom, and when I was walking past the bathtub I saw a pair of golden eyes looking at me." "What did you do?" "I ignored it and walked past it." "Were you scared?" "Yeah, they looked angry." "I'm so proud of you, but everything is Ok." "Ok."

I felt like Deacon Johnny and I were set to work together in the future. Things were just begging. I contemplated how in both Maggie's ceremonies, I was trying to honor her, and make her the direct focus, as every funeral usually does. It honors the deceased, and may have little bits of scripture, but the main focus was on the departed. I realized what a blessing the Catholic Church is, and that it put the main focus on the mass and Jesus in the Eucharist, as it should. Everything should be with the focus of God in the center. The departed have their eulogy, and family have the rest of their life to celebrate the departed.

I started to contemplate how many times I had faced the devil in the past. I know he can take many forms, but why yellow eyes, and billowing of yellow smoke in his presence. Perhaps it's because he fell from grace. There is no light in him. He displays an artificial light, and this is the reason for yellow, as it reveals a loss of power. Of course he takes on the form of red eyes too, or a beautiful man, a bull, or a dragon, but whatever form he comes… Turn to Jesus and Mary.

Jesus spoke to Blessed Alan de la Roche in a vision after he failed to renew the Dominican Rosary. Saint Dominic made the Rosary popular. Alan de la Roche was in the Dominican order, and expected to follow in Saint Dominic's footsteps. Saint Dominic was named Dominic as his mom had a vision. While she was pregnant with him, she had a vision of giving birth to a dog that came out with a torch in its mouth. It ran and set the world on fire. Dominic is a play on words Domini canis, which means; The Lord's dog in Latin. So she named him Dominic. In Alan de la Rocha's vision of Jesus, He said, "The world is full or devouring wolves, and you unfaithful dog, know not how to bark." For most of my life I studied and prayed to know God. To grow as much as spiritually possible, to fight His war. He taught me, "Worldly glory is temporary, eternal glory is forever." I merited in every way, hoping to be part of the Seraphim when I die. God has allowed me to be chained up like a vicious dog, fire burning inside me to share God and the mysteries thereof. I've seen soldiers fall, and lukewarm servants go through the motions. It kills me inside that I can't take their place, to preach the truth, and with more passion, and accuracy. I liked my jaws to attack the enemy, and this year He released me. I will catch the world on fire, like Saint Dominique and the saints before. Unleash this dog Lord…

9 798891 140257